Oak Tree Cottage

A story of love, loss and friendship

Maggie Rogers

Published by Maggie Rogers

15450

Acknowledgements

I would like to say a huge thank you to Sue Horrocks who painstakingly proofread Oak Tree Cottage for me. Thanks also to all my friends in the Nailsworth writing group, who without them I would never have written anything. Special love and thanks to my husband Terry for all his support and encouragement.

Chapter 1

A little hand rested on the folds of the blanket. Laura put her finger underneath and gently smoothed the tiny fingers around hers. She marvelled at the perfection of each nail formed so exquisitely. She looked at her baby's face, a wisp of dark hair curled onto her brow. Her eyes were closed, and her lashes created two dark crescents, resting on the flawless skin of her cheeks, pale as alabaster. A button nose, and below a beautifully formed rosebud mouth set in an attitude of gentle repose. Already there was a tinge of blue settling on and around those pretty lips, and as Laura looked a tear from her own eyes fell and trickled down the baby's already cold cheek.

'She's so beautiful,' she whispered, raising her eyes to Ben, who was standing behind her gazing down on his beautiful, perfect, silent baby daughter. Tears were gathering in his eyes but seemed trapped by his lids and didn't escape to run down his face. Ben's hand caressed the side of Laura's neck. He felt helpless, impotent; this wasn't how it was supposed to be, this wasn't what they'd spent nine months planning and waiting for.

'Would you like me to take a photograph?' The midwife, who was waiting in the corner, moved forward and nodded towards the camera on the table. Ben was planning to use it to record this happy moment, to record the birth of his, of their, first child. Neither Laura nor Ben spoke, but both looked at the midwife dressed in her blue scrubs with disbelief that she could suggest such a thing. She knew; she delivered the baby. Surely, she couldn't have forgotten in such a short space of time that their baby was dead; that this wasn't the joyous occasion they wanted to record and remember forever.

'I know it may seem strange now, but it will help, and give you something to remember her by.' The midwife found this part of her job almost as heartbreaking as the bereaved parents, but she knew that those who took nothing away to help them remember their baby often regretted it. Ben nodded and Laura instinctively held the bundle in her arms closer, as the midwife raised the camera to take photos.

'What's her name?' she asked, as she handed the camera back to Ben to check the pictures.

'Poppy,' the name was past Laura's lips before she had time to think. 'Her name is Poppy,' she repeated.

It wasn't a name on their list, it wasn't a name they'd even discussed and rejected, but when Laura looked at her forever still baby, she knew it was right.

'Poppy, that's good,' Ben said, and squeezed Laura's shoulder.

'Shall I take her so we can sort you out?' the midwife asked Laura, reaching out to take Poppy from Laura's arms.

A doctor, neither of them had noticed enter, was already in the room preparing a tray of instruments.

'I'll go and make some phone calls,' Ben leant forward and kissed the top of Laura's head. He had no desire to remain in the room while Laura was 'sorted out' but felt even less enthusiasm for the phone calls he knew he must make. Both sets of parents would be waiting eagerly for news; he wasn't sure he was up to the task but walked out of the room. He would get some fresh air first. As he left, he heard the doctor softly offering Laura his condolences, and Ben's tears finally spilled over and ran down his tired face. He rushed through the nearest outside door and leant against the wall sobbing uncontrollably.

Ben phoned his parents first, then Laura's. They were devastated of course, particularly Laura's mum who could hardly speak. She immediately handed the phone to Laura's dad, who was trying to be strong and practical, but could not quite hide the crack in his voice.

'What can we do to help, Ben?' he asked.

Ben had no idea; what could anyone do? He could hear Laura's mum sobbing in the background, and he just wanted to sink to the floor and make it all go away.

Laura's parents were at Oak Tree Cottage, they had arrived yesterday to stay for a few days to help them settle into a routine with the new baby, but now there was no new baby, so what could they do?

'Don't worry, Ben, we'll ring your parents and discuss what's best,' Laura's dad said.

Ben did not question why, he just agreed, he didn't really care what anyone did at that moment. He couldn't remember what else anyone said as his mind was numb. How could they have gone through all this for nothing? He paced back and forwards in the cold night air, he wasn't even sure what time it was, all he knew was he didn't want to go back into that labour room, he wanted to run, to scream, to turn the clock back and for everything to be different.

'Come out for a breather as well mate?' a man Ben had not noticed was leaning against the wall lighting a cigarette. 'Your first, is it?' he asked, but seemed quite happy not to receive an answer.

Ben looked at him as though he was some sort of alien being.

'First's always the worst,' the man said, blowing smoke up into the air.

Ben watched as the white wisps whirled over his head and randomly wondered if a cigarette would calm his nerves. He had never been a smoker but right now he could see the appeal.

'This is our fourth,' he said. 'Bit of a mistake this one, it's going to be the last that's for sure,' he laughed and ground the half-smoked cigarette under his heel. 'Best get back in, good luck mate,' he turned on his heel and strode back into the unit.

Ben loitered a little longer, then realising that he was freezing cold in just his shirt sleeves, slowly made his way back inside.

The doctor was sitting at a bench typing, presumably in Laura's notes, and the midwife was wiping Laura's face with a flannel and helping her brush her hair. All part of their job he thought, soon they would move on to the next patient and Laura and Ben would just become another sad statistic. He suddenly felt anger well up, he looked around the room and wondered how many babies successfully made their entrance into the world in this utilitarian room, hundreds probably more, he thought it must be quite a production line. So why not theirs, why did their baby have to die? He wanted to shout, demand answers, and shake the over-calm doctor sitting typing up his case notes.

'Ben.'

Laura's voice, barely above a whisper, cut through his thoughts and dissipated his anger in a second.

'Ben,' she said again, reaching out a hand towards him. 'Did you tell them?'

He nodded, going to her side and taking her warm, damp hand in his. He smoothed the hair back from her forehead and kissed her, his anger immediately replaced with love and a fierce need to protect her.

'We'll keep Laura in overnight so that she can see the doctor in the morning,' the midwife said.

It was already late, and Ben felt relieved, he didn't feel up to taking Laura home just yet. He didn't feel up to facing the world.

'The Registrar will be here in the morning, and he and the doctor will be able to explain what happens next.' Ben looked blankly at her, what was there to explain. Their baby was dead. They would go home just the two of them, nothing would be different, but he knew that wasn't true, nothing would ever be the same again. He nodded at the midwife who smiled kindly at him. She didn't say anymore; she recognised

4

the dazed look in Ben's eyes and knew now was not the time to discuss practicalities.

'I'll arrange for a recliner chair to be put in the room so you can stay if you want.'

Again, Ben nodded; he couldn't contemplate leaving Laura alone, and didn't want to be alone himself.

'Thank you,' he whispered in a voice he hardly recognised as his own.

Chapter 2

Over a year earlier

The estate agent smiled to himself; he was beginning to sense when buyers were serious, and this couple was making all the right noises.

'Have a wander round on your own, I'll wait for you in the garden,' Adam said. He would sit and relax for a few minutes while they looked around again, on their own. This house had been on the market much longer than expected, despite the reasonable price, which was substantially lower than a cottage like this should fetch. Cottage was a bit of a misnomer in Adam's eyes, it was actually quite a large house. There was just something about the place; it wasn't through lack of viewings or interest, it was just that buyers seemed to get cold feet and only one, so far, had progressed to making an offer, though this was withdrawn before exchanging contracts. He couldn't put his finger on what it was that stopped it selling; perhaps it was the survey, although he didn't remember any insurmountable problems being discussed, or perhaps it was because it was unlived in. The previous owners moved out a while ago and although there was still some furniture in most of the rooms, the overall atmosphere of the place was desolate and unloved. The house needed laughter and music inside to bring it back to life, Adam thought.

This couple definitely seemed different. He crossed his fingers as he sat in the sun waiting for them. After all, it was a lovely old house, in a good position, with a wonderful big garden; what was not to like? Adam hoped that in time he would own a place like this. He watched the prospective purchasers walk back round to the front of the house. Professionals of some sort he imagined, and not short of money judging by their expensive looking clothes. Expensive but not ostentatious; Adam fancied himself as a bit of a snappy dresser. He smoothed his hands down his well-cut suit, but he could tell that his client's trousers and jacket weren't from any high street store. As for the woman, her understated blue dress, high heels and long wavy blonde hair tumbling over her shoulders made her look like a model. That was the only doubt that marred his certainty about the sale; Adam couldn't quite imagine them fitting into country life. Perhaps it was a second home he thought, and hoped he wasn't going to be disappointed. He settled himself on the garden bench in the sun; closed his eyes and imagined the kudos in the office if he pulled it off, not to mention the commission. He was the newest member of the team and needed a few sales under his belt. This would be a good one.

'Let's look in the little cottage first,' Ben said, slipping an arm around Laura's shoulders as they walked away from Adam, back towards the small separate building set at right angles to the main cottage.

'This will be ideal for me; I can see clients down here and upstairs will make a perfect workroom. It'll need a few changes of course, a cutting table and sewing bench, but it's got the potential to be everything I would want,' Laura was already mentally reorganising the space. 'Look! A small kitchen. That's perfect, and is this a loo?' she asked, opening another door. 'Yes, that's good in fact it couldn't be better. I wonder what it was built for originally.'

'Didn't the agent say a dairy or storeroom or something, but I think it's been altered over the years. Looks like it might have been a granny annex or holiday let recently. Come on let's go back into the big cottage,' Ben said, eager to look around the main building again. They looked into every room in the cottage discussing what it's use would be and how it could be altered to suit their needs.

'This would make a perfect nursery.' Laura stood in the middle of an empty room next to the main bedroom. It smelt a bit musty, but probably because it had not been used for a while. She could imagine the room tastefully decorated, perhaps in a soft grey colour, with pictures or even a mural of farm animals; a chubby baby grinning up from a cot, gurgling with happiness at seeing her.

'I think the agent said that this room was only used for storage before, so it probably needs a good air and clean,' Ben said, looking at the collection of dead flies along the windowsill.

'Well, that's all easy to do,' Laura turned and looked out of the window. 'We'll have to learn how to garden,' she said, suddenly finding the prospect very appealing. 'I'm sure your dad will love to help, and mine of course. Look there's a field beyond,' she said, a vision of a pony grazing drifted into her mind, but she didn't mention it.

Ben joined her at the window.

'It's big, we might even need one of those ride-on mowers.' He had a pleasant vision of himself powering up and down the lawn, creating immaculate stripes on the grass. 'It could be fun.'

'This move feels very grown up all of a sudden, doesn't it?' Laura said.

Ben nodded, he wasn't quite sure if it was a good thing or bad thing, he wanted to have a family, and agreed that being out in the country would be better for family life, but part of him didn't want to give up their high-powered London life. Laura's enthusiasm was infectious, and he knew that there would not be a better time in his career to make a move, and he could easily work from home several days a week. He turned away from the window.

'Let's go and have another look at that room downstairs that could be my office.'

They made their way downstairs, commenting on how

they could update the bathroom, and admiring the tasteful way the previous owners had incorporated the original features into a more modern layout.

'We'd have to pull up this carpet,' Laura said, once they were in the hall. 'Wooden flooring would look good, don't you think?'

Ben nodded but was thinking more about his office. The room he was considering was along a small corridor, beyond the sitting room and down a few stairs. It already appeared to have been used as a study, there was a full range of built-in shelves along one wall, plenty of sockets and a phone line in the corner.

'Yes, this would be good, it's tucked away enough not to be disturbed, or to disturb you. Look, a proper safe! That'll be handy. It needs painting but not much else.'

Working from home regularly would make life much easier for him; at the moment just crossing London from their flat took nearly an hour.

'I'll be across in my own domain,' Laura said. 'It'll be good both of us working from home though. We'll even be able to have lunch together sometimes!'

Ben didn't reply, when he was on a roll, he didn't like stopping for anything, not even food.

'It's a funny shaped room, it's lower than the level of the garden, look.' Laura pointed to where the windowsill was almost at the outside ground level.

'We'll have to get it checked for damp and have a full survey before we commit to it, but it all looks and smells okay, considering no one's lived here for a while.'

Ben ran his hand along the wall under the window to see whether it felt damp, and although no expert he felt fairly satisfied that it didn't.

'I think this is the one, don't you? Can you imagine us living here?' he asked, turning back to Laura.

Laura nodded, her broad smile saying all Ben needed to know.

'Well, I suppose we had better go and find Adam and start the process.'

'I'm so excited; it'll be wonderful!' Laura said, and linked her arm through Ben's. Mentally she was already moving in and compiling a list of new furniture they would need to buy. They went back through the large, farmhouse style kitchen into the sunny garden beyond.

'Yes, it's just what we're looking for,' Ben said to Adam, who wasn't far off falling asleep. 'So, what now?'

'Let's go back to the office then and talk business,' Adam said, resisting the urge to thump his fist in the air. Instead, he calmly led the way back across the lawn and out to his car. The ridiculously low starting offer they put in was, to everyone's surprise, accepted, and their London flat sold quickly at a price far higher than they ever imagined.

Chapter 3

'So, if I can have everyone's attention,' Ben raised his voice slightly, and their friends who were all milling around having pre-dinner drinks stopped and turned towards him.

'I suppose tonight is going to have to double as Laura's and my leaving party; we heard this morning that everything's going through, and all being well, we move to Gloucestershire in just over two weeks.'

'Wow, so quick,' a friend said.

'Here's to you both,' another friend raised his glass.

'Yes, and to many weekends in the country for us all.'

'I'll drink to that,' said Ben, and they all laughed. 'Seriously, I hope you do all come down, it's not that far, a couple of hours outside rush hour, or there are good train links.' He felt a twinge of anxiety, he saw these people nearly every week, sometimes more, and they knew no-one where they were going. Ben loved this sleek, open plan flat, and he viewed the countryside as a playground, somewhere you went for weekends, not the real world. Laura was the one who pushed for the move; she came from Devon and hankered after fresh air and open spaces.

'Try keeping us away,' Anya, one of Laura's closest friends, said.

'We're ready to eat, come and sit down,' Laura called, as she placed another steaming dish on the already laden table. Delicious smells wafted around the room, and everyone rushed to sit down, suddenly hungry. Conversation around the table focused on the move, details about the house, the village, the actual distance from London, and inevitably the price and how much they got for the flat.

'I thought for a moment Ben was going to announce you were pregnant,' Anya whispered.

'Hopefully that comes next,' Laura whispered back. 'Once I've got my business set up.'

'Your workshop sounds amazing,' Mira, another friend joined in. 'Have you told Vicky you're leaving yet?'

'Yes of course, she's been really supportive advising me what equipment to buy and even said she'd recommend me to clients; she has contacts everywhere.'

'Aren't you nervous setting up on your own, you've worked with her since uni, haven't you?' Mira asked.

'I am a bit, but now feels like the right time, and Vicky's been encouraging me to do this for years, everything I know about dress design, cutting, sewing and marketing I've learnt from her.'

'You'll be fine, it's a fantastic opportunity,' said Anya. 'I bet you'll have clients queuing up in no time.'

'Have you got a name yet? What about Laura's Luxurious Dresses?' another friend leant across the table with a flourish.

There was a collective groan from those now involved in the conversation.

'That's awful Sam, no I'm still thinking,' Laura replied, and they spent several minutes thinking up possible names for Laura's business, which became more and more bizarre, and all were rejected.

Ben stood in the doorway, on his way back from opening another bottle of wine and surveyed the scene. Conversation and laughter flowing as freely as the wine, he really hoped they were doing the right thing.

The following couple of weeks passed by in a whirl of sorting, packing and all the last-minute tasks moving to a new house required. Although busy, Ben continued to have occasional doubts, but he never mentioned them to Laura, and they soon passed in the bustle of the move. In any case, he thought, they could always come back if it didn't work; he would keep a contingency fund until they were settled. Laura on the other hand was in her element; she almost seemed to relish the dismantling of their first home together. She talked constantly about what would go where and which things should be thrown away. Ben lost count of the number of times she told him how excited she was, and to a small extent her enthusiasm did begin to rub off on him. So that by the time the moving day came he felt less regret and more anticipation about beginning their new lives. Now the flat was empty it no longer felt like home, and he was ready to move on.

Almost before they could draw breath, they were there, sitting on packing crates in their new kitchen. The removal men had speedily emptied the van of their belongings, which seemed very sparse in the many rooms of the cottage, compared to their small but elegant flat. Ben opened a bottle of champagne, given to them by Anya before they left.

'To us, to our new home and new future,' he said, and they clinked mugs, champagne glasses being packed away in one of the many boxes.

'To us,' Laura replied. 'Sacrilege drinking this from a mug!' she said looking at the expensive label. 'Still tastes good though, I won't tell Anya.' She drained her mug and held it out for more.

As soon as the boxes were unpacked Laura wasted no time in consulting builders, and work soon started to bring the little house, as Laura now called it, up to scratch for a high-class dress designer's workshop. She oversaw most of the work herself, to the irritation of the builders, but she knew exactly what she wanted, and it had to be right. She also worked on her website and became totally immersed in all the details of setting up her business, and soon clients began to make contact.

In between work and at weekends, Ben and Laura spent

many enjoyable hours scouring shops and auction rooms for pieces of furniture to complement the age and quirkiness of the cottage, and before long it reflected their taste and style. Ben's anxieties waned as he settled into country life and realised he really could travel into central London in a couple of hours if necessary. Already, on his visits, he found the city noisy and dirty and preferred to work in his office at home.

The cottage really began to feel like home once their friends started to visit, and their plans were starting to fall into place.

'What did you think?' Stephen asked Anya, after he closed the car window and they continued to wave goodbye to Laura and Ben. They were both exhausted after spending a delightful weekend with them at Oak Tree Cottage.

'About the cottage, the countryside or Laura being pregnant?' Anya asked, blowing Laura a kiss.

'All of it really,' Stephen replied.

'Well, I wasn't surprised when they told us they were having a baby, although it was quicker than I expected. It's all such a big change for them,' Anya said, sounding less than enthusiastic.

'I guess we're all getting to that age,' Stephen gave a sidelong glance to gauge Anya's reaction.

She sat quietly looking straight ahead for a while. Having children was always something she had assumed would happen in the future, but the future always seemed some way off.

'So that's Alice and Jon moved out of London, and Bethany and Will have their place on the market,' Stephen said.

'But Laura's the first to get pregnant.'

'What about Carol and Luke they've got a baby?'

'Yes, but they aren't really close friends are they, and they already had the baby when we met them. So, Laura and Ben are the first of our close friends to be pregnant.' She rummaged in her bag for her lipstick.

Stephen didn't answer, he smiled to himself, he knew the

idea was now planted in Anya's mind; he would let it grow for a while before mentioning it again. He had surprised himself with the sharp pang of envy he felt when Laura and Ben told them about the pregnancy. He could visualise himself and Anya moving into this sort of lifestyle, of course they'd been lucky this weekend with glorious weather bathing everything in sunshine and showing the countryside off at its best. He mused as he drove, Ben's job was more flexible than his and Laura worked for herself, which made moving out of the city easier, but there were plenty of nice places within commuting distance that he and Anya could consider, in time.

'I wasn't sure about the cottage,' Anya said, after a few moments of quietness.

'No? I thought it was great, so old but with everything you need, full of character, and so much space compared to where we are.'

'Yes, I know, and they've made it beautiful, of course, but I think I prefer more modern houses. I don't know there was just something about it, I couldn't feel relaxed there,' Anya said.

'It's because you're used to London with all the noise and bright lights. Didn't you think the stars were incredible, with no streetlights around? If I were Ben, I'd buy a telescope.'

'Yes, that was good, but I still don't think I could live there. Laura's workshop was amazing though, it looked like a perfect cottage in miniature, she must have spent a fortune kitting it out,' Anya paused. 'If we did move out of London, I wouldn't want to be so remote, I'd still have to go to work.'

Stephen reached for her hand.

'We could think about it, we could explore some areas within a commuting-distance, but there's no rush,' he said.

They spoke very little on the rest of their journey, both deep in thought about the possibilities ahead. It felt as though a gear had changed and they were slowly moving in a different direction, hopefully both in the same direction, thought Stephen.

Chapter 4

Home after the stillbirth

Laura woke, not suddenly it was a gentle awakening in her own bed, she was warm but felt strangely uncomfortable when she moved, and then she remembered. The baby, her baby, their baby, was dead. They had come home without her. She wasn't a mother. They had left for the hospital, as a couple and returned as a couple, not a family, not with the baby whose arrival they so eagerly anticipated. Was it only a couple of days ago? It felt like another lifetime. Laura didn't move position; she lay rigid, numb and empty. Her stomach contracted into a tight knot, and her heart felt as though it would burst with pain. She couldn't imagine how life could ever go on; everything had changed; yet nothing had changed.

Slowly, Laura became conscious of a strange feeling in her breasts, a sort of hot tingling sensation. She put her hand up to touch them. They were hard solid spheres on her chest. Not the soft warm mounds with which she was familiar. She tentatively sat up and swung her legs over the bed; Ben stirred but didn't wake. Without bothering to put on her slippers or think about what she was doing, Laura walked along the landing and was unconsciously drawn into the room that was supposed to be the nursery. This was the first time she'd entered the room since leaving the house, in labour, full of nervous excitement. It was a nursery no longer, now it was just an almost empty room. The shock of the room's bleakness felt like a slap in the face. Ben's parents, and hers, must have sprung into action almost immediately and thought it best to remove the cot, the toys, and the drawers full of baby grows and tiny socks, before she came home from hospital. She didn't want to be ungrateful, but she wished they hadn't, it didn't feel like the right thing to do and anger began to bubble up. She wanted to hold those carefully chosen baby clothes to her chest, to smell the newness and hope that was in each garment. She wanted to caress the soft teddy and pink rabbit, specially chosen for its long floppy ears.

Much as she loved her parents and Ben's, of course, Laura was relieved when earlier in the day they all decided to go back home. She wanted to be alone with Ben, to not have to talk, or smile, or feel weighed down by anxious expressions, or excess fussing, mainly on the part of her own mother. Laura sank into the small green velour, buttoned back, nursing chair that stood alone next to the fireplace, why that particular item was left she didn't know. She looked around the walls; they were still papered in the nursery mural she and Ben took so much care to put up. At least they didn't take that down, she thought.

Laura must have dozed because she was jolted into consciousness by what felt like a sharp tugging on her breast. Momentarily confused about where she was, she reached out a hand for Ben and then realised she wasn't in bed, she was in the nursery. She felt the tugging again, it was strong and almost painful, she looked down, her nightie was soaked. She tugged it away from her body, milk was pouring, no, spurting, from her breast, she went to stand up but didn't have the strength. The tugging sensation on her nipple intensified. Laura tried but couldn't do anything to stop it. Then without warning she felt as though she was being held back in the chair and something was being dragged away from her.

'No, stop,' she shouted. 'Leave me alone.' A feeling, the like of which she had never before experienced, coursed through her body.

'Laura, darling, what is it?' Ben flung the door open and

17

pulled Laura out of the chair into his arms and held her tight. Her sobs racked against his body, and he could feel the warm milk seeping through his pyjama top.

'You're freezing, how long have you been in here?' he asked, rubbing her arms to bring some warmth to them. The room was exceptionally cold, as well, Ben noted; there must be a draught coming through the window.

'Come on let me run you a warm bath.' Ben led Laura, who's slowly subsiding sobs were replaced by violent shaking, out of the room.

'I don't know, I don't know,' was all she could repeat when Ben asked her what she was shouting about.

Sometime later he tucked her, warmer, calmer, but exhausted, back into bed and climbed in beside her. Luckily, she slept. Ben tried to sleep but gave up and made a poor attempt to read a book. Concentration eluded him, and his eyes travelled over the same line, uncomprehendingly, time and again. He watched Laura sleeping and he too wondered how they would pick themselves up from losing their baby. It was not anything he ever contemplated could happen. Becoming a parent was scary enough but now not becoming one seemed even more daunting. He waited for the hands of the clock to move, as if in slow motion, around the dial until they reached a respectable time. Then he went downstairs and rang the community midwife, relief washed over him just at the sound of her calm, reassuring voice.

'I'll be with you in about an hour,' she said.

Ben was up, showered and downstairs before Laura awoke, and was trying to decide what to have for breakfast. He wasn't really hungry and was sure Laura would refuse all offers of food. Then, after a quick tap on the backdoor, Sister Calman, Rosa, stepped into the room. She was a short, stout woman, probably in her early sixties, with a pleasant, kindly face. Her blue uniform pulled tightly across her chest; she didn't see the point of ordering more dresses, as retirement was just around the corner, and it would be a waste of money.

18

'I think Laura's still asleep,' Ben said, before even greeting her.

'That's probably a good thing,' she said, pulling out a chair and sitting down, noticing Ben's anxious expression. He stood in the middle of the kitchen and Rosa thought he looked so young and lost.

'Tell me about the night,' she said.

Ben explained as best he could, but really, he had no idea what happened, she would have to ask Laura. Rosa nodded and accepted the offer of coffee.

'I was thinking about taking Laura on a holiday. Some time away, somewhere different, I think it would do her good, somewhere warm. Adult only of course, what do you think, when is she ok to fly?' Ben realised he was gabbling but couldn't stop himself.

Rosa smiled gently at him. She understood the pain he was going through. Over the years as a midwife she had seen, thankfully not too many, but enough young couples in Ben and Laura's situation to recognise his helplessness and confusion. In a way she was pleased he was showing some emotion, as on her previous visit he was hiding behind the mask of the strong man, probably for Laura's sake, but he needed to let down his guard, let himself feel.

'I think a holiday sounds a good idea for both of you, perhaps in a few weeks, don't rush,' she said. 'Don't forget you've lost a baby as well, Ben; you need to give yourself time to grieve, time to think.'

Ben nodded, and to his horror burst into tears. Rosa stood up and gave him a hug. He sobbed into her shoulder, relishing the warmth and comfort of her support. She reminded him of when his granny would take him into her arms to soothe a cut knee or other childish trauma; he didn't want to let go, but after a minute or so, feeling slightly embarrassed, he pulled away and sat down.

'I don't know where I'm going any more, I don't feel in control, everything feels different.' Ben buried his head in his hands and silent sobs shook his shoulders.

'Think of it a bit like a train journey,' Rosa said, sitting next to him touching his arm.

'You were full steam ahead towards the parent platform, but just before you got there someone changed the points and now you've gone careering off into a dark tunnel. You can't see the end, so don't know how long it will take to get through, but you will get through, there will be light again. There may well be more tunnels, and bridges in the future, but this is the longest. Laura's on the same journey but not necessarily on the same train, so her journey may be completely different to yours, but the destination is the same.'

Ben raised his head and looked into her kind wise eyes. He would have laughed at such a clichéd analogy a few weeks ago, but somehow now, in his current position it made perfect sense.

'Yes, I get that,' he said.

He was so pleased it was Rosa looking after Laura and not the dolly-bird midwife who also worked with their doctor. The young midwife was good and fun, but somehow Ben felt she wouldn't have quite the same empathy as Rosa.

'Thank you,' he smiled, and Rosa smiled back.

'I'll go up and find Laura, if that's all right?' she stood up and made her way to the door. Ben nodded.

'She's in our room,' he said. 'I'll put the kettle on for when you come down.'

Rosa nodded, not letting on that she was busy and needed to get on to her next patient. This couple needed her now, so they were her priority. She stood up and straightened her uniform over her hips, patted Ben on the arm and left the kitchen to find Laura. Ben leant against the worktop and let out a long sigh, willingly handing over responsibility for Laura to Rosa, even if it was only for a few minutes.

After about twenty minutes Rosa came downstairs, followed by a pale, tired looking Laura. Ben put mugs of tea and a plate of toast on the table and they all sat down.

'Tell me about your baby, what did you call her?' Rosa

asked. On her first visit there were too many family members fluttering around for Rosa to talk to Ben and Laura properly. Ben took a sharp intake of breath; he wasn't sure this was a good topic for Laura in her present state but was surprised when she became quite animated and described little Poppy in more detail than Ben remembered.

'Have you got a photo of her?' Rosa asked.

'Yes, it's on the camera, Ben can you get it? I thought the midwife was being cruel when she asked if we wanted a photo of her.'

Ben took the camera from the dresser; he'd put it there out of sight when they returned from the hospital and hadn't looked at the photo since.

'She's beautiful. You could get one printed,' Rosa suggested. 'She will always be your first daughter, no matter how many children you go on to have in the future.'

'She was perfect,' Laura looked at the photo. 'Do you think it could happen again?'

Rosa looked at the two anxious faces turned in her direction, desperate for her to reassure them that everything would be all right next time. She was almost certain it would be, but she could never be sure.

'It's very unlikely. Once they know why Poppy died, the doctors will be able to advise you. Do you have an appointment?'

Laura shook her head.

'It should be in about six weeks, let me know if you haven't heard in a couple of weeks and I'll chase it up. Now, I really must go, but I'll pop in tomorrow to see how things are going.'

'Thank you, see you tomorrow,' Ben said, getting to his feet to see her out.

'How are you feeling?' he asked Laura, once Rosa was on her way.

'OK, not too bad. Rosa's advised me what to do to stop the milk coming. I don't know what it was, in the night I mean, it really felt like a baby, you know sucking?'

Ben nodded, and put his arms round Laura, he really had no idea what she meant, but assumed it must be some natural response of her body. Not for the first time he felt grateful to be a man.

'I'm sure it'll get better soon,' he said.

'Yes, once my body realises there's no …' Laura couldn't continue, she was overwhelmed by the emptiness, the sadness, and most of all the unfairness of their situation. She didn't cry, but her haunted, confused expression nearly broke Ben's heart. He didn't know what to say so just hugged her and hoped that they would both soon come out of the tunnel Rosa described.

Life carried on, what else could it do? Rosa continued to visit, and Ben in particular, found her visits a great relief. However, her visits couldn't go on forever and all too soon they were left to cope on their own. They were coping, at least superficially. Ben was trying to work and found he could forget for long stretches of time, while his head was immersed in spreadsheets and contracts. Laura, on the other hand, showed no interest in anything, it was early days, of course, but Ben grew concerned. Laura became irritated if he suggested she should try to focus on something, anything. For a while they existed in an uneasy vacuum. At last, the day came for their appointment at the hospital, when they would find out, hopefully, why Poppy had died, and more importantly how they could prevent it happening again. Laura made an effort with her hair and make up for the appointment and looked like the confident, composed woman she always used to be. Her iron grip on Ben's hand belied her outward appearance. Ben was feeling equally nervous, he felt out of his comfort zone in the world of hospitals and doctors.

The news was positive, as positive as it could be without being one hundred percent certain. The doctor a tall thin man in his fifties, told them that Poppy's death was caused by a true knot in the umbilical cord. The knot would have pulled tight during labour cutting off her oxygen supply. He explained that this was a rare condition and very, very unlikely to ever happen again. It was one of those unfortunate but highly unusual twists of fate. He reassured them that next time they would keep a very close eye on everything, and possibly deliver the baby by caesarean section. Laura's previous conviction that only a natural birth would do seemed forgotten, and she readily agreed that a future caesarean would be desirable.

They returned home, Ben trying his best to be upbeat and convince Laura that it was good news and, when it felt right, they would be able to have another baby. Laura didn't speak much, about anything. Days passed and Laura still did nothing she either drifted around the house or sat quietly lost in thought.

Ben struggled to understand what she was feeling and fought the urge to tell her to snap out of it. How could he help if she wouldn't speak, after all it was the best outcome they could have hoped for.

'Talk to me,' he said. One afternoon when Laura sat down at the kitchen table. 'I need to know what you're thinking.'

The silence hung between them.

'It was such a waste,' she said. 'So pointless and unnecessary, why did it have to happen to us? It happened once out of the blue, so who's to say it won't again - out of the blue?' Laura put her hands over her face and sobbed.

'Laura, please, don't.' Ben sat beside her and encircled her with his arms, but in a way, he was pleased, surely crying was better than blank quietness.

'You heard what the doctor said, it's very unlikely to happen again and he said they probably won't let you go into labour next time, just to make certain.'

'It doesn't help,' she said. 'I can't go through nine months again, for nothing. What if there's something about me or something I did that made it happen?' Laura stopped crying and turned to look at Ben with her tired eyes, bloodshot and rimmed with red.

'It won't be for nothing, next time it won't be for nothing.

I'm sure, from what the doctor said it was just a fluke. They'll keep a closer eye on things,' he said and hugged her close.

He hoped that he was right. He trusted the doctors; when they said they would make sure it didn't happen again. He wasn't sure how he would cope himself, if it did.

'Come on let's make something to eat, I'm starving.'

'I'm not really hungry,' Laura said.

But Ben was already on his feet opening the fridge to see what could be rustled up, and Laura quickly realised she was hungry as soon as the irresistible smell of toast and frying bacon filled the kitchen.

Chapter 5

Laura looked blankly at the young woman with a baby in a sling, standing on the doorstep. She looked vaguely familiar and for one mad moment Laura thought there must have been a mistake, and this woman was bringing her own baby back.

'Hi Laura. I hope you don't mind me calling,' the woman smiled, and instinctively placed a protective hand on her baby's back.

Laura looked at the short, not unattractive, woman who was standing on her doorstep smiling at her. Laura trawled through her memory trying to remember where she had seen her before. She looked at the woman again, she wore her hair scraped back in a clip, her nose was pierced, and both her ears were adorned with an interesting array of earrings. Of course, she did recognise her, but the last time Laura saw the woman they were both pregnant. Andrea, that was her name, Laura stared at her in confusion, why was Andrea standing at her door, holding a healthy baby?

'Andrea, I'm so sorry, I almost didn't recognise you,' Laura didn't move from the door, her hand clenched around the inner handle. She wasn't sure she was ready to be sociable and she didn't really know Andrea, and she certainly didn't want to see someone else's baby. Why was she here?

'I um, I hope you don't mind, but I wanted to come and see you. I expect all the others have been already, but…'

'No, no one's been, no one's been in touch,' Laura said. 'I suppose it's, well you know,' she shrugged. Andrea nodded.

'I wasn't sure, whether I should come, say if you'd prefer me to go.'

Laura gritted her teeth and managed to regain some composure.

'I'm glad you did, come in. Sorry, please come in,' she attempted a smile and pulled the door open wide, stepping aside to let Andrea pass.

'I didn't want to write or just ring,' Andrea said, following Laura into the kitchen. 'I wanted to come and see you and tell you in person how sorry I was when I heard your baby had died. I know there was a risk you would be out, but it's a nice day and I felt like a change of scene anyway.'

'Thank you, that's very kind. Sit down, would you like a coffee?' Laura felt genuinely touched but was suddenly uncertain how to behave. She watched Andrea unclip the sling and settle the still sleeping baby on the small sofa.

Laura became acutely conscious that no one else from the ante natal group had been in touch, it never really occurred to her before that it was odd, in fact she could barely remember them, they seemed to belong in another world. Although at the time there were a couple of women who she thought would become good friends. They had spoken of doing things together, outings with their babies, at the time it all seemed so natural and there was never any question, that for all of them, it wouldn't be as they planned. They must know what had happened to her if Andrea knew. She imagined them going around to each other's houses, sharing experiences, all without her. In their eyes Laura supposed she must seem like a failure. She looked at Andrea and again was surprised that out of all of them it was her who made the effort.

Andrea was a single mum, and at the time Laura thought of her as a bit rough and ready. She remembered that Andrea always kept herself a little apart from the rest of the antenatal group, who were all married, middle class yummy mummies, as Ben called them, and if she was honest, she was happy to be one of them. Mind you, Andrea was always ready with her opinion, and Laura remembered her hooting with laughter when they were discussing booking an appointment in the best shop in town to go and try out prams. Laura could hardly believe now how long she and Ben spent wheeling different prams around the shop, working out which configuration of car seat, pram body and wheels would best suit their lifestyle, not to mention getting the colour right. It all seemed faintly absurd to her now, what did it matter, the baby wouldn't care, they were just showing off to each other. Good for Andrea for not getting involved she thought. Laura glanced at Andrea as she filled the kettle; she could barely remember speaking to her during the classes, they didn't have much in common, but here she was, and a lump came to Laura's throat as she busied herself making coffee. She mustn't cry she told herself she must be in control.

Andrea in turn watched Laura as she pulled mugs from one cupboard and took a jug of milk from the impressive American style fridge. The kitchen looked like the sort you saw in magazines, certainly nothing like Andrea's kitchen. Laura still looked beautiful she thought, but in a pale tragic sort of way, her fair hair had less of a shine, and she wore no make-up, but then she wasn't expecting visitors. Even though she was dressed in jogging bottoms and a loose shirt she still managed to look elegant, the bonus of being tall and slim Andrea assumed. Elegance was something Andrea felt always eluded her, even at her most dressed up; still there was more to life than looking elegant. She was happy with her own style and with her lot in life, she looked at her baby and was thankful.

'So how are you, who's this little one?' Laura asked, placing a cup of coffee in front of Andrea, and looking at the little bundle that was just beginning to stir.

'This is Ralph. I named him after my granddad.' Andrea lifted the baby up and unswaddled him from his blankets.

'Do you want to hold him?' Andrea asked, in such a way that Laura knew she wouldn't be offended if she said no, but she held her arms out and Andrea passed him over.

Andrea struggled out of her rather unusual blue woollen coat; in fact, her complete outfit was interesting Laura noticed, a short plain pale brown dress over a collarless floral blouse, black tights ending in purple Doc Martin boots that were left half unlaced. Not the sort of thing Laura would ever dream of wearing, but on Andrea it somehow worked. Laura turned her attention back to Ralph, he was warm and pink, and his little mouth puckered and sucked, still half asleep. Laura put the tip of her finger to his mouth and he instinctively started to suck, the beauty of him captivated her, his utter dependence and vulnerability transfixed her, then without warning a wave of despair and unexpected jealousy swept over her. She grasped the back of the sofa and took several deep breaths.

'Are you ok?' Andrea asked, turning to touch Laura's hand. 'Shall I take him?'

'Yes, fine,' she turned away abruptly, trying to stifle an overwhelming urge to rush out of the room and keep Ralph for herself. She could imagine his soft skin next to hers, his eyes looking into her eyes with the relief of recognition that babies save for their mothers. Why should Andrea have that and not her? Suddenly she was sobbing, great gasping gulps of agony.

'It's not fair,' she got out between gasps. 'It's just not fair.'

Andrea gently took Ralph from Laura and laid him back on the sofa, before encircling Laura with her arms. Andrea said nothing, what could she say? She wasn't clever with words, so she just held Laura gently stroking her back.

Laura, whose initial instinct was to shrug Andrea off, eventually relaxed as her kindness and empathy radiated through Laura's body to calm her. Eventually she disentangled herself, blew her nose and flopped exhausted into a nearby chair.

'I'm so sorry, I don't want to make you feel bad, it's just there's, well it's like a gaping hole inside me and I feel so miserable, and such a failure. Everywhere I look; everywhere I go; all I see and hear about are babies, on the TV, in the papers, in magazines. It's as though everyone's got one except me,' Laura said.

Andrea felt tears welling in her own eyes and her heart went out to Laura who looked utterly broken. She wondered if Laura was going to cry again, but she didn't, instead a weak smile crossed her face.

'Sorry, I'm so sorry,' Laura said again.

'Don't be sorry, please. I wasn't sure whether seeing Ralph would upset you. I didn't want to flaunt him,' Andrea said.

As if on cue, Ralph interrupted them with an impatient yell.

'No, it's ok. I'm fine, really. I can't avoid babies forever,' Laura said, but wished she could.

'He's probably hungry I'll give him his bottle.' Andrea busied herself in her large bag, she eventually pulled out a ready-made bottle of formula, and without any fuss scooped Ralph up and offered the bottle to his greedy mouth.

'He's got such a strong suck; I did start feeding him myself but needed to put him on the bottle so I could go back to work. I'm sure Annabelle would be horrified.'

'Yes, I'm sure she would be, you'd be drummed out of the class for letting the side down,' Laura said, and Andrea gave a characteristic hoot of laughter.

'Remember she wouldn't even show us how to make up a bottle when I asked her to?'

'Yes, but you have to do what's best for you. I think she was over idealistic,' Laura said, feeling very relieved that Andrea wasn't actually breast feeding, she wasn't sure she would have coped watching her, her own breasts tingled at the very thought of it.

'It must be hard going back to work so soon,' Laura said, as she watched Andrea expertly wind Ralph, his little head lolling as if he was drunk.

Andrea shrugged.

'It's only part time and my mum has offered to look after

him, I'm lucky really it's all worked out so well,' she smiled.

'What do you do, for work I mean?' Laura asked.

'I'm a mechanic,' Andrea said, watching for Laura's reaction, which was the open-mouthed surprise she expected.

'No, really; how fascinating, what sort of mechanic?'

'A car mechanic,' Andrea said, and laughed.

'How did you get into that? I'm sure when I was at school it was only boys that were considered for anything remotely like that.'

'Well, it wasn't anything to do with school, it's a long story really,' Andrea looked up to gauge whether she should say more and seeing Laura's interested expression and relaxed posture she began.

'When I was ten my mum had an accident, well not really an accident my dad beat her up and she fell down the stairs breaking her leg.'

Laura gasped, but Andrea carried on almost as though she was talking to herself, and once started couldn't stop.

'It was late at night; I was supposed to be in bed, but I got up when I heard him. shouting, yelling abuse. I'm not sure what really happened I think dad was drunk, he usually was. I always liked it when he went out and it was just mum and me, we could relax, but I always listened and crept out of bed when he came home, to make sure mum was ok. He often hit her, or shouted that she was spending all his money, and saying other vile things that at the time I didn't understand. That night he seemed worse than usual, and things got more heated, I don't remember if anyone else was there, but suddenly there were police and ambulance people everywhere and dad was gone. He disappeared before they arrived. I don't even remember who called the ambulance, it might have been dad, but I'm sure he didn't even stop to see if mum was badly hurt, or alive come to that. I've never seen him since.'

'What happened to you?' Laura tried but couldn't mask the look of horrified sympathy on her face, but Andrea didn't seem to notice as she continued talking.

30

'A neighbour took me in that night, then there was talk of me going into a children's home until mum got better, but I've got a half-brother who's about ten years older than me, and he said he'd look after me. I vaguely remember a lot of discussion about it, but in the end they, Social Services I suppose they were, agreed that Billy could move into our flat until mum came home. I don't suppose they'd allow that now. He was a mechanic, and I would go to the garage after school and at weekends, and Billy and the other blokes would show me what they were doing and sometimes set me a task, to see if I could mend something. I loved it there. They all made a fuss of me; it was such a happy place. The blokes were always laughing and singing. I even loved the grease and the smell of the place. It was like a refuge, so when mum was better, which took weeks, I kept going around to the garage. I learnt so much just watching and messing about with bits and pieces, so that when I was sixteen, they asked if I wanted to be an apprentice. I jumped at it, left school and when I qualified, they took me on fulltime. I wasn't sure they'd want me back after Ralph was born, especially part time but I've been lucky, and they've been great.'

'Wow, that's some story. Did your mum ever see your dad again?' Laura asked, trying to imagine the situation.

'I don't know, I don't think so, mum eventually divorced him. Billy said once he'd heard dad went abroad, working on building sites or something. I don't care, he could be dead as far as I'm concerned.'

Laura now looked at Andrea with a mixture of sympathy and admiration; her life was way outside of the sphere of her own experience. It made her middle-class upbringing of ballet classes, brownies, and grammar school seem very staid and boring. Laura could hardly remember her parents shouting, the occasional strained conversation behind closed doors, but nothing to ruffle the peace of her childhood. Everything was always very civilized and proper.

'What about you, do you work?' Andrea asked.

'I'm a dressmaker, very girly compared to you,' Laura said.

'What sort of dresses?'

'Wedding dresses mainly and that sort of thing.'

'Designer stuff?'

'Well, I suppose so, that's what some people call it anyway,' Laura didn't want to appear too self-important.

'I do a bit of sewing, out of necessity really, nothing fancy,' Andrea said.

'Do you?' Andrea again surprised Laura. 'What sort of things have you made?'

Andrea ran her hands over her dress. 'This, and my coat,' she said.

Laura looked closely, and she hoped discreetly at Andrea's dress, it was actually beautifully made. Andrea clearly was talented.

'Not exactly designer, but I made up the pattern myself,' Andrea said.

'I'm impressed,' said Laura, and she meant it.

'Did you teach yourself?' Andrea asked.

'No, I went to college and studied art and design, and then I worked in London for one of the big designers, where I learnt more in a few months than I did in three years at college. I started doing some of my own designs a couple of years ago. I work from here now, but still do some work for my friend in London, although I haven't taken any new orders for myself for a few months because I, well I…' Laura trailed off unable to finish.

Andrea nodded, of course Laura was probably planning a long spell of maternity leave, not like her having to rush back after a couple of months.

'Did you get to see or hold your baby?' Andrea asked, keeping her fingers crossed and hoping that her question wouldn't upset Laura again.

Laura hesitated, but a feeling of relief washed over her, and she was soon telling Andrea all about her labour and the shock and despair she felt when the midwife told her the baby was dead. They even swapped labour stories and experiences, both agreeing it was nothing like they had expected, from the rapturous accounts given by Annabelle in the antenatal classes.

'I think she must have been high on something other than gas and air, when she gave birth,' Andrea laughed, and Laura agreed.

'What sex was your baby?'

'It was a girl,' Laura said. 'She was a girl,' she corrected herself. 'We called her Poppy. Would you like to see a photo of her?'

Andrea nodded.

'Yes please,' she felt a moment of anxiety, she'd never seen a dead baby before, well she'd never seen a dead person before, and wasn't sure what to expect. She arranged her features into what she hoped were an appropriate expression; the last thing she wanted was to look shocked. Andrea instinctively rocked her own warm, very much alive, baby in her arms, while Laura picked up a small photo from the dresser and handed it to her.

'She looks beautiful,' Andrea said, with an element of relief that she was able to be truthful. 'She just looks like she's sleeping. Do you know…'

'Yes, she was perfect. She died because of a true knot in the cord, rare and unlikely to happen again,' Laura said, looking at the photo over Andrea's shoulder. 'Thank you for asking Andrea, most people just avoid mentioning her, sometimes it feels as though she didn't exist.'

'I suppose people don't want to upset you. I didn't want to upset you.'

'I'm glad you did, I need to talk about her to remember she was real,' Laura said.

Andrea inclined her head towards the front of the house where a car could be heard pulling up on the gravel drive.

'Is that your husband coming home?'

'Probably. He works from home most of the time, but he needed to go to meet a colleague today.'

'Well, I suppose we'd better be going anyway,' Andrea said, and started to gather her things together.

'You don't need to rush off just because Ben's coming in,' Laura said. 'He'll be pleased to meet you.'

'I do need to get going now, or I'll miss the bus.'

Laura watched as Andrea expertly placed Ralph into his sling and hitched him onto her front.

'You will visit again, won't you? Come for lunch next time.'

'Yes, that would be lovely.'

'Hi, I'm home.' The front door banged closed and with a couple of long strides Ben appeared in the kitchen.

'Do you remember Andrea from the antenatal classes?'

'Oh, yes, Andrea, hi,' Ben looked questioningly towards Laura.

'Andrea came to see how I was.'

'That's kind of you,' Ben smiled towards Andrea, putting a protective arm around Laura's shoulders.

'I really must dash, I don't want to miss the bus,' Andrea said and moved towards the door.

'I could give you a lift if you like,' Ben offered.

'No really, the bus is fine, it's really easy from here.'

'Is it?' Laura wasn't even sure she knew where the bus stopped.

'Yes, it's only about twenty minutes. I've got an old car, but the baby seat isn't properly fixed yet, so next time I should be able to drive over.'

'Thank you so much for coming, I'll ring you soon,' Laura gave Andrea and Ralph a hug.

'Bye see you soon. Bye Ben.'

They both chorused their goodbyes and the door closed behind her.

'That was nice of her. Wasn't it?' Ben asked, hoping desperately that the visit from the odd one from antenatal classes hadn't succeeded in disturbing Laura even more than she was.

'Yes, she's quite a character,' said Laura. 'She's a motor mechanic and she can sew. It was really good to see her.'

'That's different. Did she come out on the bus just to visit?'

'Yes. I didn't realise she'd come on the bus. It was nice of her. I liked her, I'll definitely keep in touch.'

Ben smiled to himself as he took off his jacket.

'You'll be waiting a long time.'

A young man's voice, coming from behind the steering wheel of an old Jeep, made Andrea jump. She turned around and peered through the window at the grinning face of a good-looking dark-haired man about her own age, perhaps a bit older.

'I know,' Andrea said. 'I didn't realise they ran so infrequently.'

'Infrequently? Buses around here are like hen's teeth; I doubt the next one is before tomorrow. Can I give you a lift somewhere?' he asked, leaning over to open the door.

Andrea hesitated, but really what choice did she have? She didn't want to go back to ask Ben for a lift, although that was probably the sensible thing to do.

'Well, if you could just give me a lift to the main road, where I can catch a bus, that would be great.' Andrea hesitated again, wrapping her arms around Ralph. 'Perhaps I better get in the back, with him,' she said, nodding towards Ralph.

'The back's full of junk, I'm afraid,' he said.

Andrea looked and could see, several boxes, piles of papers and a black bag, full to almost bursting. He was right, there was no way she could sit in the back.

'Come on hop in. I promise I'll drive very carefully. All that stuff's heading to the tip in the morning,' he said, and patted the front seat. After hesitating again, Andrea climbed in and fastened the seat belt around both her and Ralph. Ralph opened his eyes momentarily, before closing them tight and snuggling into the folds of Andrea's coat.

'How old's the little one? My name's Adam by the way,' Adam said, holding out his hand.

'I'm Andrea, and this is Ralph he's just over eight weeks,' she replied.

'Where are you actually going?' Adam asked, as they reached the main road. 'I don't like the thought of the pair of you hanging around on a bus stop for who knows how long, and I've got nothing pressing to do.'

Andrea looked at him, she wasn't used to such gallantry and felt slightly suspicious, but his warm smile and easy charm made her feel she could trust him.

'The Greenville estate,' Andrea said, watching for his reaction.

The Greenville was a notorious council estate, normally out of bounds for people like Adam, Laura and Ben. It was the only place Andrea had ever lived and she didn't think it was too bad, not when you knew it and knew the people. Some idiots of course, but mostly just people trying hard to get through life as best they could. Adam just nodded, no look of shock or apprehension passed his face, making Andrea wonder if he really knew the estate.

'That's good, it's this side of town, but not that straightforward to get to on the bus from here, I wouldn't think.'

'It wasn't that bad coming out, but I didn't really check the times for going back.' Andrea said. 'There's probably not much call for buses between here and there.' Adam laughed; he knew the estate by reputation, but was prepared to be open minded, besides it couldn't be that bad if someone like Andrea lived there. She was so different to the usual girls he mixed with, unusually attractive and totally devoid of airs and graces.

They chatted easily for the whole of the short journey. Andrea asked to be dropped by the shops, for the first time feeling embarrassed about the blocks of flats and preferred to leave it vague as to where on the estate she actually lived.

'Thank you so much,' she said, just as Ralph gave a little squawk and started to wriggle.

'My pleasure,' Adam replied, and his smile indicated he

was being genuine. 'I hope we meet again; I'll keep an eye out for you by the bus stop.'

Andrea waved as she hurried down the street, eager to get Ralph home. Overall, she thought her trip was a success, and she would keep in touch with Laura as promised. She wasn't as stuck-up as she'd feared. In fact, not stuck-up at all, she was lovely, but so sad. Andrea felt shocked that none of the other women from the group had visited. Just goes to show, she thought as she climbed the stairs to her flat. She also secretly hoped she would see Adam again, but knew it was probably unlikely.

Chapter 6

Laura was early. She was due to meet her mother-in-law for coffee at eleven and it was now ten twenty. Parking had been easy for once, and she now had forty minutes to kill. She felt annoyed with herself for leaving home so early, but she knew Ben's mum didn't like to be kept waiting, and she knew if she stayed at home any longer, she would have made some excuse why she couldn't come. She chewed the edge of her nail and wondered what to do.

This was the first time since losing Poppy that Laura felt able to venture into town and was beginning to wonder if it was a mistake. She was starting to feel better at home, in her own little bubble, but here… She looked at her phone, but only five minutes had passed; she couldn't sit in the car for the next half hour or more. No, she could do this, she would stroll around the shops until it was time to meet her mother-in-law.

Laura was about to open the door when a woman pushing a pram walked in front of the car. She froze. She couldn't do this. With her eyes closed, she took several deep breaths. When she opened them, the woman with the pram was out of sight. Eventually, telling herself not to be so ridiculous and taking several deeper breaths, she did get out of the car. She looked around surprised that life was going on as normal. She, momentarily, couldn't understand why nothing had changed; her world was in turmoil so why was everyone else carrying on just as before, didn't they know?

It felt as though the last time she was here was in another

lifetime, surely everything must be different, but it wasn't, the same crude splash of graffiti was on the car park wall and the ticket machine was still out of order. She stood still and watched people rushing around going about their business, no one was looking at her, no one knew what a turmoil she was in, she was just an average woman on an average day in an average town. Laura looked at her watch yet again, only a couple more minutes had passed, surely that couldn't be right, she shook her wrist and looked at her watch again, of course it was right. She told herself to stop being stupid. This was a new experience for Laura, to feel less than totally confident, but inwardly she was shaking. She would go the make-up counter in the department store, maybe buy herself a new lipstick, that might give her a boost, and then it would bound to be time to meet her mother-in-law.

Walking briskly along the road towards the main shopping area, Laura started to feel calmer. She stopped to look in the bookshop window, but didn't go in. Concentrating on a book was beyond her at the moment. The next shop was one she'd frequented many times in recent months; a shop selling baby clothes and equipment. Without making a conscious decision her feet turned towards the door and she found herself in the middle of racks of tiny white, pale blue and pink babygros, dungarees, dresses and all sorts of mini outfits. She touched them letting her fingers linger over the soft fabric, as she walked in a daze around the shop. There was a gentle buzz of voices punctuated by the occasional burst of happy, anticipatory laughter.

'Can I help you?' a young sales assistant asked.

Laura jumped, 'No, no thank you, I'm just looking,' she said.

The girl smiled, 'let me know if you need anything.'

Laura nodded, she felt embarrassed, exposed. The girl must know she didn't have a baby; she had no right to be in the shop, she felt a fraud, a failure. She should leave, but something kept her there, looking, touching, longing.

'Excuse me, can I get past please?' A woman with twins in a double buggy smiled a tired, bedraggled smile at Laura, but the smile wasn't returned. 'It's a bit difficult to manoeuvre in these tight spaces,' she said.

Laura didn't reply but stepped aside to let the woman pass. She stared at the woman and irrationally felt a surge of anger towards her, how dare she have two babies, and to not even look as though she was enjoying the experience.

'Thank you, I never expected two,' she said, almost apologetically.

Laura watched her struggle and noticed that the woman, actually she was hardly more than a girl, looked worn out, big dark circles around her eyes, she was dressed rather scruffily, and her face was devoid of make-up. Her appearance almost roused a tiny spark of sympathy in Laura.

Laura stood rooted to the spot for several seconds after the woman and her precious cargo had passed, and it was only when she saw the sales assistant making her way towards her again that she moved. Hurrying towards the exit Laura suddenly stopped next to a navy blue and red pram, it was very like the one she and Ben had chosen, seemingly a lifetime ago. She touched the handle; all her hopes and expectations flooded back, and nearly choked her. She gasped there was a baby, a real baby, in the pram. She felt confused why was there a baby in a pram that was for sale? In a pram identical to the one they had bought. Laura gripped the handle and looked around, there was no one nearby.

'Poppy,' she whispered, and reached into the pram to lift the sleeping baby into her arms and turned away.

'Hey, what are you doing?' A woman, presumably the mother, and the shop assistant seemed to pounce on Laura. The baby was snatched from her arms, and in panic Laura fled from the shop.

She ran without looking back, adrenaline controlling her limbs, she turned into a dark narrow alleyway that ran between two shops. Gasping for breath and terrified, she didn't notice the short flight of steps inside the alley, leading up to the street behind and tripped, falling to her knees. Pain shot up her legs and she cried out in surprise and pain. She crumpled into a heap at the bottom of the steps and stayed there shaking uncontrollably. Slowly she raised herself up into a sitting position on the cold concrete floor, which was filthy with rubbish and stank of urine. An emotional torrent flared through her body and in total frustration she banged her head into the wall, rocking agitatedly until the rough surface broke open the skin on her forehead.

Laura raised her head, opened her eyes and was momentarily fascinated by the scarlet globules clinging to the rough grey concrete, she gave a guttural moan as a red-hot pain seared across her forehead. Then banged her head harder against the wall, the physical pain taking the place of her mental anguish, and oddly it seemed to soothe her, to be her only reality. How long she sat there, seconds, minutes, she didn't know, but she had no inclination to move, all thoughts of her mother-in-law chased from her mind.

'It's ok, come on now, ok let's just sit here,' a woman said, her voice penetrated into Laura's consciousness. She became aware of a hand on her shoulder, gently pulling her head away from the wall. Laura looked again at spots of her own blood on the grey dirty surface of the wall and felt a mixture of disgust, fear and shame. She looked at the woman, a police or security officer, and suddenly felt afraid as the implications of the commotion in the shop hit her.

'That's it, just sit here a minute,' the woman gently guided Laura to sit on a cold stone step beside her and handed her a tissue.

'Just tell me in your own time what happened in the shop,' she said.

Laura looked at her; she looked like a woman in her fifties, and despite the uniform looked kind and not in the least threatening or authoritative.

'I don't know, I didn't …'

41

'Laura, Laura, oh my goodness, are you all right?' Ben's mum burst into the alleyway and scooped Laura into her arms before anyone could move.

'I'm Esme Jefferies, Laura's mother-in-law,' she explained. 'Whatever is going on? I saw Laura running from the shop when I was down the road. What has happened?'

The security woman briefly explained the situation, as far as she understood it. Esme nodded as she listened, then quietly explained Laura's circumstances across the top of Laura's sobbing head, which was pressed into her shoulder.

'I see, how awful for her. I'm sure the baby's mother will understand when I explain everything. There clearly was no malicious intent.'

'Malicious intent, I should think not indeed. I must take Laura straight home, she needs looking after, if that's all right with you?'

'I thought…Poppy… I wouldn't…' Laura couldn't form a coherent sentence, so let Ben's mum take control.

'No of course you wouldn't Laura dear, come on let me take you home.'

'That's fine but before you go, I better just take some details, you know, just in case.'

'Yes of course,' Esme scribbled down both Laura's and her own contact details. 'Might be best to ring me first if there's any need for clarification.'

'I'm sure everything will be ok, I'll explain the situation,' the security officer said. 'Best get Laura home now.'

Esme nodded her thanks while looping her arm through Laura's and leading her out of the alley.

'Take care Laura,' the officer said, suddenly overcome with emotion herself, she sank back down onto the steps, memories of her own infertility came flooding back, not as traumatic as a stillbirth of course, but now she thought about it she could remember the pain and empty feeling acutely. Her heart went out to Laura and she would do everything possible to put the other young mother's mind at rest, after all nothing really happened the baby didn't even stir. She watched as Laura was led away by her mother-in-law.

Esme steered Laura along the road in a business-like manner, despite feeling quite shaken herself. Her daughter-in-law was never anything other than poised and immaculately turned out, but now Laura, head down stumbled along beside her. Dirt on her coat and a rip in the knee of her trousers. Several people stared as they walked past, and an older woman even tutted, probably assuming Laura was drunk. It took all Esme's self-control not to retaliate.

'I wasn't going to do anything. Ouch that stings,' Laura said later, as she sat in her own kitchen while Esme dabbed at her forehead with an antiseptic wipe.

'Keep still dear, I need to get this grit out.'

'I wasn't going to do anything, to the baby I mean. I wouldn't have taken her, I just didn't think,'

'I know dear,' Esme made appropriate soothing noises, as she bustled about filling the kettle, after she finished administering to Laura.

'For a moment, I thought it was Poppy. I wanted it to be my baby. I just wanted to hold her, I wouldn't have taken her or harmed her, or anything, I just…' Laura's voice trailed off, and big fat tears gathered on her bottom lid and slowly spilled over, silently running down her cheeks.

'I know darling, no one thinks you were going to take the baby,' Esme said, but could imagine the momentary terror of the other young mother when she saw Laura reaching into her pram.

'It's all right, Laura dear, it's all right. People understand it's all part of your grief.

Things will get better with time, you wait and see, time is the big healer.'

Esme was aware that she was talking a lot, but wasn't sure what else to do, so she put the tea things down and just held

Laura and patted her back while offering what she hoped were comforting words. All the time willing Ben to come back home.

By the time Ben did return Laura was calmly peeling vegetables at the sink.

'Oh, hello mum,' he said, with a question in his eyes. Not that he wasn't pleased to see her, it was just that he knew Laura was meeting his mum in town and didn't expect to see her here.

'Everything all right, good shop?' he asked generally.

'I had a bit of a funny turn,' Laura said, leaning against the sink.

'What sort of a funny turn?' Ben asked Laura but looked towards his mother for an explanation.

'I'm fine now I don't need the doctor. I'm fine,' Laura said, moments later, after Esme explained the situation to Ben.

'Thanks mum,' Ben said, as he followed his mum out to her car a while later.

'I would give the doctor a ring if I was you, I was very worried at the time,' Esme said, climbing into the driving seat. 'Best to be sure. She's clearly not herself.'

Ben nodded but wasn't certain what it was he was supposed to be sure of, or what a doctor could do. In the end he rang Rosa instead. To his surprise and relief, she said she would talk to the doctor, explain the circumstances and ask him to visit.

The doctor's visit was fleeting but efficient. Mild postnatal depression aggravated by grief was his diagnosis and a prescription for antidepressants his solution.

'Make an appointment for Laura to see me in a couple of weeks,' he said on his way out. 'Call the surgery if you're worried before then, but it's all quite understandable in the circumstances. She will get better.'

Ben was worried, very worried, and the doctor had done little to reassure him, but he felt he couldn't delay this busy man any longer by unloading his own feelings. He felt sure his mother had made light of the episode, to try to protect him, or more likely to protect Laura, but looking at Laura's cut head and bruised knees he wondered what really had happened, and hoped it was all just a misunderstanding as she had said.

He knew nothing about postnatal depression, mild or otherwise and was determined to tuck Laura up in bed early, before spending time searching for more information on the Internet. Much later Ben slid into bed beside Laura, knowing more about postnatal depression, a condition he's never heard of before, than he had ever wanted to. He felt more confused on the one hand, but more hopeful on the other, and was keeping his fingers tightly crossed that Laura's condition would be the milder version. He lay awake into the small hours mulling over everything until falling into a fitful sleep, next to a deeply asleep Laura.

Chapter 7

'Laura, what are you doing?' Ben pushed himself up on his elbow; it was dark, and he had no idea of the time. He could see Laura standing at the end of the bed, but in the dim light he could not see what she was doing. He could just make out that she was turned away from him looking towards the bedroom door.

'Laura?'

'Can't you hear it?' she remained staring towards the door.

Ben climbed reluctantly out of the warmth of their bed and went to where Laura was standing. Every part of her was on alert and Ben could see, as his eyes adjusted to the glow of the moonlight, that Laura's knuckles were white where her hands were gripping each other.

'Darling, what are you doing? Come back to bed, you're freezing,' he started to rub her cold, naked arms.

Laura shrugged Ben's hands off, without turning to look at him.

'No, listen, there, did you hear it?' she said.

'No, I didn't hear anything. Come on, come back to bed.'

'There,' she stiffened. 'You must be able to hear it now.'

Ben shivered and gently tugged on her arm. Laura didn't move.

'It's a baby, crying, you must have heard it!'

She strained her ears, every part of her body ached for the baby, its cry was so plaintive, so feeble, but she knew it wasn't Poppy. At last, she looked at Ben, how could he not hear it, he must be able to, or else he was lying.

'No really, there's nothing, come on,' he tried again to steer her back to bed.

'I don't believe you,' she pulled her arm away from his hand, and walked towards the bedroom door. She threw an agitated look back at him before making her way across the landing. Then stopped outside the closed nursery door.

'Listen, there, don't tell me you didn't hear that,' she said, flinging the door open, and stepping inside.

Ben, following immediately behind her, felt an icy blast of air and went to close the window. It was already closed. He made a mental note to check for draughts in the morning. Laura swirled round and pointed to the small built-in cupboard.

'There, listen, it's coming from in there.'

'No, honestly. I really mean it; I can't hear anything.'

She pushed past him and yanked open the door. It was empty. She stared in disbelief at the empty shelf, one small coat hanger swinging in the draught. Laura crumpled and sank onto the chair.

'I did hear it, it was in there, you must believe me,' she looked up at Ben with wide staring eyes, willing him to say he heard the cry as well.

'Don't look at me like that, you don't believe me, do you?'

'I don't know, it's probably a cat or a fox in the garden, they cry like babies. It's all getting mixed up in your mind.'

'It wasn't a fox it was a baby; I know how a fox sounds. If it was a fox, you'd have said I can hear a fox, not that you couldn't hear anything,' she said.

'It's a baby, not Poppy. I don't know…' she stopped and stared into the empty cupboard. 'Perhaps it's behind,' she tugged at the shelf.

'No, Laura, stop it, come on now, let me get you back to bed. There's nothing behind the cupboard, it's built in.'

Ben at last succeeded in turning her away from the cupboard and steered her out of the room. She was trembling, and Ben wasn't sure whether it was from cold, fear or anger, but he knew he was afraid. Afraid for what was happening to Laura. His heart was thumping hard for many minutes after they both settled back into bed, what would happen if she didn't start to improve soon? He had no answer.

The next morning Laura slept late. Sunlight was filling the room with a, golden glow when she awoke. She reached out her hand, but Ben's side of the bed was empty. The events of the night gnawed away at her mind and she was reluctant to get up. She felt safe in bed.

Eventually she pulled on her dressing gown and made her way to the top of the stairs, stopping to look at the nursery door, which was now firmly closed. Now she was up, and all was quiet, she was less certain about what it was she had actually heard, but she was certain that it wasn't a dream or a fox. Neither was it her imagination, but how could it really be a baby? It couldn't be, that was madness! Laura hesitated, took a step towards the nursery door and was about to open it, when Ben's voice reached her, coming from the sitting room. She stood still straining her ears, she could only hear his voice, definitely only his, he must be on the phone. She touched the door handle but then changed her mind and turned back to the stairs.

Quietly opening the sitting room door Laura edged into the room. Ben, fully dressed, was standing with his back to her looking out of the window, his phone pressed to his ear, but he sensed the door opening behind him.

'I'll have to go, speak soon, bye,' Ben turned towards Laura and smiled.

'Who was that?' she asked.

'Just mum and dad, they send their love,' Ben replied.

'Were you talking about me?'

'Well not about you, they asked how you were. I said you were still asleep.'

'You were talking about me, weren't you? I know you were. Telling them I'm hearing things, that I'm going mad. That's why you hung up as soon as I came in.'

'No, honestly, that's not true,' he crossed the room and reached out to touch Laura's arm, but she moved away and stood glaring at him across the room.

'They're concerned about you; *I'm* concerned about you,' he said.

'Why? Because you think I'm hearing things, making things up.'

'No of course not, come and sit down a minute. It's natural to feel upset, your hormones …'

'Don't talk to me about hormones, it has nothing to do with hormones. I heard it, I heard a baby. I think you're lying if you didn't hear it; you're trying to make me look an idiot. You think I'm going mad, all of you. Well, you can go to hell.'

'Laura, please.'

'Don't touch me, leave me alone. You don't understand what it's like,' Laura was about to storm out of the room, but her legs didn't move. Part of her wanted to leave immediately, but another part of her wanted to either stay and argue or rush into Ben's arms. She wasn't usually so argumentative, in fact she wasn't argumentative at all, and she felt confused. An inner tussle ensued. One demon's voice urged her to walk out of the room slamming the door. That would show him, how dare he talk about her behind her back. She didn't need his or his parents' sympathy; she was fine on her own. The other voice in her head was more conciliatory, and was appalled by her outburst, where did it come from it just wasn't her? She wavered between one and the other, deep down knowing what she should do, but it wasn't that straightforward. She felt as though she was on self-destruct.

Ben moved first and slumped on the sofa, he felt lost and more than a little concerned about Laura's state of mind. He loved her, of course he did, more than anything, he wanted to protect her and make the pain go away but at this precise moment he wanted more than anything to walk out of the house and keep going. Their lives seemed to be unravelling in slow motion and there was nothing they could do to stop it.

He didn't walk out, instead he just glanced out of the window at the expanse of lawn and the large oak tree and longed to be back in London. To hear the bustle of life going on in the street below, to know there were friends around the corner. He felt alone, he wanted his old Laura back, and he wanted to go back to the time when they were relaxed and laughed at the world together. They rarely argued, bickered sometimes, of course they did, but they were more spirited debates, nothing like they were experiencing now. Never before had he heard Laura speak so coldly. He felt lonely and out of his depth.

After a few seconds, that felt like many minutes Laura's demon lost, only just, and she sat down next to Ben.

'I'm sorry,' she whispered. She felt weak and drained and more than a little confused.

Ben nodded but didn't look up; he was struggling not to feel angry and didn't reach out to hold her as he normally would.

'I lost a baby as well, I do understand, or at least I'm trying to,' he said.

'I know, I'm sorry, I don't know what came over me,' Laura reached for Ben's hand.

For a second his hand lay motionless, until slowly he curled his fingers and squeezed Laura's.

'We need to get through this together, support each other, not fight,' he said, looking up.

Laura nodded; neither of them mentioned the crying baby, both hoping in their own way that that aberration was gone. Laura rested her head on Ben's shoulder, and he stroked her hair. They sat quietly holding each other for what felt like an eternity.

'Breakfast?' Ben asked, at last. It was late and he was getting hungry.

'I'll get it,' Laura said, and jumped to her feet, grateful the moment had passed and determined to be more in control of her emotions in future. A proper breakfast, that would make them both feel better.

Ben wanted to ring Laura's mother, to ask her to come and stay, after the episode in the night, but Laura refused. What she needed was time and space, and much as she loved her mother, she didn't want her fussing around the place. Ben, on the other hand, felt he needed support and would have welcomed her presence, welcomed someone to share the responsibility, but didn't want to upset Laura further by suggesting it again. Laura spoke to her mother often on the phone anyway, and Ben hoped his mother-in-law might pick up something from Laura's tone and suggest visiting herself, but it didn't happen. Laura told him that her mother was encouraging her to try to go out and do things that felt normal. Laura wasn't sure she could visualise normal anymore but thought she was probably right. Not that she could really think of anything 'normal' she wanted to do.

Her mother had suggested going to a big supermarket, as it might be easier to go somewhere where you're less likely to meet people you know, she had reasoned, but Laura shuddered at the thought. Last time she was in the supermarket, towards the end of her pregnancy, the shop was full of mothers with babies sitting in the little seat at the end of the trolley. Then she had smiled warmly at them and they returned her smile, all knowing she soon would be one of them. One woman even wished her good luck, as she acknowledged Laura's bump. They would still all be there, but now she would feel like an outsider, not someone about to join the club. No, a supermarket was definitely off limits. She decided to walk into the village, that was fairly normal. Not that it was something she routinely did before. Ben's enthusiasm when she mentioned she might go to the shop for a paper seemed a bit excessive. Was it such a big deal?

Chapter 8

Right, she said to herself locking the door behind her and putting the keys in her bag. She would buy a few things and come home, what could be easier? She felt shaky and her confidence was at rock bottom, but she calculated that she was less likely to meet people with babies in the village shop, and with any luck at this time of day there would be few people around. Hopefully she could get there and back without seeing anyone at all, it would defeat the object she knew, but at least it would satisfy Ben and her mother. The sooner she ventured out, the better she would feel, or so Ben and her mother kept telling her. The first time will be the worst her mother said, but she didn't know about Laura's disastrous attempt at meeting Ben's mother. Nothing could be worse than that she supposed.

Laura walked slowly along the lane, keeping her head down most of the way, she couldn't understand how Ben seemed to have slotted straight back into normal life, as though nothing had happened; he even talked about going to watch rugby with his friends this weekend, and she felt irrationally hurt and betrayed. Deep down she knew he was really grieving as much as her, he just seemed to be able to manage it better, or perhaps he was able to hide his feelings better than her. They did talk, the doctor had said they should talk about what happened, but there was a limit to how much they could, or wanted, to talk about it. Although, for Laura it was the only topic on her mind, the first thing she thought about when she woke, and every night before she slept. She was analysing every second of the labour and birth, to see if she could pinpoint the moment, the moment when her baby died and if anything could have changed the outcome. She knew it couldn't, it was just one of those rare flukes, but she couldn't stop torturing herself, maybe it was her fault after all, and the doctors were just covering it up. When Laura did talk to Ben about it, he was reassuring, but she knew that he didn't want to keep engaging in the minute analysis of Poppy's death, in the way that she wanted. Surely it was quite an easy thing for a baby to swim around and loop through the cord. Ben would not be drawn, so she decided to just stop talking to him about it.

It didn't take long to walk along the narrow road towards the centre of the village; it was barely more than a hamlet with only the one small shop, which was now run by volunteers, a pub, church and tiny primary school. Laura could only recall one previous occasion when she had walked into the village to the shop, and that was towards the end of her pregnancy when she found sitting still difficult. Luckily the primary school was a bit further along beyond the shop, so Laura didn't have to pass it. She shut out of her mind how many times she had imagined walking along the road to the school, with a skipping child beside her, eager to meet their friends.

She pushed the shop door open. A bell jangled to alert the person serving, not that they could miss anyone entering the shop, it was so small. A customer was already there, talking to the shop assistant.

'Well, if you ask me that place is cursed, there's always some tragedy or other, and do you remember when…'

'Elsie, shh,' Grace, behind the counter, interrupted the woman in a sharp whisper, and imperceptibly inclined her head towards the door and Laura.

'What? Oh dear, er well,' Elsie turned, and stumbled over her words when she realised it was Laura who had entered the shop.

'Hello, my dear, it's good to see you again,' Grace said, her face flushing in embarrassment, self-consciously shuffled papers on the counter.

'Well, I'd better be off, lots to do,' Elsie picked up her shopping and scuttled, head down, past Laura out of the shop.

Laura stared after her, she hadn't missed Elsie's comments and the not-so-subtle whispers when she entered, followed by the awkward mumbling. She was certain Elsie was talking about Oak Tree Cottage, why else would she rush out alarmed when she saw Laura.

'What did she mean, 'cursed'?' Laura asked.

'Oh, you don't want to take any notice of Elsie she's got too vivid an imagination for her own good,' Grace tried to smile reassuringly.

'But she was talking about my house, wasn't she?

'Don't you worry about Elsie she's full of stories. Anyway, how are you dear, such a difficult time for you,' Grace said, whilst not denying that Elsie was talking about Oak Tree Cottage.

Laura swallowed hard, determined not to cry in the shop, and show how piqued she was by the comments of the other woman.

'I'm not too bad, thank you.'

'That's the spirit, it'll get easier you know.'

How would she know Laura thought, looking at Grace with some distain. Yet there was something about the older woman's expression that touched her.

'I lost a baby, he was born early, survived a couple of days. You never forget, but it does get easier.' Grace spoke as though answering Laura's unspoken question.

'Oh, I'm sorry, I didn't know. I hope you're right, but I can't imagine that yet.'

Grace nodded, her heart went out to Laura, she recognised her pain. The new couple in Oak Tree Cottage was how she usually thought of Laura and Ben, even though it was well over a year since they moved into the village. Nice young couple she thought, although she didn't really know them, Ben used to call in more often to pick up a paper or a sneaky bar of chocolate, but she hadn't seen him for a while. There was something in what old Elsie said, no one seemed to live untroubled in that house. She wouldn't mention anything about it to Laura of course.

'I'll just take this, please.' Laura placed a bottle of milk and a packet of biscuits on the counter.

'Give yourself time to grieve dear,' she said, patting Laura's hand as she took her money.

'Thank you, did you...' Laura hesitated. 'Did you have more children?' she asked.

'Eventually, I ended up with four, although it took me a while, I was too scared to try for another for a year or so. I couldn't bear the thought of losing one again. Three girls and a boy, all grown up now and I'm soon to be a granny, but I never forgot my little Eddie.'

'Poppy, that was my baby's name, she never lived, it must be even harder to lose a baby that lived.'

'I don't know about that dear, it's hard either way.'

'I suppose so, thank you for telling me, sometimes it feels like I'm the only one it's happened to,' Laura said.

'Yes, I remember feeling very isolated at the time,' Grace was about to continue, but the door swung open and a couple of workmen came in wanting drinks and crisps and directions to a house that was being renovated nearby.

Chapter 9

Laura knew which was Elsie's cottage. She had noticed her hanging washing on the line or picking vegetables from the small, neat garden when she was driving past. What was to stop her walking that way now and perhaps talking to her if she was outside? No one was outside the cottage as Laura walked up to it, but the front door was ajar. She hesitated, she should get back home, but something stopped her continuing on her way, and before she made any conscious decision her hand was pushing the gate open and she was walking down the path. Her brain quickly caught up with her feet and she turned to retrace her steps.

'Hello there, miss,' an elderly man, presumably Elsie's husband, was standing at the corner of the cottage. 'Can I help you?'

Laura looked at him and was about to apologise and leave, when she thought, what the hell!

'I was looking for Elsie,' she said.

'Well, look no further, she's inside. Come on in, come on now, don't be shy,' he pushed the front door wider and ushered Laura inside.

'Elsie, visitor!' he called. 'I'm Gerald, by the way. You're the young lady from Oak Tree,' he said. It was a statement rather than a question, but Laura nodded anyway.

She followed Gerald straight into an old-fashioned sitting room. As her eyes adjusted to the dim, internal light, she made out a room crammed full of too big, old-fashioned, shabby floral furniture, arranged around a wood burning stove and enormous television. The television seemed out of place and Laura was surprised to see a range of electrical gadgets underneath it, so they were obviously keeping up with technology. A tabby cat stretched itself along the back of one of the sofas, pulling threads as it flexed its claws. The room had a faint fishy smell, possibly to do with the cat or more likely yesterday's dinner.

Elsie bustled out of the kitchen, drying her hands on a tea towel. She stopped, not able to hide her surprise, and some alarm, at seeing Laura.

'Well, hello and what can I do for you?' Elsie asked.

'I heard what you said, in the shop,' Laura said.

Elsie didn't speak, she just looked at Laura, then nodded towards a chair, put down her tea towel and sat down herself.

'I just wondered what you meant,' Laura perched on the edge of a small wooden framed armchair opposite Elsie.

'Now don't you go filling the poor girl's head full of nonsense,' Gerald said, and assuming this was going to be women's chat he returned to the garden.

'Oh, he's right it probably is nonsense, nothing for you to worry about,' Elsie didn't quite meet Laura's gaze.

There was an awkward pause, Laura felt uncomfortable and now she was there she wasn't sure she wanted to hear Elsie's stories. Elsie felt ashamed and wished she had kept her mouth shut in the shop, but how was she to know Laura, of all people, would walk in?'

'Please I'd like to know. I um, well I've heard things, in the house. Everyone thinks it's in my mind because of, well because…' Laura paused and looked at Elsie.

'Because you lost your baby,' she completed for Laura. 'I'm very sorry dear, really I am, it must be a difficult time for you.'

'Yes, thank you, it is difficult, but I hear a baby crying, in the house, no one else hears it. I don't know, the doctor says it's postnatal depression, but it sounds so real.'

Laura looked down at her feet, an acute feeling of embarrassment washed over her, what on earth possessed her to tell Elsie, a virtual stranger, all this?

'I've always lived round about, not always here; Gerald and I moved to this cottage about fifteen years ago, but I was born in the vicinity,'

Elsie paused to pick up the cat who was now clawing at the carpet by her feet.

'As kids we used to think your cottage was haunted, it was different then, much smaller, more like this place. People have knocked it around and extended it over the years.'

'Haunted by what?' Laura asked, aware of a strange feeling growing in the pit of her stomach.

'Well, we never really knew, you know what kids are like always making up different stories. But there was always talk of strange goings on in there, years and years ago, incest, suicide and so rumours and stories grew.'

Laura just nodded although her brain was whirring. Elsie carried on.

'We used to run past on our way to school and dare each other to run into the wood.'

'What wood?' Laura interrupted.

'There used to be a big wood around here and your cottage was just on the edge. Even when I was young many of the trees had already gone, felled for one reason or another, but it was still big enough to be dark and scary to kids. My brother reckoned there was a ghost in the woods; he used to hide behind a tree and jump out making us scream.' Elsie chuckled to herself.

Laura sat quietly, waiting for her to continue. She didn't think there was anything to laugh about.

'I can't remember when most of the trees went and the garden was walled off, a good few years ago,' she said, suddenly remembering Laura was there. 'You've still got the big oak of course. It wasn't called Oak Tree Cottage then, most places didn't have names, just known by the name of the people that lived in it. They all have names or numbers now though. I suppose Oak Tree Cottage was a logical choice for your place.'

'But in the shop, you said you thought it was cursed?'

'Just a figure of speech, dear, nothing more.'

'But something must have made you think that?' Laura said, trying to swallow, but her mouth felt dry.

'Well, it's just no one ever seems to stay there long. I can't remember how many people have lived there, some can't have had time to hang their coats on the hooks, let alone put pictures up.'

Elsie looked up at the array of pictures and photographs adorning the uneven walls of her small room.

'Why did they leave?' Laura asked, following her gaze to the multitude of pictures showing weddings, babies, and family groups, many with a beaming Elsie and Gerald in the centre.

'Oh, now that I *don't* know, least not for all of them. Now, there was one family; not long after they moved in a child fell out of the tree and broke her neck, lived, but they moved, needing specialist equipment and things like that. Another couple split up; he was having an affair with a girl in the village. Quite a scandal that caused! Then another family moved in, and not long after the father died of a heart attack, then a baby died,' Elsie was getting into her stride.

She stopped, suddenly noticing the look on Laura's face.

'Of course, you can't blame the house for that, just a lot of coincidences, I dare say. it was all a long time ago. Just me adding two and two and making five.' She nodded and smiled, what she hoped was a reassuring smile in Laura's direction.

'A baby died? Was that the owners before us?'

'Let me think, I'm not sure. It was empty a while. No, I think there was, yes that's right, the people before you were foreign, French or something. They didn't fit in. Well, they wouldn't, would they. Went back to France, I think. I don't think they had any children, funny couple.'

Anxious as Elsie's tale was making her feel, Laura couldn't help an inner smile at Elsie's obvious disapproval of French people living in the village. She wondered if she and Ben drew the same disapproval as such outsiders, Londoners, moving into the village. Laura made some enquiries about Elsie's own family, indicating the photos on the wall and after a polite interval made her excuses to leave.

'Well nice to meet you dear, I hope everything works out for you.'

After the dim sitting room the bright daylight made her eyes water.

'Don't take too much notice of all them ghost stories, kids' stuff, that's all.'

Gerald who was standing by the side of the cottage, misinterpreted her action for wiping away tears. He must have been hovering close enough to hear Elsie's tales.

'My Elsie likes a good gossip, but there's no harm meant,' he said. Laura smiled and hoped he was right, but she felt troubled by Elsie's stories. Gerald walked up the path with her but didn't say another word; he was a kindly looking man, dressed in muddy blue threadbare overalls that must have seen many seasons in the garden. Gerald just nodded as he opened the gate, stepping back to allow Laura to pass through.

'Just wait a tick,' he said, and hurried back down the path soon to return with a bunch of purple sprouting broccoli. 'They're early this year but taste good. Just steam for a few minutes, that's what my Elsie does,' he said. 'Good source of vitamins for you.'

'Thank you, that's very kind.'

She would have liked to engage Gerald in conversation and hear his view of the residents of Oak Tree Cottage, but just as she was wondering what to say, Elsie's voice called from inside and he turned and made his way back down the path.

'Take care now,' he said, over his shoulder, as he made his way back to Elsie.

Every detail she'd heard was mulled over on the walk home. She was about to find Ben and regale him with everything that had happened, but something made her hesitate, perhaps she'd tell him later, or perhaps she'd just keep it to herself. Instead, she made a cup of coffee and took one to him in his study, and just told him about Gerald giving her the broccoli. He was, Laura thought, over enthusiastic about it, but she realised he was just relieved that nothing untoward had happened to her on this outing.

'I'm going to be away for a couple of nights next week,' he said, looking up from his computer as Laura put his coffee on the desk.

'Oh,' she leant against the wall an involuntary shiver running down her back. Ben often stayed away with work and Laura never thought twice about being at home alone, but now…

'Why don't you go and stay with your parents?' he asked, reaching for her hand. 'You know your mum would love to spoil you for a few days.'

'Yes, I might. I'll give her a ring,' she said, hurrying back to the kitchen before he caught the look of panic on her face.

Chapter 10

Laura parked her car on the quay and climbed out, she wanted a few minutes to herself before going to her parents' house. She breathed in the fresh cool air and could already feel her body start to relax. It was early in the year, so not too busy along the quay, but despite the weather the ice cream van was parked in its usual spot. She bought a ninety-nine and licked it as she wandered along taking in all the familiar sights. It was just that, the familiarity of the place, that helped her to relax. She had been born here and knew the place like the back of her hand, although she did notice a new shop and some recent renovations since her last visit. Somehow, she felt she didn't have to be fully adult here, she could revert and let her parents take the strain.

The tide was coming in quite rapidly, and the boats that drunkenly straddled the sand at low tide, were now again afloat and bobbing happily in their preferred environment. Just looking at the water helped somehow to put things into perspective. It always had that effect on Laura, she remembered after arguments with her parents or fall outs with friends, coming down to the quay and watching the sea, whatever mood it was in always helped to calm her. Leaning against the rail she was lost in thought as she savoured the delightful creaminess of her ice cream, which was in danger of melting and running down her arm if she didn't finish it quickly. The water was working its magic. How could she be so melodramatic as to think that their cottage was haunted. With the effect of distance, the idea seemed ridiculous, she really did need to pull herself together.

A women's Gig team were setting off from the jetty, rowing against the incoming tide. Laura felt the familiar twitch in her arm as she remembered her time, as a teenager, in the team. It was hard work and often cold, especially as they trained in all weathers, but the camaraderie and excitement of competitions made up for it. She watched as the boat made tortuously slow progress towards the mouth of the estuary. They would head back when the tide was high and the water slack, making it faster and easier on tired muscles. She popped the end of her cone into her mouth and sat on a bench, people watching for a while, she was in no real hurry, her mother wasn't expecting her before one o'clock and she was enjoying this time to herself.

She watched for a while a man crabbing with his young son and smiled at the child's squeals of triumph when he pulled his line up with a crab clinging to the end. Last time she sat here was with Ben, several months ago, although it felt like the distant past. She was heavily pregnant, and they had dreamt about the times to come when Ben would be crabbing with their son or daughter. Laura realised she was remembering that occasion without feeling distraught, or even envious of the man and his child. Thank goodness, perhaps at last she was starting to recover.

She strolled further along, pulling her jacket close to ward off the chill of the wind, to where a group of young lads were egging each other on to jump off the quay into the water. Even with the tide fully in it was quite a long drop. First one went, to a cheer from the onlookers, he soon bobbed up and called to the others to follow saying it was fine and not even too cold. Laura was sceptical about that, but they did all have wetsuits on, which in her day would have been considered cheating. She had done it once or twice, but only ever in the summer. It had always been more of a male pursuit, showing off to the watching girls. Laura watched as this group of boys one by one jumped in, swam to the steps and ran back to take their turn for another go, all except one boy who kept moving to the back of the queue. There was no gaggle of admiring girls; they were jumping to impress each other, or, possibly, Laura, and an older couple who'd stopped to watch.

'Come on Benzo don't be a wimp,' a boy called from the water.

The boy called Benzo, a nickname Laura presumed, stared reluctantly at the water, her heart went out to him, she wanted to say don't do it if you don't want to, stand up to them; but instead, she gave him what she hoped was a smile of understanding and empathy.

'Benzo, Benzo,' a couple of the boys chanted, and with a sudden rush and eyes screwed shut, Benzo launched himself off the quay and landed in the water with an almighty splash. Within minutes he was running back up the steps and with a whoop jumped in again. His grin was one of joy and relief; he was now one of them.

'Well done lad,' the older man said, as he and his wife walked on along the quay. 'You wouldn't catch me doing that, not even when I was your age.'

Benzo beamed and seemed to grow in stature.

'Come on how about a mass jump to finish,' another boy said.

Laura and the older couple paused to watch as the half dozen boys flung themselves into the water together, creating a splash that only just missed soaking the three of them.

'Not sure it's that safe,' the older man said. 'But I guess boys will be boys. They could be doing worse things.'

A look at her watch told her it was time to go and she turned towards her car; she was ready now to be embraced into the cocoon of her parents' home, and ready to enjoy her mother's home cooking.

'Darling come on in, lovely to see you. How was your journey?'

Before Laura could greet her father, she was overpowered by two over excited Red Setters who bounced, barked and wagged in delight all around her.

'Hello Rolo, hello Dexter, good boys,' she patted their glossy heads and gently pushed them back down onto four paws, before turning back to her dad.

'Hi Dad, not too bad, thanks. Where's mum?' Laura leant forward to kiss him. He rolled his eyes.

'She's with Mrs Soames down the road, great drama as ever, she tripped in the kitchen, called your mum and she's been there ever since. Mum's called an ambulance and Mrs Soames' son, so she should be back as soon as one or other turns up. Anyway, come on through to the conservatory we can have a drink while we wait.'

Laura smiled, her mum always seemed to be the one people called in a crisis and Laura knew she would be in her element. In some ways she felt grateful to Mrs Soames because it meant there wasn't a big emotional welcome, which inevitably would have ended in tears.

'Here you are,' her father handed her a big glass of red wine. 'Good journey?' He asked again. 'Not too many roadworks, I hope.'

'No, it was easy, luckily.'

She stood looking out through the small conservatory that her parents had built, many years ago, along the back of the house. It made the most of the stunning view out over the quay and to the sea beyond and was where they spent most of their time. It was where they used to retreat to, when Laura brought friends home to play her records, very loudly, on the hi-fi in the sitting room.

It was strange how she appreciated her family home far more now she no longer lived there; as a teenager she just took the view and the town for granted. It was a great place to grow up, and she honestly couldn't remember a time when she was bored, but also, like most of her friends, she couldn't wait to get away to somewhere more exciting. Most of them went off to university and then found jobs and settled all over the world, or so it seemed. Very few either remained or returned home, but now looking around Laura was struck by how beautiful it was. Perhaps one day she and Ben could live by the sea, she thought.

About half an hour later Laura's mum burst into the room full of the drama of Mrs Soames' fall.

'You should see her leg, well it must be broken in at least two places, the poor dear was distraught. The ambulance men were wonderful, and her son arrived just in time to follow them to the hospital. I really don't know how much longer she'll be able to live there on her own, that's the second fall this year,' she took a gulp from the offered wine glass and sat down, before turning and beaming at Laura.

'Laura, darling, I'm so sorry I wasn't here, but you know how it is when these things happen. How are you, how was your journey?'

Laura leant over and gave her mum a kiss.

'I'm fine and the journey was fine. I stopped for an ice cream on the quay.'

'You always were fond of those ice creams and I've got a big tub in the freezer. Now are you hungry? You must be starving; I'll get some lunch, a bit late I know, but never mind.'

Her parents asked about Ben and how they were both coping, but there was no big emotional scene, for which she was grateful. She wondered whether her parents, or more likely her father, had agreed on this strategy before she arrived.

Laura's old childhood bedroom was now refurbished and redecorated into a neutral guest room; her single bed replaced with a new double. There was no evidence of Laura's pop posters and horse pictures on the walls, or her dressing table that was always strewn with experimental make-up, but there was still a feeling of familiarity about it. It was still her room. Here she didn't have to pretend, didn't have to explain. She leant on the windowsill looking out into the night, the sea shimmered in the moonlight and across the estuary, she could see the familiar intermittent flash of the lighthouse. As a teenager her desk was placed under the window and she spent many hours staring out to sea daydreaming, when she should have been doing her homework.

A gentle tap on the door pulled her back to the present and as she turned around, her mother opened the door and came into the room.

'I just came to see you were all right, before going to bed,' her mother said.

Laura nodded and was determined not to cry, but the kind, worried expression on her mum's face brought a lump to her throat and an involuntary cascade of tears were released with big sobbing gulps.

'Oh darling, Laura, come here,' her mum pulled her into her arms and Laura buried her head in her mum's shoulder.

Her mum smoothed Laura's long hair and remembered the days when she would brush it until it shone, amid Laura's protests and then she would plait it ready for school. Laura was always a pretty child but her hair, which she never cut short, was in those days her best asset.

'There, there now, come and sit down,' her mum steered her towards the bed and they both sat down.

'Tell me how you're feeling,' her mum said.

Laura poured out all her pent-up emotion and fears and untypically her mum said very little, just nodded and listened, all the while holding Laura's hand, occasionally squeezing it until Laura stopped talking and eventually yawned.

'I really don't think I've got postnatal depression, do you?'

Her mum shook her head.

'I only said to your dad earlier that I didn't think you were depressed, sad yes, but that's to be expected. Unless it's the medication the doctors given you. Ben told us he'd given you some antidepressants, perhaps it's them working.'

Laura said nothing. She was surprised Ben had been talking to her mum without telling her.

'I rang Ben,' her mum said, as if anticipating Laura's thoughts.

'I just think I'm improving. Being here helps.'

'Yes, a bit of distance can often put things into perspective, not that you've got it out of perspective, it's been a dreadful time, but you know what I mean.'

'I know. Thanks mum.'

'Well, you know you can stay as long as you like and you can come anytime, and Ben of course.'

'I'm meeting some old friends on Tuesday, then I think I'm ready to go home. Ben will be home on Thursday.'

Her mum smiled and patted the bed.

'Come on hop into bed, let me tuck you in like I used to.'

Laura climbed under the duvet and her mum kissed her forehead.

'Sleep well darling.'

'Night mum, and thanks.'

Laura slept deeply and dreamlessly that night, waking up refreshed and looking forward to enjoying a few more days being looked after and with no responsibilities.

The weather was dry with a strong fresh breeze, and Laura relished the freedom of long walks along the beach with Rolo and Dexter, sometimes alone and sometimes with her father. They talked about everything and nothing, and Laura was surprised by how intuitive her dad seemed regarding her feelings over the loss of Poppy. He usually left all the emotional dealings to Laura's mother. After another couple of days with her parents Laura headed for home stronger and with a more positive outlook. Her heart was still aching with the loss of her baby, she was sure she would never totally get over her, but now she felt it was somehow part of the rhythm of life and she could begin to look forward to a better future.

Ben was busy in the garden, surrounded by tools, a wheelbarrow full of weeds and piles of branches, when she arrived home. She smiled to herself at the sight; he was easing comfortably into the country lifestyle.

'Darling, have you had a good time? How are your parents?' Ben crossed the lawn and hugged her.

'It was good, very relaxing. How was your work trip?'

'Not bad, I got home late last night and have been tidying up the garden today.'

'I can see, it looks amazing.'

'Drink?' Ben asked.

Laura nodded.

'I was just about to make a coffee, but now you're here do you fancy a G&T or glass of wine?' Ben asked, already heading towards the kitchen.

Laura nodded.

'Glass of white please.'

'Sit down I'll bring another chair. That's something else we need, nice garden furniture.'

They sat chatting about their respective trips and planning what else could be done with the garden, in a way that would have seemed impossible a week or so ago. Ben was full of plans for a summerhouse in a corner of the lawn with a built-in barbeque beside it.

'That's the part of the garden with the evening sun, what do you think?'

Laura nodded, and Ben continued to make suggestions for other improvements, jumping up to pace out an area or point things out to Laura.

'You know what?' Laura said, when he sat back down. 'I think I'll start picking up a bit of work tomorrow, or at least sort out my emails and update my website, let people know I'm back in business.'

'Great idea,' Ben smiled, and reached out his hand. 'Things are going to be OK, I'm sure of it.'

He felt as though a light was starting to flicker at the end of a tunnel, he knew it was still early days, but this was the first time since they lost the baby that Laura had even mentioned work or started to look forward rather than back.

'Cheers,' he said, raising his glass, stretching his feet out and surveying with pride the progress he'd made in the garden. He didn't say anything to Laura, but he'd identified one area of the garden that was going to be perfect for a swing and climbing frame in the future.

'Cheers,' Laura replied. In her mind she could imagine a little boy, maybe two, or a girl, running up and down the lawn, kicking a football, but she didn't say anything to Ben.

Chapter 11

Laura screwed up her nose.

'But we don't even know them very well,' she said.

'We do a bit, we've spoken to them, well I have a few times, and this is a good chance to get to know them properly. They seem really nice.'

'I don't want to get into the dinner party scene again. That was one of the things we said we wouldn't miss from London.'

'I don't think, come round for a bite to eat, indicates a dinner party,' Ben said.

'It had better not.'

Laura remembered the anxieties she went through trying to plan, shop and cook for the dinners. She wasn't a natural cook, although her friends seemed to think she was. She could follow a recipe and had an eye for presentation, which seemed to be more than half the battle. Remembering whether anyone was vegetarian, vegan or allergic to anything was a nightmare, and it seemed every time people came round someone else couldn't eat something or was into some new fad.

When they first lived in London, the regular dinner parties were a source of excitement for Laura. She took great care preparing her menu, sourcing the right ingredients, and making their little flat look lovely, to welcome their friends. The evenings had been relaxed, and it was more about being with friends and having a good time than about the food. Then fairly quickly everything got out of hand. Friends of friends and work acquaintances became involved and the stakes were raised. The dinner parties became bigger and more exotic. The fun and laughter went out of the occasions, at least for Laura, who hated the competition and one up-manship that took over. She began to dread them, and she knew others, her closest friends, felt the same, but they all seemed trapped on the merry-go-round, no one wanted to be the first to get off. Laura knew she couldn't face that again.

'So, shall I text William and say we'll be there?' Ben asked.

'I suppose so, but I warn you if it is a dinner party and we have to reciprocate, you're on the cooking.'

'It's a deal, I want to start cooking more anyway,' he said, as he dodged out of the way of her playful punch.

They walked the short distance from their cottage up to the old farmhouse, perched on the hill, well hardly a hill more an area of raised ground behind the village. Old hawthorn hedges lined the narrow lane, in a month or two they would be bursting into flower and wildflowers would probably adorn the verges. Grass was growing through the middle of the road breaking through the tarmac and Ben idly wondered who was supposed to maintain it. The last of the early sun-shine was rapidly fading, and the only sound was the tweeting of birds as they prepared to settle for the night. It was a tranquil spot, and made Ben remember why they had decided to move to the countryside.

'Isn't it peaceful?' he held his arms wide. 'Do you fancy getting a couple of bikes?' Ben asked.

'Bikes? I haven't been on a bike for years.'

'It would be so much nicer here than riding around London with all the fumes, and safer,' he said.

'You never did ride around London.'

'I know, but that's why, it would be great round here, don't you think? We could go for picnics. It would keep us fit.'

Laura snorted and Ben put an arm around her waist and pulled her towards him so he could kiss the top of her head.

'What was that for?' she asked.

'For nothing,' Ben replied.

The farmhouse appeared very old and rambling, and, built out of local stone, it sat comfortably in its surroundings. There was an old barn and several outhouses to one side, but there was little evidence of any farming activity in progress, and there was definitely a lack of farmyard smells. As they approached the house, they could see that the gardens were beautifully tended, which made Ben's efforts at tidying up their garden pale into insignificance. He was about to comment when William opened the impressive oak front door.

'Hi, lovely to see you both, come on in! I did wonder about sitting outside for a drink as it's still quite warm, but it will be dark soon, so probably better to stay in.'

William leant to kiss Laura on the cheek and shook hands with Ben. His rolled-up shirtsleeves and jeans immediately put Laura at ease, and she was pleased she hadn't dressed up too much and felt quite comfortable in black trousers and a loose pink top. That was the other ridiculous thing, in London everyone was always supposed to be decked out in the latest fashion, not that that was a problem, in fact she enjoyed that aspect, but it just added to the overall pretence and stress.

'The weather seems quite exceptional for this time of year,' said Ben.

'It probably means we're in for a cold spell in a few days, anyway, come on in,' William ushered them into a cosy sitting room. The furniture was quite a mismatch, some large dark wood pieces, clearly antique and probably quite valuable, and three large, rather shabby sofas that just asked to be snuggled up on.

Claire appeared, also dressed in jeans, wiping her hands on a tea towel, with a beautiful brown and white spaniel trotting at her heels.

'I'm so pleased you could come. Sit yourselves down; I'll get some crisps to nibble on. This is Gem, by the way,' Claire said, patting the dog on her head.

Laura and Ben exchanged a knowing glance; crisps were

definitely frowned on as the cheapskate of nibbles in their previous existence, where only fiddly handmade canapés would suffice.

'This is beautiful,' Laura said, as she walked over to the window and looked out onto the terrace. Crumbling pots and urns jostled for space and Laura imagined them overflowing with flowers and shrubs in the summer. Steps led down from the terrace onto a large lawned area divided by paths and borders.

'We're not really gardeners, more potterers, most of this was set up by William's mother years ago. We just try and keep it under control, although I think we are getting better with practice,' Claire said, putting a bowl of crisps on the large coffee table before joining Laura at the window.

'We are totally clueless when it comes to our garden. We've let it go a bit wild, but Ben recently started to clear it up, so it's looking better. I'd like to turn it into a proper cottage garden sometime,' Laura said.

'Laura wants it to look like something out of Homes and Gardens, but I think it might be beyond me,' Ben said.

'No, I don't. I just want cottagey flowers and shrubs.'

'Come and look, there's still just about enough light,' William beckoned to Laura and Ben to go through the French doors and join him on the edge of the terrace.

'You can just see your house from here,' he pointed down the slope of the lawn, and over a field where several ponies grazed.

'And there's the castle, you can just spot it between the trees,' he pointed in the opposite direction.

The church and most of the rest of the village was visible around to the side and front of the house.

'I always say we know what's going on in the village before they do,' said Claire.

'It's a great vantage point,' said Ben.

'Did you know the people who lived in our house before us?' asked Laura, following Claire back into the house.

'Only by sight, they didn't mix much. They worked away, didn't they?' Claire called across the terrace to William.

'Who?'

'The people in Oak Tree Cottage before Laura and Ben, I can't even remember their names?'

'Yes, French couple, odd pair, didn't know much about them really. The place was empty for a while before you bought it.'

'They left it in a bit of a mess,' said Ben, accepting a crisp from a proffered bowl. 'But I suppose that might just be how an unlived-in house seems. Anyway, we definitely want to become part of the community.'

'Well in that case, do you play cricket?' William asked.

Claire raised her eyebrows and turned to Laura as the men started discussing the merits of the local cricket team.

'How are you coping Laura, since the baby?' Claire asked.

Laura was surprised by her direct question, but pleased that it was out in the open, so many people hedged about, or avoided, mentioning anything at all.

'I'm up and down; I don't really know how I feel most of the time. I suppose I need to be getting over it soon.'

'I don't think you ever really get over something like that,' Claire reached a hand across to touch Laura's. 'I don't mean you'll always feel this bad, just that it will become manageable; you won't ever forget her.'

'Have you, I mean did you…?'

'Three early miscarriages and then one at about four months, but that was well over thirty years ago. Traumatic enough but nothing like you've been through. We have two strapping sons now,' Claire said.

Laura picked up a slight catch in her voice and was surprised again by how many women had lost babies or been through the trauma of miscarriage, yet rarely was it spoken about. Before she lost Poppy, she never knew anyone who'd lost a baby, and it certainly wasn't discussed in any classes or baby books that she read, it was a hidden taboo, and certainly nothing she ever contemplated would happen to her. Claire must be in her mid to late fifties to have two sons about thirty. It was difficult to tell her age by looking at her. Laura also noticed that she hardly wore any make up and envied her clear smooth complexion, she hoped the clean country air would have the same effect on her. The two women became deeply engrossed in a conversation about babies and feelings, and Laura was pleased with herself that she didn't get over emotional. The men, not expecting or wanting to get involved, wandered back out onto the terrace, to give them a bit of space.

'Is this a working farm?' Ben asked William.

'Not anymore sadly, it's been a working farm in my family for generations, but our boys weren't interested, and it became too much for me. I've got a few hobby sheep, chickens and the like but nothing commercial. The cows, down there, belong to another farmer, it's quite good I get to see them, but he does all the work.'

'What do your sons do?'

'Paul's a session musician, a guitarist mainly, he's off all over the world playing with well-known bands, or so he tells me, and does studio recordings. Graham does something technical, to be honest I don't really have a clue what he does but it pays well; he's in Stockholm now.'

'Doesn't sound like you can see much of them?'

'No, not as much as we'd like but they come back as often as they can, or when they want some home cooking. Talking of which we better go in and eat.'

By the time the two men walked back across the terrace and into the sitting room Claire and Laura were already in the kitchen.

'Ah, here you are, I thought we'd eat in the kitchen. You don't mind, do you?' she asked Laura and Ben. 'The dining room only really gets used at Christmas and big dos and to be honest it's a bit chilly in there.'

'No, the kitchen's great, thanks,' Ben replied.

The simple steak and vegetables were delicious, and the conversation was as easy and varied as though they were all old friends, and for the first time since moving Ben felt they were with like-minded people. He smiled to himself as Laura's laugh rang around the kitchen, she was evidently captivated by some tale of Claire's.

'More wine?' William refilled Laura's glass in response to her nod. 'Ben?'

'Thanks, it's so good not having to drive.'

'Damn, who can that be?' William put the bottle down and went to answer the phone in the hall.

Claire placed a huge cheeseboard on the table and popped a grape into her mouth as she sat down.

'Tuck in,' she said.

Chapter 12

'Well would you believe it?' William sat back at the table a couple of minutes later and took a big slug of wine.

'What's happened?' Claire asked.

'The Browns can't keep Colin.'

Laura raised a quick eyebrow towards Ben who was busy cutting cheese trying to appear as though he wasn't listening. Laura was certain neither of their son's was called Colin perhaps this was another relative. She followed Ben's lead and cut some cheese, feeling uncomfortable by the sudden irritation in William's voice.

'Well why not? I had a feeling about them right from the start, didn't I say?' Claire asked.

'He's been made redundant, well lost his job, sacked probably, so they've got to move in with her mother and they can't take Colin.'

'Well, I suppose being made redundant isn't his fault; they'll have to bring him back here. Did you say that?'

Laura shuffled nervously, she was surprised that William and Claire were being so frank and open in front of her and Ben.

'Yes of course I did, they'll bring him over tomorrow, goodness knows what we'll do with him,' William said.

He took another swig of wine and looked at Laura and Ben, with a strange expression on his face, which Laura interpreted as embarrassment.

'I don't suppose you two fancy a puppy, do you?' William asked.

'A puppy?' Laura and Ben echoed together.

'Yes, Colin, he's one of Gem's puppies.'

Laura and Ben both tried hard to stifle a giggle.

'You thought Colin was a person, didn't you?'

'Well, we weren't really sure, but I'm glad he isn't, poor chap.'

'Easy mistake to make; what idiot calls a puppy Colin? I thought they looked clueless when they came to choose him,' said William.

'Well at least they came back to us and didn't just sell him on,' said Claire.

'True. He's not really a puppy as such, what is he nine months old now?'

'Nearly nine months,' said Claire.

'We did say once we were settled, we should get a dog,' Ben looked at Laura, and by her expression he knew there was no way Colin was going anywhere other than to their house.

'I love dogs I grew up with them. We always had German Shepherds when I was young, but now my parents have two nutty Red Setters.'

'Yes, highly strung dogs Red Setters. Well, Colin, if he's anything like Gem, will be quite calm.'

'He should be house trained by now, hopefully.' Claire said.

'We'll have to go shopping tomorrow Ben, to get all the stuff he'll need. I think Colin's quite a cool name; anyway, he's probably too old to have it changed now.'

They all looked at Laura and smiled; Ben reached across the table and squeezed her hand.

'Looks like Colin's got a new home,' he said.

'I've asked them to bring his bed and leads, food, toys and any other things they have for him, so you won't need much.'

'Don't you believe it,' said Ben. 'Laura never overlooks a shopping experience, even if it is for a dog.'

'We could bring him down to your place tomorrow afternoon after they drop him off, or do you want to come and check him out up here first?'

'No bring him down,' Ben and Laura said in unison.

Laura chattered happily all the way home about what they would need to do in preparation for Colin and how she always wanted to have a spaniel. They went to bed that night exhausted, perhaps a little drunk, but happy to have something other than their grief to fill their minds.

The next day they returned from the local pet supermarket with, what felt like to Ben, half the shop's stock, all essential according to Laura. Ben couldn't help comparing this trip with the last time Laura was so excited over a shopping spree, which was when they were looking for baby equipment.

Later in the afternoon they heard a car door slam and within seconds a small brown and white whirlwind entered their lives. His back was mostly brown with a few white patches and white legs, his head and ears were brown with a white streak down his nose. Two large brown eyes, ready to melt anyone's heart sparkled brightly and his mouth was open as if in a permanent smile. His long brown feathery tail was a constant wag.

'Hello Colin, you're gorgeous,' said Laura.

'He's quite a live wire,' said Claire, dumping a dog bed and bag of belongings on the kitchen floor. 'This is what they've been feeding him on, but I've brought some of Gem's food, which is better quality, so it's worth swapping him over gradually.'

Laura looked at the scruffy bed and decided she would dispose of it after a few days, when he was used to his new home and replace it with the new one that fitted her décor better.

'Colin, here boy,' Laura called.

Colin, who was busy sniffing every corner of the kitchen looked up and ran towards Laura and jumped up nearly knocking her off balance.

'Ah, ah, Colin. Good boy, now sit,' she said.

To everyone's surprise Colin sat and looked up, focusing

on Laura's hand, which held a biscuit. 'Good boy,' she bent down and patted his head at the same time as giving him the biscuit.

'Well, it looks like he's going to be very happy here. Now the Browns assured me he was house trained, but I have my doubts that he's been trained in much else,' Claire said, as she watched Colin put his front paws on the kitchen worktop and sniff to see if there was anything that took his fancy within reach.

'Down, Colin.'

Colin put all four paws on the floor and bounded towards Ben, looking for a reward for being a good boy.

'I'll take him in the garden, come on Colin, let's see what's out here.'

Colin bounded after Ben.

'Coffee?' Laura asked Claire.

'No thanks, I must get back. I'll ring you in a couple of days we can take Colin and Gem for a walk together, ring me if there are any problems with him.'

'I'm sure he'll be fine, he's a lovely boy.'

Frantic barking from the garden took Laura and Claire to the kitchen window, they could see Colin standing under the oak tree, hackles up and growling between barks. He was backing away then jumping forward.

'Squirrels,' said Claire. 'He probably hasn't seen them before, the Browns lived on an estate in town.'

'Colin, here boy,' Ben called, he flung the ball hitting the tree and it ricocheted back across the garden with Colin in hot pursuit.

'He's happy now. Well, I better be off,' Claire walked out into the garden. 'Bye, Ben,' she shouted up the garden.

Ben waved with one hand and threw a ball for the tireless Colin with the other.

'I don't think we'll need bikes to keep us fit now,' Laura said, catching the ball and throwing it down the garden for Colin to chase, as she walked across the lawn to join Ben.

Apart from being reluctant to sleep in the kitchen on the first night, Colin quickly settled in and soon it was difficult for Ben and Laura to remember life without him.

Chapter 13

Laura pushed her phone into her pocket and walked across to her workshop, for the first time in many weeks. She'd said yes to Vicky before giving herself time to think, and now she was beginning to wonder if she'd done the right thing. It was one thing saying she was starting to think about going back to work, but it felt quite different now there was a real client in the pipeline. Was she ready? There was only one way to find out.

She unlocked the door and stepped inside. Everything was left in pristine order, Laura hadn't really thought in detail when she became pregnant about how long she would take off, she was going to play it by ear, but had anticipated at least six months before starting work again seriously. This was sooner than expected. She closed the door behind her and took a deep breath; in a way it felt good to be back, the smell of fabric still lingered lightly in the air. The reception room, where she met clients, was warm and inviting and Laura started to relax. This was her domain. Here she felt in control.

Deliberately, she'd kept the space baby free, this was her workplace, and although when she was pregnant, she often envisaged a gurgling baby in a bouncer or playpen in the corner, she knew babies and dressmaking didn't go together. In here there was nothing physical to remind her. Going upstairs to her cutting and sewing room she smiled at the tidiness, which was in complete contrast to how it looked when she was working. Then the frenetic activity seemed to fill the space with life and muddle, although in reality Laura was a tidy worker. 'Tidy as you go, and keep everything in its place,' Vicky always stressed to her apprentices, and Laura carried on in that vein in her own workshop. Thinking about Vicky made Laura remember the phone call a few hours earlier that had prompted her come over in the first place. Vicky came straight to the point, as she always did.

'Darling, I know you're not officially working, but I'm up to my eyes and there's a new client in your neck of the woods, Lady Carlton-Prior. Her daughter Lucinda's getting married and they're looking for a one-off dress. How would you feel about taking them on?'

Laura's first instinct was to refuse, she wasn't ready and had said so to Vicky, who didn't reply straight away, just left a short pause to give Laura time to move on from her knee jerk reaction. Laura was certain Vicky was passing on this client to encourage her to move on, and not just because she didn't have the capacity to deal with the commission herself, but Laura wasn't sure she was ready to take on proper work just yet. Vicky knew about Poppy, of course, and her support and love for Laura and Ben was genuine, so Laura knew she wouldn't push her if she wasn't ready, but when would she feel ready? Thinking about it made her feel confused, she wasn't sure about anything anymore, it felt as though something inside her was different, she didn't feel like the same confident, in control Laura, that she used to be.

Wandering around, Laura opened and closed drawers and cupboards, touched silks and threads, uncovered one of her sewing machines and ran her hand across its smooth surface, as if she was refamiliarising herself with the tools of her trade. Eventually she sat down at her desk and picked up her pencil, she started to doodle different styles of dresses, quickly becoming absorbed. A one-off dress Vicky had said, Laura smiled to herself, she knew many brides-to-be who came in wanting a unique dress, who by the time they tweaked and altered Laura's design, ended up with a version of the latest in-vogue fashion style. Laura didn't mind as long as they were happy with the end result, but she hoped that Lucinda Carlton-Prior might be more adventurous. As she drew, Laura's confidence rose, of course she could do this. She felt ready, excited at the prospect. Hopefully, Vicky's recommendation would be followed up, and Laura would receive a phone call from the Carlton-Priors. She put her pencil down and decided that if they didn't make contact, she would more actively market her business; she felt ready to get back into the swing of it.

'Laura,' Ben opened the front door to Laura's workplace and called up the stairs.

'Up here, come on up.'

Ben bounded up the stairs two at a time. He felt too big and masculine in this predominantly female domain and usually kept away, afraid he might touch something delicate and bejewelled and damage it.

'Hi, everything ok?' Ben asked. 'I wondered where you were.'

'Yes fine, Vicky rang; she's too busy to take on a new client and wondered if I would like to work with them. The name sounds very county, but they're fairly local,' Laura replied.

'Is that good? Is it what you want to do?'

'I wasn't sure at first, but I'm hoping they'll get in touch. It could be interesting, not to say lucrative. Yes, I want to do it.'

Ben pulled Laura into his arms. 'I'm so pleased,' he said. 'What will you do if they don't ring? Did Vicky give you their contact details?' He said hoping that this move forward wouldn't come to nothing.'

'I thought about that. I'll let people know that I'm open for new commissions.'

'Fancy a glass of wine to celebrate?'

'Certainly do,' Laura replied, she was about to switch off her computer and follow Ben, when Colin bounced in through the open door, ran upstairs and began charging around the workshop.

'Out, out, go on, this is definitely out of bounds to dogs,'

Laura shooed Colin back down the stairs and out into the garden where he charged up and down barking, inviting play.

'He's completely mad,' said Ben. 'Good job you didn't have yards of white fabric everywhere, can you imagine?'

'Don't, it doesn't bear thinking about, I'll just have to make sure the bottom half of the door is always shut so he can't get in,' Laura said, feeling pleased she'd decided on the stable door.

She picked up a muddy ball that Colin had deposited on the floor and followed him out into the garden where he was waiting for someone to throw it. She threw it across the lawn and Colin hurtled after it, picked it up and ran back dropping it at her feet and bouncing excitedly waiting for her to throw it again.

'Doesn't he ever get tired?' asked Ben.

That evening was one of the most relaxed at the cottage since Poppy's stillbirth. Ben looked across at Laura curled up on the sofa with, a now thankfully peaceful, Colin lying beside her with his head on her lap and felt they had turned a corner.

Chapter 14

The top half of the workshop door was open, so that it looked more welcoming, and Laura busied herself inside putting her portfolio and several magazines on the table. She paused to flick through her photographs and felt a surge of pride, along with a buzz of excitement but was also unusually nervous. Before she became pregnant, she was beginning to build her business, and her confidence working on her own, was growing rapidly. She was eager and motivated and knew that Vicky was on the end of the phone if she needed her, but Laura was determined to make it on her own and prided herself in not needing any help. Vicky had visited in the early days and been very impressed with the set-up. At that time Laura's belief in herself had been sky high. Now she felt differently, she no longer felt invincible and was beginning to wish that her first new client wasn't someone quite so high profile.

Pacing around the room, waiting, Laura gave herself a firm talking to; of course, she could do this; she'd done it before; she was a good seamstress and hadn't yet found a client she couldn't deal with. Time was ticking on, where were they, she needed to get going again. What if they didn't turn up?

A crunch on the gravel indicated a car, and Laura watched from the window, as a black Range Rover swept into the parking space to the side of the garage. Two people stepped out; the driver a tall elegant looking woman in her late forties, who matched Laura's idea of a stereotypical country lady. She wore trousers with smart ankle boots, an expensive looking tailored tweed jacket over a cream jumper, and her bobbed honey blonde hair was held in place with a velvet Alice band. The other younger woman, presumably the daughter Lucinda, was also tall, with the willowy ease of the young and privileged. She was dressed in skinny dark jeans, trainers and a sweatshirt, and looked around with an air of someone being taken against their will to see an elderly aunt. As they crossed the drive, Laura opened the door wide and smiled warmly in their direction.

'Good afternoon, I'm Laura, please come in,' she stepped inside followed by her clients.

'I'm Alexandra Carlton-Prior and this is Lucinda, my daughter, the bride to be,' Lady Carlton-Prior extended her hand, which Laura took in a business-like shake.

Lucinda nodded in Laura's direction. 'Hi,' she said.

'Please, take a seat', Laura indicated two comfortable leather chairs strategically placed by the coffee table. 'Can I get you both a drink?'

'Thank you, coffee, for us both, white no sugar,' Lady Carlton-Prior replied, sitting down and straight away picking up Laura's portfolio and starting to flick through.

'You worked with Victoria English I understand. What made you set up on your own?' Lady Carlton-Prior asked, putting down the portfolio when Laura returned with a jug of coffee.

'Yes, I worked with her for many years. I decided to set up my own brand when my husband and I decided to move to the country. Vicky has encouraged and supported me through out. Have you had clothes made by her studio in the past?' Laura asked, feeling as though she was being interviewed.

Lucinda imperceptibly shrugged her shoulders and flicked her eyes towards the ceiling; Laura wasn't sure it was in impatience with her mother or the conversation in general.

'Not myself, I know of her, of course, she has a good reputation I understand. My usual designer suggested her for

Lucinda, but then Victoria recommended you. Apparently, she's very busy.' Lady Carlton-Prior said.

She cast her eyes around Laura's domain and as far as looks could tell, her expression showed approval, although it was difficult to gauge. Laura wasn't sure on first impression whether she was going to warm to Lady Carlton-Prior, and Lucinda seemed to be in a permanent sulk. She wondered whether Vicky actually knew anything about them, and presumed not, or she might not have been so keen for Laura to take them on. Well, if nothing else it will be a challenge she thought, pushing doubts away and becoming business like.

'Lucinda, tell me about the wedding and the sort of dress you are looking for.' Laura addressed herself to the bride to be, but Lady Carlton-Prior replied before Lucinda opened her mouth.

'We'll be using the local village church for the service followed by a reception at home, possibly a marquee but I do find them rather vulgar, but it does depend on numbers. I would like Lucinda to have a traditional dress, but she, of course, has other ideas. Anyway, one thing that is important and beyond debate is that Lucinda will wear the family veil, it's been worn by generations of my family, and so of course, I expect Lucinda to keep the tradition going.'

Laura looked across at Lucinda, who with her legs crossed and arms folded was turned away from her mother. Her body language was screaming to Laura that she wasn't going to do anything her mother demanded and Laura, feeling sympathy for her, could understand why. How on earth Lady Carlton-Prior persuaded her to attend the appointment in the first place seemed like a minor miracle, and Laura felt that making progress on anything was going to need more than a miracle, of any size. Perhaps this commission, if it did happen, wasn't going to be as enjoyable as she hoped.

'Do you actually have the veil with you?' Laura asked, more in hope than expectation. Neither Lucinda nor her mother appeared to have a bag large enough to conceal an antique veil, and Laura felt nothing would be able to proceed until she had seen it.

'Yes, of course, it's in the car,' Lady Carlton-Prior said.

Laura sensed that she was about to ask her daughter to go and fetch it, but to her relief Lady Carlton-Prior rose to her feet and said she would go and get it herself.

'Is a traditional wedding dress your vision?' Laura asked Lucinda, once they were alone.

'Mother is driving me absolutely mad; she's gone into overdrive; I'm beginning to feel that I have no say in anything. I sometimes wonder who the actual bride is, me or her!' Lucinda replied.

'I don't think that is so unusual, I've met lots of mothers who have a set idea about how their daughter's wedding should be, but my aim is for every bride to walk down the aisle in a dress of their dreams, so you need to be the one who feels happy with it, not just your mother. Hopefully we can win her over as well.'

Lucinda grinned and nodded, and Laura felt that there was the beginning of a connection, Lucinda wasn't the sort of girl who would let a domineering mother have her way, but Laura envisaged a few fireworks along the way.

'Here it is,' Lady Carlton-Prior said, when she returned and unwrapped acres of tissue paper to reveal an exquisite ivory lace veil.

'Goodness, that's quite beautiful. May I?' Laura held out her arms and the veil was ceremoniously passed over.

She took a couple of steps and shook it out so she could see the full extent of it.

'Antique Brussels lace with Point De gaze Roses, is that right?'

'Yes, it is, how clever of you to recognise it,' Lady Carlton-Prior said, smiling for the first time.

'It has a timeless quality; I'm sure it will fit well with any design, traditional or modern. How old is it?' Laura asked, as she carefully refolded the veil and handed it back.

'I'm not sure exactly, eighteen hundred possibly but all the Carlton-Prior women wore it, including myself, although of course I was marrying into the family, but there were no other females in the line. It's quite fragile now although in good condition, so hopefully a few more brides will be wearing it.'

'I think it's in excellent condition, it's obviously been well looked after,' said Laura, and was rewarded with another charming smile from Lady Carlton-Prior.

She turned to Lucinda and was relieved to see that she was nodding and didn't outwardly appear to be rejecting the idea of the veil.

'Tell me Lucinda, do you have any particular type of dress in mind?'

'This is where it gets difficult,' said Lady Carlton-Prior, crossing her long legs and looking at her daughter, and once again answering before Lucinda could speak.

'Well, Lucinda, why don't you talk through your ideas. I'll just jot down some thoughts as you talk,' Laura said, hoping she didn't sound too rude to Lady Carlton-Prior, but she really wanted to hear Lucinda's viewpoint.

'I want something a bit different, not just a variation on the traditional big white or cream dress.'

Lucinda's mother gave an only just audible tut.

'Go on,' encouraged Laura.

'I haven't got any fully formed ideas, but I quite fancy trousers, or something along the lines of *The Lady of Shallot*.' Lucinda said.

Laura's pulse quickened; this really could be a unique commission.

'You can't possibly wear trousers,' said her mother. 'Can she?' she asked, turning to Laura for back up.

'Well trousers aren't unheard of as an alternative wedding outfit these days, and they can be made in many different styles,' Laura replied, and was treated to an almost hostile glare from Lady Carlton-Prior, and a carefully suppressed smile from Lucinda.

'Ridiculous, and what about this Lady of Shallot idea, anyone one would think she was going to get married in a field.'

'That would be preferable,' Lucinda said.

Laura had the uncomfortable feeling that she was being dragged into a long running argument between mother and daughter and was desperately trying to think of ways to remain neutral. She felt fairly confident that Lucinda would stand her ground and not be bullied into the dress her mother wanted, but she suspected that mother would be footing the bill, but only for what she considered an appropriate dress.

'It would be possible to incorporate a style of trouser under a more traditional overdress, that could be taken off for the evening reception,' Laura suggested. 'By the Lady of Shallot, are you thinking of the flowing sleeves?' she asked Lucinda.

'Yes, sort of floaty,' Lucinda replied.

'Do you have any images,' Lady Carlton-Prior swept her hand over the table of carefully arranged magazines.

'I'm not sure if there are any actual trouser outfits but do have a flick through while I try to do a couple of sketches.'

Laura moved to her easel and quickly produced a couple of rough line drawings. One showed loose trousers and a fitted strapless top, with a dramatic overdress, which was clasped at the waist. The sleeves were long and wide and there was a flowing train. Another sketch showed harem style trousers and simple top under a floaty dress, which draped and tied around the waist and was reminiscent of a Greek goddess.

'These are just ideas, but sometimes it's easier to start with an idea and then we can adapt it, or we can come up with something entirely different.' Laura stood back letting Lucinda and her mother study the sketches.

'Yes, they look good, I'm not really sure what I was thinking of,' said Lucinda. 'I like the idea of an overdress, those sleeves are good, and that collar and I quite like both styles of trousers,' she pointed to aspects of both sketches.

Lady Carlton-Prior looked silently at the sketches for what, to Laura, felt like an eternity.

'Hmm, well I suppose they could look like potential wedding dresses; they are better than I imagined, I rather like that idea,' she pointed to the same flowing overdress that Lucinda indicated. 'But it would depend what they look like in reality,' she said.

'Of course, any design would be made as a mockup first. Would you initially like me to do a range of drawings and send them to you, to look at, and we can go from there?' Laura asked Lucinda.

'Yes, that makes sense,' Lady Carlton-Prior agreed, answering again for her daughter.

'Yes, thank you. I'll give you my email address before we leave,' Lucinda said.

'Would you like another drink, while I take Lucinda off to do some measurements?' Laura asked.

Lady Carlton-Prior refused, but settled back into a chair with a magazine, while Laura took Lucinda upstairs. She didn't usually take clients upstairs for initial measurements but was desperate to separate mother and daughter for a few minutes. She chatted to Lucinda as she wielded her tape measure and recorded all the details she needed.

By the time they left Laura was much clearer about Lucinda's likes and dislikes and the type of fabric and colours she liked. Lucinda being tall and slim was going to be an excellent model and should, hopefully, look good in almost any style of dress or trousers. She waved them goodbye and was itching to get to work on some more detailed designs for their approval. Her enthusiasm was well and truly back on course. There was also a hint from Lady Carlton-Prior that the bridesmaids' dresses could also be commissioned, if the designs looked suitable, despite Lucinda's protest about not wanting bridesmaids.

Chapter 15

A few weeks later, Laura, sitting in her workshop, was deep in thought. Her business was booming and most of the time she was feeling better in herself. To her surprise, after a couple of further tense meetings with Lucinda Carlton-Prior and her mother, a design that seemed to satisfy them both had been decided upon. Laura was now engaged in making the design toile, in a light muslin, so that tweaks could be made before it was cut out in the proper fabrics. She sat at her desk doodling new designs; there was no doubt she would need help. She flicked through her order book, not only was she making Lucinda's outfit, but there were four bridesmaids and a flower girl, not many by society wedding standards. Too many according to Lucinda, or Lucy as she asked Laura to call her, when they were last talking on the 'phone. She would be happy with just her best friend.

This wedding alone was a big commission for Laura, but when Lady Carlton-Prior asked her to make a special dress for her to wear to the evening reception, it took on huge significance. A London designer, a name, rather than a person Laura knew, who apparently had already made several outfits for different occasions, was making Lady Carlton-Prior's outfit for the wedding itself, but she was happy enough with Laura's work to ask her to make her evening dress. It was hopefully just out of loyalty to the other designer that she hadn't been asked to make the daytime wedding outfit as well. She felt it was a bit of a test and if she could impress her, then Lady Carlton-Prior could well put more business her way. She didn't like to think about the consequences if she didn't make a good impression, but she was again feeling confident in her own ability.

Since changing her website to say that she was now open for new commissions, work had been coming in. As well as the Carlton-Prior wedding Laura was also working on a smaller wedding, and refashioning some beautiful pieces that, since losing weight, no longer fitted their wealthy owner. The small wedding was a local affair and the young bride's joy at having a bespoke designer dress, made her a delight to work with. Laura looked forward to their appointments and took pleasure in adding little extras and suggesting ways of accessorising her dress, to bring out the best of her small features and petite figure. Not that she didn't look forward to Lucy's appointments, it was just they were less relaxed if Lucy's mother was in attendance; although Laura made sure she gave both clients an equally high-quality service.

Laura mapped out her workload, she could manage, just. The dates worked but it would be hard. It would be nice to have someone to bounce ideas off and help with some of the basics, but who? Perhaps she should ring Vicky for advice. This was the downside of setting up on her own, it was exciting, and she loved the freedom, but she did miss the hustle and bustle and sometimes complete madness of Vicky's studio.

'I think I'll advertise for someone to come and work with me,' Laura said to Ben that evening, when we they were in the kitchen preparing their evening meal.

Ben smiled to himself, relieved that Laura was, almost, back to being her old self. He glanced at the photo of Poppy on the dresser and although he still felt a pang, the horror of that time was at last fading.

'Good idea. What about asking Andrea?' he suggested.

'Andrea? She's a car mechanic.'

'I know, but didn't you say she was good at dressmaking?'

'Yes, but …' Laura continued laying the table, thoughts

whirling around in her head. Andrea, good to her word, had kept in touch and been back over to see Laura a few times. Her visits had been easy and even seeing Ralph was a pleasure. No one else from her antenatal group came near. There was a card of condolence signed by a few of them, which to Laura smacked of duty. She felt they were embarrassed, or frightened that she might somehow contaminate their perfect world, or at least the image of motherhood, that she was sure they were presenting to everyone outside. She could imagine their little self-depreciating laughs as they declared they never realised how difficult it would all be, but how wonderful, Tom or Joe or whoever, was at supporting them. Part of her irritation with them, was the strong suspicion niggling in the back of her mind, that she would have been the same, never setting foot outside unless she was immaculately groomed and not admitting to anyone that life was less than wonderful. She sighed, who knew, perhaps she was being unfair, and she supposed the reality was probably very different for all of them. Certainly, she remembered Andrea saying that she barely had time to get dressed in the first couple of weeks, let alone put-on make-up, but then Andrea wasn't like the others.

Andrea! Of course, she came back to why she was thinking about Andrea. She was a good seamstress, from what Laura had seen. On several occasions Laura was surprised and impressed with clothes Andrea told her she'd made for herself and for Ralph. They weren't the style of garments Laura designed and made, but Andrea obviously had some basic skills that could be developed. More importantly she liked Andrea, she was down to earth and funny, and clearly hard-working, but she was a mechanic and enjoyed it. She might not want to give it up to do fairly menial work in a sewing room.

'You could ask her, before you advertise,' said Ben, as he fried onions, tomatoes and mushrooms to go with some juicy looking tuna steaks that were sitting on a board next to the pan.

'I suppose I could ask her, but I doubt she'll want to, she works with her brother close to where she lives. Coming here wouldn't be very convenient. That smells great! How long will it be? I'm starving!' Laura said nodding towards the pan.

'Couple of minutes, pour some wine and it'll be ready.'

A couple of days later Laura pulled her car up outside a small garage and climbed out, looking around in confusion. She was sure this was the name of the garage Andrea had mentioned. It was in the right area, but this place was closed. Laura looked closer and peered through a side window, not only was it closed but also, judging by the lack of equipment inside, it was completely shut down. A sturdy padlock on a chain held the large front doors together. There was no information, not even opening times, on any of the pieces of paper stuck to the windows. She stood in front of the doors and stared around; she knew Andrea lived on this estate somewhere but had no idea of her address. She pulled out her phone to see if she had transferred Andrea's phone number. Her number wasn't there, Andrea had always called her. It must be recorded in received calls Laura thought, and began searching the list.

'Closed down. Week or more ago,' a youngish man walking passed the garage called to her.

'Yes, I can see! I'm looking for someone that used to work here, Andrea ...' Laura suddenly realised she didn't even know Andrea's surname.

'Yeah, Andrea Willis, her brother ran the place. Good mechanic, for a woman,' he said.

'I don't suppose you know where they live?' Laura asked.

'Car broken down. I'll 'ave a look if you like?' he said, nodding towards Laura's car.

'No, my car's fine thanks, I'm a friend of Andrea's.'

'Not much of a friend if you don't know her name or where she lives,' he said. 'You from the council, or social, are you?'

'No, I'm not. I'm genuinely a friend, but we haven't known each other long.' She was irritated at having to explain herself to a complete stranger, and thought that he wasn't going to tell her Andrea's address, but after looking her up and down and glancing longingly at her car, he nodded towards one of the two storey blocks.

'Cabot House, first floor, number six,' he said. 'See you then,' he called over his shoulder, as he carried on his way towards a small rank of shops.

'Yes, thank you,' Laura replied, and climbed back into her car.

She parked in a space beside the block but felt uneasy, there were so many reports on the news about drugs and violence, as well as cars being damaged or stolen on estates like this. Scanning the area around and satisfying herself that no one was loitering or watching her, Laura made her way to the nearest staircase. It was spotlessly clean, which surprised her. From newspaper articles and television programmes she always imagined these stairwells would smell of urine and be littered with rubbish and used syringes. She began to feel foolish and ashamed for being taken in by media stereotypes. Number six was the first flat at the top of the stairs. Laura kept her fingers crossed as she rang the bell, hoping that Andrea would be at home. All was quiet inside, and she was about to turn away disappointed, when the door opened and Andrea, Ralph in her arms, was standing in front of her.

'Laura, what a lovely surprise, come on in.'

Andrea's genuine pleasure at seeing Laura on the doorstep chased Laura's doubts away. She stepped inside and followed Andrea down a short corridor into a small sitting room. Laura looked around, everywhere was tidy, if sparsely furnished, and the walls were adorned with some fascinating artwork.

'My scribbles,' Andrea followed Laura's gaze towards a particularly intriguing piece.

'You're full of hidden talents! They're very good did you teach yourself?' Laura asked.

'Partly, and I used to go to a local art group, before this young man came along. My mum is my greatest fan, well probably my only fan,' Andrea said. 'Take a seat, would you like a coffee?'

'Thanks, that would be lovely.' Laura sat on the sofa and watched Andrea carefully place Ralph in a bouncy chair before she disappeared into the tiny kitchen. Ralph stared at Laura with big round brown eyes, and she stared back.

'Hello little one,' she said, and smiled and was instantly rewarded with a gummy smile back.

'There you go, it's only instant I'm afraid,' Andrea placed two mugs of coffee on the table.

'I went to the garage first, thinking you would be there,' said Laura.

'Ah, you saw it was closed then.'

'Yes, is it closed permanently?'

'Probably, it's a long story. My brother, Billy, turned out to be not as honest on the financial front as we thought. I don't know the full extent but fraud, embezzlement, money laundering, you name it he seems to have been up to it,' Andrea said. 'We thought maybe it was just a mistake at first, that he would be able to explain, but it seems not, he's up to his eyes in trouble and there's definitely no mistake.'

To Laura's surprise she looked angry rather than embarrassed.

'Mum's gone with him to the police station today for more questioning, but he'll have to go to court, and who knows, probably to prison, serves him right. I could kill him.'

'Oh dear, I'm really sorry.'

'He's an idiot, it was a good business, he's cost everyone their jobs and God alone knows what the guys will do, or me come to that, there isn't much work around here, but sorry you don't want to hear about all my problems. Were you…?'

'Well, the reason I came to see you might be relevant to your problem,' said Laura.

'Really?' Andrea looked interested.

'I wondered if you would like to come and work with me. I need someone to help now my orders are growing, and I was impressed with your dressmaking skills,' Laura looked at Andrea, hoping she wasn't sounding patronizing.

'Go on,' Andrea leant forward her interest piqued.

'It wouldn't be quite full time to start with and it would be fairly basic work initially, but well, if it works, and I get busier…' Laura looked up at Andrea's paintings while she tried to think of a better way to put it; she wasn't very good at this side of business.

'You mean I wouldn't be designing my own range of clothes?' Andrea pulled a face.

Laura felt a moment of panic, perhaps she'd made a mistake, and she hadn't really imagined Andrea touching the designer gowns, not at the beginning anyway.

'Don't worry, I'm joking,' Andrea said. 'I wouldn't expect to be more than a dogsbody at first.'

'No, not a dogsbody, definitely not that. More an assistant.'

'I would love to work with you, really, even if the garage was still going it would be really tempting, but as it is I can't think of anything better.' Andrea looked away and Laura wondered if she was wiping away a tear.

'It would all be proper, contract and all that sort of thing,' she said, suddenly realising she would need Ben's help to make sure she did actually do everything properly. Employing another person would mean all sorts of paperwork that was new to her. She could always ring Vicky for advice if Ben didn't know what to do, she thought.

Andrea made another coffee and the two women talked in more detail about the job, and, more importantly for Andrea, the salary, which she was happy with. Ralph making demands to be fed eventually ended their conversation, and Laura prepared to leave satisfied that they agreed about everything.

'Thank you so much Laura, it's a real lifeline as well as something I've always wanted to do. I can't wait to tell mum.'

'Thank you for saying yes. I'll see you on Monday morning.'

Laura skipped down the stairs back to her car; she had a good feeling about Andrea and was looking forward to them working together. She felt confident she'd made the right decision, turned on the car radio and sang all the way home.

Chapter 16

Ben looked at the clock, twenty-two minutes past three, it was dark not even a glimpse of moonlight to cast a shadow. He couldn't see her, but he knew Laura was standing on the landing outside their bedroom door, he could hear her rapid breathing and his heart sank, not again, just when she seemed to be making such good progress. He must have felt her moving and getting out of bed in his sleep, just enough to rouse him, and now he was wide-awake.

Lying still, Ben strained his ears to hear. Nothing. Perhaps he was wrong, he hoped he was wrong, she might just be in the en-suite, but then he heard her move on the landing. He waited, lifted his head so he could hear more clearly, again there was nothing. Ben didn't want to leave the warmth of the bed, but he knew he would have to go and investigate. Reluctantly, he swung his legs over the side, slid his feet into his slippers and padded towards the door.

'Laura,' he whispered. 'Come back to bed.'

Now that his eyes were accustomed to the dark, he could see her silhouetted against the window. She was standing still, not just still he could tell she was rigid, just outside the closed nursery door. She didn't move, or even look in his direction at the sound of his voice.

'Laura,' Ben said, louder, as he reached her and touched her arm. 'What are you doing? It's the middle of the night and cold.'

'Shh, don't make a sound, listen, there, can you hear it?'

Ben felt a wave of nausea sweep over him; he couldn't bear

the thought of her sinking into depression again; he thought she was over this. In fact, this was the first time to his knowledge that Laura had heard noises from the nursery, since the arrival of Colin. Colin's presence was so therapeutic for them both, but he would be curled up in front of the woodburner in the kitchen now. Perhaps they should let him sleep upstairs; it might help to calm Laura. All these thoughts whirled through Ben's head in a couple of seconds as he stood by Laura's side.

'There, did you hear?' Laura put her hand out towards Ben. 'Can you hear it?'

'No, I can't hear anything. Come on Laura, it's freezing you'll catch a cold, come on back to bed.'

'Listen, there, a baby crying. You must be able to hear it. I don't believe you can't hear it.'

'Honestly, Laura, there's nothing, I can't hear anything, I promise I wouldn't say I couldn't, if I could.'

'It's in there. I know it is. Ben, please, go and look.'

Ben threw open the door with more confidence than he suddenly felt; he rubbed the back of his neck, which annoyingly was starting to prickle. He flipped the light switch.

'There, it's empty,' he said. 'Come on, let's get you back to bed.'

The sudden bright light made them both blink, but it illuminated every corner of the room, even into the cupboard, its doors still wide open from Laura's last frantic search of the room. Laura hesitated behind him, stepped into the empty room and crumpled onto the chair sobbing.

'Oh Laura, darling, please don't. Come on we'll get through this together,' he knelt beside her and encircled her with his arms. 'Trust me there isn't a baby here, there isn't anything in here, come on back to bed.'

Ben helped her to her feet and steered her gently back to bed, he climbed in beside her and was asleep again as soon as his head touched the pillow, his breathing deep and rhythmical. Laura lay not moving beside him, her mind was too active to let her sleep. Her whole body was on alert, listening hard, to pick up any sound in the night, but all she could hear was Ben's steady breathing, it was even too early for the birds to be singing. She felt irritated that Ben was able to fall asleep so easily, she wondered whether he was really telling the truth, despite what he said. She found it hard to believe he really couldn't hear the baby or, was he just pretending, to try and stop her getting anxious, but that didn't work because if he was telling the truth then she must be going mad.

Maybe it was all in her mind, maybe she was ill, the doctor and everyone else thought she was. Mild postnatal depression he'd told her in a kind but I've-seen-it-all-before tone. Laura didn't believe him, she wasn't depressed, grieving yes, of course, but she was starting to slowly move on, she was working again and functioning well, meeting people, taking Colin out. She wasn't depressed she was doing just fine; she wasn't dwelling on Poppy, well not all the time. When she was staying with her parents, she seemed fine, and they didn't think she was depressed. It must be the cottage. Laura thought about the antidepressants in her bedside drawer that she hadn't taken, she didn't need them, she was certain of that. She wasn't the sort of person to pop pills for everything. She didn't want her mind to be dulled by drugs all the time. She assured herself that the crying from the nursery was nothing to do with depression, she didn't know what it was, but even if Ben couldn't hear it, it wasn't in her head; or was it? She tossed and turned, doubts flooding her mind as she fell in and out of restless sleep. What if she was ill, what if she was going mad? Should she take the prescribed pills? Should she go back to her mother? Her mind was awash with thoughts and contradictions, and strange dreams did nothing to restore her inner peace.

Chapter 17

Laura slept late the following morning and by the time she emerged, tousled, into the kitchen Ben was up, dressed and reading the Sunday paper with Colin snoozing by his side.

'Coffee and toast?' he asked, getting to his feet as she entered.

Laura nodded.

'Please,' she said, patting Colin who also jumped up and was bouncing around her.

'How are you feeling?' Ben asked.

'Ok, I'm fine, really I am. It's just that, well, it just feels so real in the night,' Laura pulled out a chair and sat at the kitchen table.

'I know, everything seems different, worse, at night,' he said.

Colin stopped bouncing and laid his head on Laura's lap. She stroked his silky ears while she watched Ben make her breakfast.

'I'm going to make us a proper Sunday lunch today,' Laura said, after she'd eaten her toast and drunk a strong cup of coffee.

'Are you sure, do you want to?'

'Of course, you wait and see. You can take Colin for a walk, and I'll surprise you with my special roast.'

Ben was sceptical, but didn't want to discourage any semblance of normality, not that Laura cooking Sunday lunch was normal, in fact he couldn't ever remember her doing it. He thought back with a pang to the leisurely Sundays they used to have. *It* felt like a lifetime ago. They would get up late after toast and coffee in bed with the papers, then wander down to a café for a late brunch, perhaps meet up with friends, have a walk in a park or visit a museum or gallery. Usually followed by an evening in, curled up on the sofa watching TV or listening to music, while nibbling on exotic delicacies picked up from one of the many foreign food outlets that were springing up everywhere; but of course, that was London. He doubted the village shop even opened on a Sunday let alone sold anything deliciously exotic.

An hour or so later Ben pulled on his coat and picked up Colin's lead. Laura was showered and dressed and seemed to have put the night's episode behind her, although Ben thought she looked tired and pale. He kissed her cheek and watched for a moment as she assembled vegetables, and placed the chicken, brought over by Claire a few days earlier, in a roasting pan. He quickly tried to assess whether she was going to be all right while he was out, and could see no reason why not, so he called to Colin to join him. Colin was by his side in an instant, waggy-tailed and ready to follow anywhere.

'We'll eat about two thirty, don't be late,' Laura called, as they set off.

Ben walked quickly beyond the village and climbed a hill, which gave him a vantage point in both directions. It was a steep climb, but he relished the physical effort, the air was clear and cold and the view from the top was worth the effort. Colin was in his element, sniffing in the bushes and racing after the ball Ben threw for him. He sat on the wall smiling at Colin's exuberance. Laura would love it up here, he thought, but for now, guiltily, he was enjoying being on his own with just Colin for company. In one direction he could see the river and distant Welsh hills, and in the other he looked down on the village and over to William and Claire's farmhouse.

The village pub seemed to be beckoning him down for a drink, and he didn't resist. By the time he reached the pub he was glowing with the effort and cold, and the anticipation of a thirst-quenching pint made him hurry to the bar.

'Ben, good to see you,' William was standing at the bar, pint in hand. 'What can I get you?'

'Pint of Jolly Cobbler please,' said Ben, now feeling warm he peeled off his jacket and pulled up a barstool, he was pleased to see William.

'Good walk?' William stroked Colin, who was now extremely muddy, but still welcome in the pub.

'Excellent,' Ben took a big slug of beer. 'Went up the hill opposite your place, great views.'

William nodded in agreement.

'You can see for miles on a clear day like today. It's a while since I've been up there, must make the effort, but Gem's not quite as lively as Colin here,' he looked down at Colin who was jumping up at the bar to see if anything edible was in reach. Ben pushed Colin's feet off the bar with a sheepish grin to the barmaid as she leant over and wiped the mud away.

'Sorry,' he said. 'Lie down Colin,' and to both his and William's surprise he sighed and settled himself on the floor. The two men talked dogs, countryside, sport, and two pints later when William asked after Laura, Ben related the events of the night before, and about the previous time when Laura thought she heard a baby crying. He didn't intend to, and felt slightly disloyal, but the beer loosened his inhibitions and he needed to talk. William was sympathetic and he felt, like Ben, that it was all probably linked to her grief, and depression. He suggested asking Claire to call in sometime to see if Laura felt like talking to her.

'Tell her not to tell Laura I told you, but yes that would be good.'

'She'll be very discreet.'

After a while the men made moves to leave, dinner was beckoning to them both. William left first, leaving Ben to finish the last dregs of his beer. Ben was just putting his coat back on when a man, the vicar as it turned out, pulled up the stool beside him. Ben was surprised to see the vicar in the pub on a Sunday and wasn't sure he wanted to enter into a conversation with him. Ben had nothing against him, he'd heard he was a good chap, played cricket and joined in village life, but Ben wasn't a churchgoer, well, not even a believer and he hoped the vicar wasn't going to try to persuade him to join his congregation.

'Aiden Jones,' he held out his hand.

Ben shook it. 'Ben Jefferies,' he said, zipping his coat up.

'I hope you won't think I was eavesdropping, but I couldn't help overhearing your conversation with William, about your wife hearing a baby crying.'

Ben felt slightly alarmed, he didn't want their problems known all over the village, cautiously he nodded but said nothing.

'You're in Oak Tree Cottage, aren't you?'

Ben nodded again, wondering what might come next.

'It's just your wife isn't the first person to say she's heard a sound like a baby crying. A lady who lived there a few years ago mentioned something, but it's probably nothing,' he said, noting Ben's expression. 'A fox outside, or you know what these old places are like for creaks and groans, like I say it's probably nothing and I think I tried to reassure her of that at the time, but if ever you want to talk the vicarage is right behind the church.'

Ben felt apprehension rising as Aiden was talking, he wasn't sure he wanted to hear what he was saying and didn't know whether it made him feel better or worse. He couldn't think what to say in response, so just stared with a blank look on his face at the vicar. Aiden wasn't an old man, early fifties perhaps, with an open friendly face. He seemed quite down to earth and sane, not someone liable to flights of fancy, he might well be the sort of bloke, in other circumstances, Ben could have enjoyed a pint and chat with. He tried to analyse why the dog collar put him off but couldn't reach any reasonable conclusion.

'Thanks, but I'm not, well I'm not really religious,' Ben said.

'That's not a problem, my offer's still open, and if ever you want to chat you know where to find me.'

'Yes, well, thanks I'll bear it in mind.'

Ben made his way home feeling slightly confused and uncomfortable and decided not to mention the vicar's comments to Laura. He wasn't sure it would help her at all to learn that other people thought they heard a baby crying, and after all, he decided, there couldn't be anything in it, just coincidence. There must be a logical explanation, if it was real, he would have heard it as well, and he definitely had not. He was surprised and irritated that the vicar even mentioned it; he must have an ulterior motive, he thought, and by the time he reached the cottage had convinced himself that was the case.

The smell of roast chicken filled his nostrils as soon as he opened the kitchen door, and he realised that he was starving. Laura, her long hair piled on top of her head was busy stirring something on the cooker, and all thoughts of the vicar disappeared. Laura was flushed with the heat and Ben was struck by how vulnerable she looked. She turned round and smiled and was greeted enthusiastically by Colin whose nose twitched in delight at the smell of the chicken.

'Not for you,' Laura said, as Colin nuzzled his way between her and the cooker. 'Good walk?' she asked Ben.

'Really good, we went up the big hill, you know the one the other side of the village; we must do it together some time, there are great views from the top. Then I dropped into the pub and had a pint with William.'

'Sounds good, how's William?'

'Good, he sends his love.'

'Can you open a bottle, better be white with chicken. It won't be too long.'

'Smells wonderful, I'll just go and get cleaned up first.'

'I've made pudding as well,' Laura said, as he left the room.

Ben hesitated outside the nursery about to go in, but decided not to and pulled the door closed, he definitely wouldn't say anything to Laura about what he'd heard.

Chapter 18

Laura banged her hand on the table and let out an audible groan, the pencils bounced, and coffee slopped.

'You OK?' Andrea looked up from where she was sorting threads and trimmings into drawers.

'It's these accounts, I just can't get my head around them,' Laura replied.

'Can I help, I'm reasonable at figures?' Andrea asked, walking across and leaning over Laura's shoulder.

'You can if you like, it's just this lot here, I can't get them to match and add up. I get a different figure every time. This column is supposed to be the same as that one.'

'OK, let me have a look. Why don't you take a break?'

'I will, thanks Andrea. I think I'll go for a walk, try to clear my head, is that all right?' Laura stood up and smiled weakly at Andrea.

Andrea nodded, and murmured her agreement, as she settled into Laura's chair.

'I'll probably be gone by the time you get back, I can't be late picking Ralph up,' she called, to Laura's retreating back.

Laura raised her hand in acknowledgment. She hurried across to the cottage and into the kitchen. The warmth from the burner, where Colin was curled up, came out to meet her as she opened the door and stepped inside. She knew there was more money in her account than her calculations showed, and as soon as she received the final payment for another recently completed dress, she would be well in credit, even after paying Andrea and her suppliers. She shook her head, this was definitely the downside of self-employment. Hopefully, Andrea would be able to spot where she was going wrong. She would have to do as Vicky suggested and hire an accountant.

It was a cold morning, but at last the rain had stopped and the sun was successfully struggling to find a gap in the clouds. The mellow stone of the cottage was taking on its familiar golden glow; the colour of the stone was one of the aspects that attracted them to the cottage in the first place. It looked so warm and welcoming.

'Walkies Colin,' Laura called. She pulled on her wellies and fleece, which was difficult with Colin bouncing around her, excited at the thought of an unexpected walk. She shoved a couple of poo bags and biscuits into her pocket and set off across the lawn to the back gate, Colin eager at her side.

They crossed the field and onto the lane, the rain overnight and now the warmth from the sun left the air full of the fresh scent of wet grass and Laura breathed in deeply. It wasn't quite the same as the sea air at home, but it was good. The tarmac on the road shone like a silver ribbon winding off into the distance, the aftermath of rain in London was never like this she thought.

Laura walked slowly up the lane, Colin running ahead, sniffing in the hedges and disturbing the occasional pheasant, his tail a constant wag. She really hoped the walk would clear her head; she desperately wanted to get the paperwork finished today. She hoped Andrea could sort it out. Already, after a fairly short time, she knew employing Andrea was a real success, not only was she a good seamstress, but they were becoming good friends. She was so different to any of her London friends, but Laura felt totally at ease with her and they shared a sense of humour. Andrea was straightforward with no edge to her and Laura felt her precious business was all the better for having her.

As she walked further up the lane, her vision was beginning to dance, in the strange way it did before the onset of a migraine. Perhaps it was just the glare from the wet road, and it would go in a minute. She walked on a little further then sat down on a rough dry-stone wall that formed part of a bridge spanning a small stream. She closed her eyes, if she sat still for a few minutes with her eyes shut, the headache might not develop, if she was very lucky.

'We'll just wait here a minute Colin.' Colin trotted up to her side and laid his head on her thigh, tail still wagging.

'Good boy just sit for a moment,' Laura patted his head. He sat patiently waiting until Laura was ready to continue their walk. After a few minutes Laura tentatively opened her eyes. The dancing waterfall effect seemed to have eased, and there was no familiar, and dreaded, drilling pain behind her eyes. Thank goodness, she thought relieved, the last thing she needed today was a bad headache.

Cautiously, she raised her head, the lane was no longer shining wet with the rain, in fact it now looked like it was covered in mud. Laura looked closer and to her surprise realised that it wasn't covered in mud, it *was* mud. How could that be, tarmac can't disappear in a few minutes? She closed her eyes again, opened them and looked, not just at the lane by her feet but the whole stretch, it was definitely mud and not only that, it was dry mud.

Feeling confused, she stood up and looked around, at what should be a familiar scene. The usual trickle of a stream under the bridge was now a small river, flowing quite rapidly between tree-lined banks. She was certain the banks were just grass or bare mud before, but now there were mature trees including a large willow, which dipped its branches close to the water's edge. The bank was quite steep in places, and further upstream Laura could see a small boat moored to a wooden pontoon. She turned around and looked back towards the cottage, she could see an unfamiliar small building, a barn of some sort. A large deciduous wood was blocking her view of Oak Tree Cottage. The hairs on the back of her neck stood on end and she gasped for breath, reaching out to the wall to steady herself. Looking the other way Laura could see the tower of the church and a few cottages but nowhere near as many houses as there should be. On the hill to her right William and Claire's farmhouse looked as solid as ever, but the barns were missing, and Laura suddenly realised that the telegraph poles and electricity cables were also missing. She pulled her phone out of her pocket - no service. Panic and confusion began to flood through Laura's body, and she thought for a moment she was going to be sick. She reached for Colin, for reassurance and sat back down, and as she did, he gave a short howl and raised one of his paws towards Laura.

'Jesus Christ, Colin, what's going on?' She sat back on the wall and took some deep breaths. She must make sense of what was going on. She must keep calm.

There was nothing that made sense; the only conclusion she could reach was that she was actually going mad. She really must have postnatal depression, or worse, and it had finally claimed her mind. It was her own fault for not taking the antidepressants; but she didn't feel mad. Surely if she was mad, she wouldn't think she was mad.

She closed her eyes again, squeezing her lids tight before opening them and looking around. The scene was the same, familiar but totally different, how could it be? She stood up, she needed to go back to the cottage, once she was there everything would be all right, she just needed a lie down, go to sleep and then everything would be back to normal, it must be some strange new aberration of a migraine. She would take the antidepressants, and everything would be fine.

'OK Colin let's go home,' she took a few shaky steps along the lane, but Colin didn't move.

'Come on, good boy,' Laura called. She couldn't cope with Colin playing up as well.

Colin edged towards her, his hackles were up, and his tail was tucked between his legs. Laura's stomach contracted; didn't dogs have a sixth sense? Colin knew something was wrong; he moved to Laura's side and howled again, an eerie haunting sound.

'Don't do that Colin, please, we'll go home, and everything will be fine,' Laura spoke quietly to him and stroked his head. She pulled his lead out of her pocket and with trembling fingers clipped it to Colin's collar. The last thing she needed at this moment was for him to run off in fright. She turned to walk down the lane, but stopped, a cloud of dust was rising in the distance and moving towards her. As she stared, rooted to the spot, the dust revealed a person on horseback, galloping along the lane towards her.

'Quick,' Laura tugged on Colin's lead and the pair of them inelegantly, at least on Laura's part, half climbed, half fell, over the low wall into the field, partly so they weren't mown down by the horse and partly to hide. The horse and rider came thundering passed; oblivious of Laura crouched down behind the wall. The man was riding so fast Laura doubted he would have noticed even if they were standing in the middle of the lane. She turned and watched him disappear, as she was enveloped in the dry dust kicked up by the horse. She coughed and instinctively brushed herself down, while continuing to stare after him along the lane.

Fear momentarily turned to fascination; he looked like someone out of a Jane Austin novel, a Mr Darcy no less. He rode a white stallion and was dressed in cream riding breeches, leather boots, a long green tailcoat and top hat. Laura imagined him wearing a white frilly shirt. Part of her degree had been studying aspects of fashion in history, and Laura's love of horses made her choose riding habits. She felt certain the rider was dressed in typical Gentleman's Regency attire. He was obviously an aristocrat of some sort.

As a child, well more a young teenager, she used to go riding as often as possible and competed in gymkhanas on a borrowed pony. Her bedroom wall was festooned in rosettes and photographs of horses. One of Laura's hopes when she and Ben decided to move to the country was that she would be able to take up horse riding again, even have a horse of her own. She last rode several years ago; it was on an unsuccessful pony trekking holiday in Wales, with Ben, not long after they met. She'd twisted his arm to go and he, not wanting to disappoint her, pretended he knew how to ride. She remembered the trip with affection. It was only unsuccessful on the horse riding front, mainly because Ben fell off and broke his finger, but not on the romance front. After that holiday they became a couple, on the condition that Laura never persuaded Ben to go riding again. She sank back down on to the grass and leaning against the wall was momentarily lost in memories, the sun was warm and in other circumstances she could happily have dozed for a few minutes.

Chapter 19

Colin pawing on her arm and his quiet whimper brought Laura back sharply to her present situation. She must get home. She pulled herself up and looked to the left and right along the lane before climbing back over the wall. All was quiet, unnaturally quiet, there was no distant hum of traffic or whirring of chainsaws, or other sounds that usually made up the soundtrack of daily life in the village. Crows were cawing in the trees but otherwise there was nothing.

She walked back along the lane looking for the stile back into the field that backed onto their cottage. She walked to where she thought it should be but became disorientated, there was no stile, neither was there a field, just trees.

A bit further along the lane there was a worn track through the wood, Laura hesitated for a moment then tightening her grip on Colin's lead decided to follow it. The air was filled with the fragrance of leaves and seemed fresher than Laura remembered. Twigs snapped under her feet releasing an earthy, woody aroma. She suddenly realised the trees here were in full leaf, yet earlier when she left home, they were only beginning to show signs of buds and the leaves were just reappearing.

She walked cautiously along the path having lost her bearings, until the trees thinned a little and she could see the side of Oak Tree Cottage ahead of her. She was about to rush forward so this ordeal could end, but she stopped almost before she'd started. Something wasn't right; she moved forward slowly, making sure she kept out of sight. As she neared the cottage, she became incapable of moving any further, and felt the blood draining from her face, she looked at her feet, now heavy as lead, almost expecting to see it seeping through her shoes. She crouched down and shaking put her head between her knees to stop herself fainting.

Clearly, through the quiet air, came the sound of a baby crying, a faint distressed sound that chilled her to her core. It was exactly the same cry as she heard at night. She pulled herself to her feet and was about to run in the opposite direction when she heard a scream, followed by another, it sounded like a young girl, not a child, but not a woman. She dug her once immaculately manicured, now just clean and short, nails into the trunk of the nearest tree to steady herself. Colin gave a low growl and Laura noticed that his hackles were up again. She put her hand on his collar, and they crept cautiously round to the back of the cottage, keeping their distance at the edge of the wood.

The cottage was much smaller. There was no kitchen or dining room extension, only a side wall with an old wooden cart leaning up against it. There was a small outbuilding on the site where Laura now had her business, and where Andrea should now be working on her accounts, but it bore no resemblance to her pretty two-story workshop. She saw but struggled to register these differences as she pulled Colin back into the trees, which now covered almost the whole area of what was currently her back garden. There was a small unkempt area nearer the cottage where vegetables were growing with difficulty amongst the weeds, and a few scrawny chickens scratched in the earth.

Laura's eyes were fixed all the time on the cottage, insanely she half expected Ben to come out of the cottage and tell her it was all a joke. She was quivering inside, but every cell in her body was on full alert. The baby crying, and girl screaming, stopped. But the following silence was almost as disturbing. Laura strained her ears to hear any sound from the cottage, she could hear nothing, and she wondered if she'd imagined it, but Colin's rigid stance and rumbling growl indicated he was still picking up sounds from inside.

The silence was finally broken by raised voices, muffled at first then louder. The small wooden door halfway along the back wall was thrown open and a girl ran out. She looked about fifteen or sixteen and appeared completely dishevelled, her hair hung in a brown and tangled mass onto her shoulders, and her face was as pale as the moon. Her apparently once white, now grubby shift had what seemed to be bloodstains over the back, soaking down to the hem. She wore black boots unlaced, which almost caused her to fall as she ran from the house towards the wood, and where Laura and Colin were standing behind a tree. The girl was oblivious to everything around her and didn't notice Laura standing within a couple of feet of her, as she ran deeper into the wood. Laura felt the urge to follow but was distracted by angry words being exchanged by a man and woman back in the doorway of the cottage. The man was physically restraining the woman, who seemed nearly as upset as the girl, her daughter maybe. She was struggling to release his hand from her arm; so presumably, she could follow after the girl into the wood. The man was shaking and pulling the woman quite violently, and when he raised his hand Laura gasped, sure he was about to strike her. She couldn't make out what was being said, but suddenly, with a shove, the woman was back through the door and it was slammed shut. Again, silence descended, more stifling than before, and a sudden squawk from a chicken made her jump.

Laura leant against the tree, her heart was hammering in her chest and tears began running down her cheeks in a steady torrent. All she wanted to do was go home, but she didn't know where her home was anymore. She didn't know what to do, this was madness, she must be hallucinating, but how could hallucinations be so real, and if she was hallucinating why was Colin so disturbed?

After a few minutes she made her way further back into

the wood, she couldn't stay here anymore, and she became determined to find the girl. Certain that she held the answer to the baby Laura heard crying in the night. The girl was nowhere to be seen in the wood; the trees weren't dense, but they grew randomly with thick undergrowth, making progress slow, and Laura could only imagine the girl must have made her way straight through.

She soon lost her bearings and felt uneasy in the gloomy overbearing atmosphere of the wood. Pushing through stout shrubs, barely noticing scratches from brambles, she reached a small clearing, with what she assumed was a large badger sett at one side. Colin suddenly barked and pulled on his lead. Laura saw a black boot on the floor and caught a glimpse of bloodstained fabric halfway up an oak tree, with a small foot dangling beneath. She panicked and started to run, dreading what it meant and not wanting to look up to confirm her worst fear. It felt like she ran forever, never seeming to reach the edge of the wood, Colin sticking close by her side. In her haste she fell, tripping over a fallen branch and crashed to the floor, she wasn't badly hurt but lay where she landed sobbing so hard her ribs hurt. When would this nightmare ever end? She struggled to sit up, and examined her knees, muddy but no harm done. Colin rested his head on her shoulder and licked her ear; she hugged him close and let her tears soak into his soft coat.

'What are we going to do?' she whispered. 'Thank God you're with me.'

Colin licked and gave a first tentative wag in reply.

After a few minutes Laura straightened herself up and got to her feet.

'Come on, let's get out of here,' she said to Colin, and walking this time, made her way to where she could now see sunlight, indicating the last of the trees.

Chapter 20

Laura found herself on the side of a larger, but still basically mud lane, although there had been some efforts to lay stones down in places. She tried hard to work out where she was, this must be the road that now eventually reached the motorway junction, but without any familiar landmarks she couldn't be certain. She stood inhaling deeply until her heart rate was almost back to normal. There was a field opposite that looked like it sloped down to the river and just as she was about to cross over a cart, pulled by a small horse came round the bend. There wasn't time to hide so she stood back from the lane and tried to look inconspicuous, hoping the cart would carry on past.

'Whoa,' one of the two men sitting on the cart shouted to the horse as he pulled sharply on the reigns. The men stared at Laura, and she stared back not quite sure what to do or to make of them. They looked like they were in fancy dress about to go to a Ceilidh. One of them, the younger one, was wearing a loose creamy coloured cotton smock with a round domed, light-coloured, brimmed hat. The other man was wearing black trousers tucked into long socks with old brown boots, a crumpled loose shirt and a tatty waistcoat, with a flat cap of sorts on his head. The mutual staring seemed to last for ages, until the horse impatient to be moving stamped its foot on the ground.

'Whoa there. Youm not from round 'ere,' the older man stated rather than asked.

Laura shook her head, uncertain whether to laugh, or cry, or run away as fast as she could.

'Where you be from then?' the younger man asked, leaning across and eyeing Laura suspiciously. Laura opened her mouth to answer but wasn't sure what to say, but before she could speak the older man answered for her.

'One of them fair people, or actor types, I be bound. Lost is e?'

'Sort of,' Laura answered.

'Up e gets then; we be taking this lot t' castle.'

Laura hesitated, but the man held out his hand, she accepted it and he pulled her up on to the cart. There wasn't a seat as such, they were sitting on filled sacks, and there were more sacks and a couple of barrels in the back. The man pushed Laura across, so she was sitting in the middle between them. Colin, without hesitation, once he saw Laura climbing up, jumped into the back of the cart and settled himself on a sack. They set off with a lurch, the small horse showing surprising strength as he pulled his load over the uneven road. The sun was now quite warm, and Laura pulled down the zip of her fleece to cool herself down.

'What be that?' the younger man asked, pointing to Laura's jacket. 'Did e see that?' he asked his companion. The reigns were pulled to slow the horse down.

'Show 'im,' he said.

Laura pulled the zip up then back down again, both men stared in amazement.

'It's called a zip, look it fastens the front of the jacket together,' she tugged on either side to demonstrate how firm it was.

'Well, I ain't never seen the like, do it agin.'

Laura let both of them pull the zip up and down. The fabric of her fleece equally fascinated them.

'Soft as a lamb.'

'It's called a fleece,' Laura said.

'I ain't never seen no fleece that colour, where be it from?'

'It was made in China,' Laura said, and despite everything couldn't help feeling amused by the look of awe and reverence that came over their faces.

'An' them boots, that ain't leather be it?' the older man nodded towards Laura's green wellingtons.

'Rubber, it'll be common here soon.'

'Rubber?' he bent to touch Laura's boot. 'Rubber, that from China too, never seen nowt like it before, 'ave you Will?'

'What?' the younger man was still absorbed by the workings of Laura's zip. He turned his attention to her boots.

'Rubber, you say, from China. Look no seams nor laces,' said the older man.

Laura nodded.

'You'm from China?' the man called Will asked.

'No, I've never been to China, but they make lots of clothes and …' she was about to say electrical goods but realised that would be too difficult to explain. 'And different fabrics,' she finished.

They continued to question Laura as the cart made its way along the lane, intrigued by everything she wore, the way she looked, and the way she spoke. In the end they convinced each other that her exotic clothes, and very strange dress for a woman, were down to the fact that she belonged to the fair. She didn't contradict them and was even beginning to enjoy herself. She managed to ascertain from their discussion that George IV was on the throne; so, wracking her brain for school history facts, and the clothes of the horseman, guessed the year must be around 1820 or a bit earlier. She didn't ask directly, not wanting to raise even more questions about where she was from and why she was there. Questions she would have very much liked the answer to herself.

Chapter 21

As the castle came into view Laura wasn't sure whether she was reassured or confused that it looked exactly as it did when she and Ben visited it. A guided tour round the castle was one of their first outings, after moving into the cottage. She remembered it was finished in the twelfth century and was the oldest lived in castle, by the same family, in the country. She wracked her brain for any other information, she remembered Queen Elizabeth I visited sometime in the sixteenth century and Edward II was murdered there a couple of centuries earlier, none of which would help her in her present predicament.

'Who lives in the castle now,' Laura asked.

'It be William Berkeley, calls is self Earl Fitzhardinge,' the younger man said in a tone that made Laura think he wasn't too impressed by the Earl.

She wondered if he was the man on the horse who galloped passed her earlier. His appearance would fit with the title. The cart stopped on the lane at the edge of the castle meadow, she could see in the meadow a gathering of carts and makeshift tents and stalls. The two men looked at Laura, who didn't move, but just sat staring at the scene ahead of her.

'Best get down 'ere, we be going up t'castle courtyard,' the older man nodded first towards the fair and then towards the castle. Laura was reluctant to get down, she was anxious about being on her own again, but the older man gave an impatient tut and twitched the reigns, eager to complete his delivery. She climbed past Will and slid to the floor. Colin was by her side as soon as her feet touched the ground and without more ado the cart rolled on. Laura watched it jolt its way along the lane towards the castle and resisted the urge to run after it. She felt even more lonely, the brief interlude on the cart now only served to make her more anxious. This was ludicrous, what was happening couldn't be real and yet it was so vivid. Surely if it was a dream or in her imagination she would have woken up, or it would have stopped, by now.

Laura didn't want to attract attention to herself so made her way across the lane and into the trees and bushes lining the bank of the river, thankful for the cover they gave her. She felt weary and didn't know what to do next, after a short time she found a secluded spot, slightly raised above the meadow, where she sat down and surveyed the scene in front of her. She felt it was important not to fall asleep, but wasn't sure why, if she did, she might wake up at home, but somehow, she couldn't risk losing control, not that she felt in control of anything.

A hubbub of noise and activity was coming from the fair people who were grouped along one side of the meadow, with several carts, and men on horses, milling around in the middle. Fires had been lit and wisps of smoke rose up and drifted over the site. Along with the smell of smoke there was a pungent aroma of humanity, mingled with meaty smells, that Laura presumed was food cooking on the fires. From what Laura could see it appeared to be mainly women grouped around the fires chatting and stirring pots. They were a bit too far away to be sure. In an area nearest the road, groups of men, dressed in a similar way to the men on the cart, were standing around and lining up in front of a table, where another two, more official looking men were sitting. Laura presumed it was some sort of hiring event, probably for farm labourers. On the far side of the meadow and closer to the castle were the tents and stalls that she'd noticed from the road. This seemed to be either a travelling fair or possibly a circus, as near to the tents she could see jugglers practising, and someone else walking on his hands, who cartwheeled then sprang to his feet and lifted a woman onto his shoulders.

'Hello.'

Laura jumped as a small boy, probably about seven years old suddenly appeared around a tree. He plonked himself down beside her and grinned.

'Hello,' said Laura, studying her new companion closely.

He was a scruffy little boy and reminded Laura of the young pickpockets in Oliver Twist.

'Who are you, I ain't seen you before?' he asked, absently stroking Colin.

'I haven't been here before.'

He nodded, accepting this as a reasonable explanation.

'Are you with the fair?' asked Laura pointing towards the caravans and makeshift tents and stalls.

He nodded again. 'I ride the horses,' he said.

Laura raised a doubting eyebrow.

'I do, look,' he suddenly swung into a handstand, then rested his head on to his arms and waved his legs around. He then sprang in one movement onto his feet and did a back-flip landing on one leg and bent over backwards until his hands gripped his ankles.

'See I do that on the back of a horse.'

'That's very clever,' Laura was genuinely impressed, if a little doubtful that he could do that on a horse. 'What's your name?'

'George, like the King, he's dead now but the new King is gonna be George as well, so that's all right, I'm still like King George. What's your name?'

'Laura.'

'Who's that like'?

'I don't think I was named after anyone in particular,' Laura said.

'You talk funny, where you from?' he asked.

Laura thought, where was she from at this moment in

time? Nowhere she could sensibly explain to George.

'I'm from London,' she said at last.

'I'm gonna go to London one day, to see the Tower of London,' he said, rolling over on the grass. 'Join one of the big circus's and make me fortune.'

'That sounds exciting.'

''Ave you got summat to eat?' he asked, sitting up again.

'No, sorry, I haven't, only a few dog biscuits,' Laura produced a couple of biscuits from her pocket and Colin immediately sat up expectantly.

'Dog biscuits, you mean biscuits for him?' He nodded towards Colin. 'Biscuits special for a dog?' His look of total incredulity made Laura laugh.

'He's called Colin, look,' Laura showed George a small bone shaped biscuit; he took it from her and studied it carefully. Laura thought he was about to eat it himself, but he looked at it longingly and gave it back to her.

'Watch this,' Laura said, getting to her knees.

'Colin, sit.'

He sat.

'Colin, paw.'

He lifted his paw and Laura took it in her hand.

'Good boy,' she said and gave him a biscuit.

'Can I do it?' George asked.

Laura handed George a biscuit and he put Colin perfectly through his party trick.

'Wow, 'e should be in our show. Come see my dad,' George leapt to his feet. 'Come on, 'e can be in it tonight, an' you.'

'No, I can't, Colin and I can't stay we have to go?'

'Go where, back to London?'

Laura nodded, her stomach contracting as she realised she didn't know where to go and soon it would be starting to get dark.

''Ave you got any more?' he asked. 'Any more biscuits?' he said, when Laura raised an eyebrow. She put her hand in her pocket pulled out a couple and handed them to George. She expected him to put Colin through his party tricks again, but instead he nibbled the end.

'Tastes good,' he said stuffing the rest into his mouth.

Laura was about to stop him eating the other one, but she didn't suppose it would do him any harm. He didn't look as though he was used to healthy nourishing food, and she was sure none of the ingredients would harm him. Suddenly a shrill whistle sounded across the field.

'Me dad, I best go, it's nearly time to get ready,' he jumped to his feet. 'Bye, bye Colin,' he patted Colin's head. 'Sure you doesn't wanna be in it?'

'Sure, thanks, bye,' Laura said, and watched him skip across the field towards a man holding two horses; perhaps George really did ride them.

Once again, she felt acutely lonely after he'd gone, but she took hold of Colin's lead and retreated into the trees, she didn't want anyone coming to look for her, not at the moment anyway. Laura dithered for a while, she was tempted to make her way round towards the castle, maybe see if there was a way in, even find some clothes to change into, so she wasn't so conspicuous, but she quickly convinced herself that was a stupid idea and eventually decided to follow the river back towards the village. She pulled blackberries from the bushes as she went and suddenly hungry stuffed them into her mouth. Blackberries, it must be September, but how could it be?

Chapter 22

Away from the fair Laura quickly became lost again. The castle was hidden by the trees, and nothing else looked familiar. She tried to pull herself together; the river must go towards the village, just as it did in her real life, so all she needed to do was follow it. She had no idea what to do or where to go, even if she did reach the village, there would be no familiar places or faces. What if this was her life from now on? No, she shook her head, that couldn't happen, it was impossible, ridiculous. With no other ideas she decided to follow the river and take it from there.

Laura stumbled as she walked, her vision was playing tricks again and her head felt as though a drill was boring into her temple behind her left eye. She knew this time closing her eyes wouldn't stop the migraine developing. Climbing up the bank she found herself back by the small stone bridge. She clung to the wall, leant over and was sick down her fleece and into the water below. She moaned and slid down onto the stone surface of the bridge, she no longer cared whether anyone saw her, she no longer cared what happened to her. Putting her head in her hands she squeezed her fingers against her temples trying to subdue the pain. She needed her bed, her tablets; most of all she needed Ben, and to go home. Sobs escaped and wracked her body sending even more spears of pain through her head. Colin stood watchful, beside her, his tail occasionally wagging with anxiety; he was on high alert ready to protect his mistress.

'Laura, Laura, what's up, are you all right?'

Laura slowly opened her eyes and at first couldn't work

out what the big black shape in front of her was, the sun glinted off the side but surprisingly didn't add to her aching head, in fact her head felt slightly better. She blinked and started to get to her feet but slumped back down.

'Laura?'

Comprehension slowly took shape and Laura recognised Claire standing beside her black Land Rover.

'What's happened to you?' Claire asked, kneeling on the road beside Laura.

'I'm not sure,' Laura whispered.

'Come on let me take you home,' Claire put a hand under Laura's arm to help her up. 'Is Ben at home?' she asked.

'No, I don't think so.'

'OK, come home with me and I'll give Ben a ring.'

Claire helped Laura into the front seat and Colin leapt into the back, he settled on the seat with a sigh of relief that at last someone else was in charge. Back in her homely kitchen Claire made Laura sit in the old armchair by the woodburner.

'Here let me take your fleece,' Claire screwed her nose up, looking at the odd dark streaks of vomit down the front. 'What have you been eating?' she asked.

'Blackberries,' Laura replied, struggling out of her fleece and pulling on the jumper that Claire offered, it smelled faintly of Claire's perfume, which Laura found comforting. She shrunk down into the depths of the chair and stared blankly into the orange glow of the fire, welcoming its warmth. She felt as though she was still in a dream, detached from the real world, but at the same time relieved to be in familiar surroundings at last.

'Blackberries, at this time of year?'

Laura didn't answer, she felt too numb to try to comprehend the last few hours. Claire wracked her brain to think what other dark berries were around at this time of year, hoping that Laura hadn't eaten anything poisonous.

'Never mind, you just sit quietly. I'll make some tea,' Claire bustled about but kept a wary eye on Laura in case she was sick again. Laura took a sip of the sweetened tea, 'I don't take sugar.'

'It's what you need right now,' said Claire, and Laura didn't argue.

Claire rang Ben, he was on his way home and would come straight to their house, but he would be at least an hour. William came in through the kitchen door followed by a draught of cold air just as Claire put down the phone.

'My it's getting chilly out there,' he said, as he headed for the burner to warm his hands.

'Hello there Laura, good to see you,' he raised his eyes to Claire for answers, as he realised with one glance that all was not well with Laura.

'I picked Laura up in the lane, I don't think she's well, but I'm not sure what's happened. Anyway, Ben's on his way.'

William sat in the other chair and took in Laura's distressed, dishevelled state.

'Right then Laura, what have you been up to?' he asked, not unkindly, but Claire cringed behind him at his direct question.

'I don't know, I can't make sense of it, I'm not sure,' She spoke so quietly that William leant forward to hear.

'Try and tell me.'

Laura started to tell her tale, talking slowly and at times barely above a whisper, but once she started, she found she couldn't stop until she reached the point where Claire found her on the bridge. Claire, who'd perched herself on the arm of William's chair part way through Laura's tale, now exchanged a sideways glance with him, neither of them at all sure what to make of what they heard.

'My head,' Laura leant back resting her head and rubbing her temples. 'The migraine's coming back,' she said.

'The fire's lit in the sitting room, would you like to go and lie on the sofa until Ben gets here?' Claire asked. Laura nodded.

Claire helped her into the other room, where she guided

her to the sofa and covered her with a blanket. Colin followed close behind and lay on the floor. She returned with a large plastic bowl, and put it on the floor, incase Laura was sick again. The sitting room was the same room with large, dark, old-fashioned furniture that Laura and Ben had been entertained in before. The fire was roaring in the hearth, but the heat barely reached the sofa, and she was grateful for the heavy blanket that she tucked round her neck.

'Ben's on his way, and I'll pop back in to check you're OK in a little while, but try to get some sleep,' Claire said, wondering if she was doing the right thing leaving Laura alone. Laura nodded, but was half afraid of sleeping, or at least afraid of waking up and finding she was somewhere else again.

'Now don't you get onto the sofa,' Claire warned Colin. He wagged his tail in compliance, but as soon as Claire was out of the room he was up and rested his head on Laura's feet. His weight on her legs soothed Laura and she drifted into dreamless sleep.

'Well, what do you make of that?' Claire asked William, when she returned to the kitchen.

'The brain can play funny tricks when you're not well,' he shrugged, picking up the paper and turning to the crossword. 'Hopefully Ben won't be long,' he chewed the end of his pen in contemplation. He wasn't good with cerebral problems; give him a broken bone any day. Claire smiled; William could cope with any manner of illness and emergency involving animals but when it came to people, and women in particular, he was hopeless. She remembered fondly how useless he was when their second child was born at home, she'd yelled at him in-between pushes to think of her as a cow giving birth in a field. It worked, and he safely delivered their son before the doctor arrived.

Ben arrived within the hour his face etched with anxiety.

'Where is she, is she all right?'

Claire related the events of the afternoon, including Laura's strange story in as much detail as she could remember.

'What do you think it means?' he asked. 'She's always suffered with migraines but nothing like this, it sounds a bit weird. Do you think I need to get the doctor? It's probably linked to losing the baby, don't you think?'

'I would, could be the baby,' said William. 'It all sounds a bit odd to me.'

'Yes, probably sensible,' Claire agreed. 'Try not to worry, I'm sure she'll be fine.'

Laura smiled sheepishly at Ben, who brushed away her apologies. He thanked William and Claire as they climbed into their car, eager to get her home so that he could call the doctor.

'It could be linked to the baby, couldn't it? I mean I don't know much but hormones can be tricky blighters,' William said, as they watched Ben's car drive away. Claire smiled at William and tucked her arm in his.

'It brings things back, doesn't it?' he said.

'Yes, it's a difficult time for them. Poor Laura, she must be going through hell. I don't know about you, but I could do with a drink.'

'Good idea, you stay here I'll bring a glass out.' William headed for the kitchen while Claire sank into a chair on the terrace. She remembered the gnawing pain of loss after her miscarriages, particularly the last one. At four months the baby, a girl, was well formed. She would have loved a daughter, not that she didn't love her boys, of course, but, well there was something about mothers and daughters. She sighed. She knew William felt the loss as much as she did. Just a day or two after it happened, he said he was off to do something on the farm. Claire went out to escape the oppressive walls of the house and found him sobbing in the barn. It was the only time he'd shown emotion like that, and as he sobbed in her arms he'd repeated 'my little girl' several times.

'Here you go.' William handed Claire a glass of red wine and settled into the chair beside her. It was chilly, but they both preferred being outside when possible. 'You know what Laura was saying, about the men on the cart?'

Claire nodded.

'Well, I was just thinking, it reminds me of that old story of my Great Grandfather's, my Grandmother used to tell, do you remember? About the strange woman from China?'

'No, it's not one of the many bizarre family tales I recall.' Claire laughed. William's family were full of tales and folklore. She supposed it was because generations of his family had lived on the farm and passed stories down to one another, but they gained embellishment with each telling.

'I'm sure it's one of the ones my Grandmother wrote down. I think it'll be in one of the boxes in the loft.' He drained his glass and put it on the table before standing up.

'You're surely not going up in the loft now, are you?'

'I need to check it out. Anyway, it might help Laura.'

Claire somehow doubted that, but knew it was pointless to stop William now he was on a mission. Thirty minutes later, Claire had retreated to the fireside in the kitchen, William reappeared.

'Look, here it is,' he held out a small leather-bound notebook. 'Read this, it's not exactly the account Laura gave, but pretty close.

Claire read the beautifully handwritten pages. Handwriting really is a lost art, she thought. It only took her a few minutes to read. She closed the book and look up at William, who'd been watching her intently as she read.

'Well?' he said.

'You're right, it isn't exact, but it's uncannily like Laura's story.'

'I think we should tell her; it might set her mind at rest.'

'I'm not sure about that, it might freak her out. I think it would me. It's all very odd.'

'But don't you think she needs to know?'

'I'm not sure, let's think about it again in the morning.'

William agreed, took the book from Claire and settled down to read more of his grandmother's tales from the family. There was nothing else as strange as his Great Grandfather's story about his Great Uncle Will.

Chapter 23

Ben walked to the car with the doctor, he was a tall thin man in his mid-forties with receding dark hair and a long sharp nose. He looked tired, Ben thought, and seemed a little distracted, probably overworked, but even so he felt slightly dissatisfied with the doctor's explanation of migraine and postnatal depression. Ben had a sneaking suspicion that the doctor didn't have a clue what was wrong with Laura. He jumped, too quickly, on the fact that Laura hadn't been taking the antidepressants he'd previously prescribed for her. He stressed that she must take them, and that Ben must make sure she did. Ben felt guilty that he didn't know she wasn't taking them; in fact, it never crossed his mind that she wouldn't, but assured the doctor that he would check in future. He felt very doubtful that not taking the tablets was the primary cause of Laura's current condition, but what did he know, he wasn't a doctor.

When Ben voiced his doubts and pressed for more of an explanation a flash of impatience crossed the doctor's face, with a barely suppressed sigh he said he was almost certain that Laura had either dreamt or imagined the crying. Her strange episode, as he called it, was a bit more unusual but he thought because she was actually in the same place when it started and when Claire found her, that it was probably again just a vivid dream or some sort of hallucination.

'Make an appointment for her to see me in a couple of weeks.'

He got into his car and was about to drive off but instead

he climbed out again, crossed the drive and put a hand on Ben's arm.

'I'm sorry,' he smiled, and fiddled with his tie. 'I know you were hoping for more definitive answers, but Laura's hormones are all over the place at the moment. I feel certain she will get back to normal in time. You can ring me or make an appointment earlier if she doesn't seem to be improving. Like I said there are other things we can try if necessary, even though Laura is reluctant to consider them, she might not… Well anyway call if you're concerned.' This time he got into his car, slammed the door and with a nod and smile drove out of the gate, spraying gravel as he went.

Later after the doctor's visit Ben flopped onto the sofa with Colin. Laura was asleep upstairs: thanks to some medication the doctor administered. He didn't know what to think. Laura had been so much better lately, happier and her work was going well, and it was a few weeks now since she woke saying she could hear a baby crying. He felt disappointed; were they back at square one, or worse?

He spent what felt like hours reading everything he could find on the Internet about hallucinations caused by migraine and postnatal depression. There were some accounts of visual hallucinations with migraine, but they were more odd flashes of something out of the corner of an eye, not the full-blown story about people and places that Laura described. The reports linked to postnatal depression were more vivid but again not Laura's lucid recollection of events.

Ben crawled into bed much later, exhausted, and not really reassured. Laura was deeply asleep and didn't stir when he pulled the duvet across. He lay awake beside her, wondering if she was developing some more significant mental illness. His Internet wanderings seemed to point more in that direction.

He must eventually have slept soundly, for the next thing he knew was the morning sun pushing through the curtains. Laura was still asleep, and he carefully rolled out from under the covers and went downstairs to make some coffee and let

Colin out. Laura felt Ben get out of bed but didn't move. She lay quietly, going over and over in her mind the events of the previous day. It felt as real to her now as it did at the time, and her memory was as vivid as ever, despite the sleeping pills, or whatever concoction, the doctor had given her. Surely it couldn't all be in her imagination? That was what the doctor implied, but it was impossible, she was never an over imaginative or excitable child, she could use her imagination to see designs but that was different and down in most part to her training. She shuffled and turned to lie on her back, what if it was, what if she was mentally ill, some sort of madness that she would have forever? No, she didn't feel mad. She made herself think about normal things; her work, the dress for Lucinda, she was aware of everything but couldn't raise any interest or enthusiasm, perhaps Andrea could finish the dress. She knew deep down that was ridiculous, but her conscious mind didn't care. She just wanted to stay here, warm and safe in bed and not be compelled to do anything or go anywhere. She turned on her side and pulled her legs up into the fetal position, and sucked a strand of her hair, something she hadn't done for many years.

Maybe she dozed, she wasn't sure, nor did she know what time it was, the sun wasn't shining now, and the light was the dull grey light that sometimes lingers from morning until night. She lay very still and listened, there was nothing, she was relieved and relaxed a little, there was no baby crying, but then became anxious that she couldn't hear any sounds at all. Laura pushed herself up on one elbow, the room looked normal, but something was wrong, the silence pressed down on her. Panic began to well up inside, what was going on? She strained every part of her body and was about to get out of bed, when she heard a door close downstairs.

'You stay here Colin, good boy,' Ben said, as he closed the kitchen door behind him. Laura sank back on her pillow in relief, but she wasn't ready to answer Ben's questions or listen to his ponderings yet. She was certain by now he would have worked out an explanation to satisfy himself. Pulling the duvet up close she closed her eyes and pretended to be asleep. Ben walked quietly across the bedroom and looked down at Laura, he stood there for a minute or two. He knew she wasn't asleep; he'd spent too many nights awake beside her, as she slept soundly, and knew what her sleeping breath sounded like. He wondered whether to speak, or sit on the bed, to see if she would respond, but in the end decided to leave her, she clearly wasn't yet ready to face the world, or even him.

An emotion welled up inside Ben; it felt like a physical lump. He leant on the bedroom windowsill with one hand, and pushed the other clenched into a fist, to his chest. What was going on, this wasn't how it was supposed to be? He looked back at Laura, unmoving under the covers and he struggled to suppress a seed of anger. What was she playing at? Why hadn't she taken the tablets prescribed weeks ago? Was she ill or was this all some strange charade? He had no answers, just knew Laura was different, different from the carefree, ambitious, glamorous Laura of their London days. Perhaps they should go back, give up on country life, go back to where they used to be happy, but he knew even as he thought it, that going back wasn't the answer. A bark from the kitchen brought him back to the present and he went downstairs to let Colin out into the garden.

Chapter 24

Ben was leaning against the sink when Claire and William appeared and tapped on the kitchen window making him jump.

'Hi, sorry it's a bit early,' said Claire, glancing between Ben in his pyjamas and the clock, which said ten forty-five. 'How's Laura?'

'No, it's not too early, I'm late. She's still asleep. Come in, coffee?'

'We don't want to intrude but William's remembered something. Yes, coffee would be great, thanks.'

William and Claire sat at the kitchen table, while Ben busied himself making coffee. It was a lovely light room, even now the weather had turned dull, but the atmosphere felt tense and oppressive. Claire glanced at the tiny photo of Poppy propped on the dresser and tried to imagine how she would have coped, if she and William had lost a full-term baby. Her imagination could hardly stretch that far, the pain must be indescribable it was no wonder Laura was depressed. As Ben poured three cups of coffee the door opened and Laura came in, looking dishevelled but surprisingly beautiful. Her tangled hair rested on the shoulders of an oversize jumper that she'd pulled on over a pair of blue flowery pyjamas.

'Hi, I thought I heard voices,' Laura said, nodding her head as Ben raised the coffee pot. 'Please, black.'

'How are you feeling?' Claire asked.

'OK, actually quite good, thanks, and at least I'm in the

right century,' Laura replied, twisting a strand of hair tightly round her finger. She pulled out a chair and sat down, smiling brightly at all around the table. She was determined to be all right.

Ben looked at her feeling surprised and quizzical, but his shoulders lowered slightly in relief when he studied her face, she did look fairly normal he thought, considering what she'd been through. He reached across and took Laura's hand giving it a squeeze.

'William's remembered something,' Ben said, looking towards William, confused about what he could have remembered that would be relevant to their situation, but he liked William and smiled encouragingly.

'Sounds intriguing,' Laura said. 'What is it?'

William hesitated, Claire wasn't sure this was the right thing to do, but he'd persuaded her that his story might help Laura. He now felt doubtful and didn't want to cause Laura more upset. Claire was usually right in these sorts of situations.

'Come on then William, tell them your Great Grandad's story about the Chinese lady,' Claire said.

Laura and Ben exchanged glances. Laura shuffled in her chair stifling the sudden urge to laugh. 'Sounds even more intriguing.'

'Well,' William began, and the others leant forward to listen.

It reminded Claire of when her boys were young and William would tell them rambling yarns after tea, and they would both lean, elbows on the table, head in hands and hang on their father's every word.

'Well, it's nothing really, but when I was a kid my Grandmother lived with us, up at the farm. All our family, generations of us has lived up there. I think we might be the last though, I can't see our boys taking it on. Claire gave him a get on with it look, and he smiled sheepishly in response.

'OK, I know, so one of my Great Grandad's favourite stories was a tale that his Great Uncle told, about a Chinese lady that they met on the lane. I didn't give it a thought yesterday, but after you'd gone, I remembered, and the similarities to Laura's story are uncanny,' William fiddled with his watch, this all felt highly implausible.

'It's possible that the telling of the story over the years has warped the details a bit,' Claire interrupted.

'So, what is it?' Laura asked.

'Well, apparently my Great Grandad's Great Uncle and another man met a woman in the lane, they were on the cart, going to the castle,' William continued. 'Delivering grain or something and probably milk.'

Laura sat bolt upright and concentrated hard; she clenched her hands around her cup of coffee so tightly Ben took it off her in case it broke.

'So, when would that have been?' Laura asked.

'It must have been early to mid-eighteen hundred, isn't that right William?'

He nodded slowly as if mentally counting back over the years.

'Yes, that's about right. Now then, we've always referred to it as the China lady story; I think my father even told it to our boys, do you remember Claire, and they weren't overly impressed. None of us ever really took it seriously, it's a bit vague really.'

'Oh, do get on with it William, or do you want me to tell it?'

'No, Claire, don't rush me; let me tell it my way. So apparently this lady was dressed like a man, you know trousers, boots that sort of thing, but they knew she was a woman because of her hair and the way she spoke. She was wearing a coat as soft and white as snow, which opened and closed like magic when she ran her fingers up the front,' William was at last getting into his stride.

'My fleece is blue, but they did comment on how soft it was and were totally fascinated by the zip. I told them it, my fleece, came from China,' Laura said, musing over the details.

'That could be how the story has evolved to her being a

Chinese woman,' said William. 'The similarities are striking, don't you think?'

Laura nodded, but Ben remained still and quiet. He wasn't sure whether this was better than thinking Laura imagined the whole thing.

'Did your Great Grandad say anything else?' Laura asked.

'Well, the story changed from time to time, depending on who was telling it, and who was listening. Sometimes she was a witch; sometimes she spoke in a foreign language. Another time animals surrounded her, but they ran away when they saw the horse and cart coming along the lane. I don't remember anything being mentioned specifically about a dog, though. The only consistent part of the story has been about the magic opening and closing of her coat and her being from China.'

William took a gulp of now cold coffee; he looked around slightly embarrassed, particularly when he looked at Laura who was hanging on his every word.

'To be honest we took his Chinese lady story with a pinch of salt, no one really thought of it as anything more than a bit of a yarn. I haven't thought of it for years but a few things you said yesterday just triggered it in my mind,' William looked around and shrugged; he didn't really think he was being very helpful and was beginning to regret telling the story.

'But what does it mean?' Laura asked. 'It can't mean that I'm the Chinese lady, that would mean I've been back in time, that's nonsense. Isn't it?'

She stood up and went to the door opening it to let Colin, who was standing impatiently on the step, back in.

'Colin was in the back of the cart out of sight, they didn't really say much about him,' she closed the door and walked back to the table, where she stood looking from one to the other.

'What if it happens again, I couldn't cope with that.'

No one replied, what could they say? They just sat, all with their own private thoughts.

'Did your Great Grandad say she was seen again, did anyone else see her?'

William shook his head.

'That's all I know, I'm afraid.'

'Of course, it could all be just stories, you know made up to amuse the kids,' said Claire, now beginning to feel even more uncertain about the wisdom of telling Laura. 'You know how these stories grow in families.'

'No, I don't recall anything like it in my family, do you Ben?'

Ben shrugged, like Claire he was beginning to wonder about the wisdom of telling Laura this tale.

'No not really, I suspect it's just an interesting coincidence. Quite amusing though, anyone for more coffee?' Ben busied himself gathering mugs and putting the kettle on, wracking his brains for something to change the subject and lighten the now slightly tense atmosphere. 'Laura why don't you ask Claire her opinion on the sitting room curtains?'

'Oh yes, I'd love to see what you're doing.'

Laura led Claire out of the kitchen and both Ben and William sighed with relief.

'Sorry Ben, I hope I haven't made things worse for Laura.'

'Don't worry, she's in a very strange place at the moment, who knows your story might even help,' he said, but doubted very much that it would. By the time William and Claire left, Laura outwardly, at least, appeared quite relaxed and only mentioned the China lady story again in passing, with a laugh.

Chapter 25

Laura came down the stairs, quietly, not for any particular reason, it just so happened she didn't have any shoes or slippers on, and she was walking slowly, so made no sound. She was in a sort of daydream, trying to make sense of everything and constantly failing.

'I'm worried mum, really worried.'

Laura stopped and listened, Ben was talking to Esme, his mother, he must be on the phone. She could take the couple of steps across the hall to the kitchen and she knew he would change the subject, or she could wait and see what he said next. To her surprise, Esme answered clearly. Ben wasn't on the phone; Esme was here, in the kitchen.

'I know darling we're all worried. What does the doctor say?'

Laura took a step closer to the door, it wasn't properly shut, and she just hoped Colin wouldn't sense her presence and give her away.

'He didn't really give an opinion on Laura's actual story, just said it was a bit strange, probably accounted for by postnatal depression and grief,' Ben said.

'But that's what he said before, after that episode in town. Doesn't he say anything about treatment or timescales?' Esme had been an auditor in a big firm and always wanted precise answers. To her life was more or less black and white and she couldn't cope with uncertainty. There was a pause and Laura could hear Ben tapping the table, something he did when he was nervous or unsure. He probably was weighing up how much to say to his mother. She leant closer to hear what he did say.

'He did say if things got worse or Laura experienced more of these episodes that she might benefit from some Cognitive Behaviour Therapy or, as a last resort, a short spell in hospital, but he didn't really say much else. I don't know mum; I don't know what to do or think anymore.'

Laura retreated to the stairs and clung to the bannister. Poor Ben, he sounded so low and anxious, but she almost didn't have room in her head to worry about him. All she could think was that he and the doctor must think everything that had happened was in her mind. She wondered if Ben had told Esme about William's story of the Chinese woman, she hoped he hadn't but even if he had, what difference would it make, they clearly thought she was ill or mad.

'Have you phoned Penny?' Esme asked.

'No, Laura asked me not to, I don't think she wants to worry her.'

'I'm not sure, I think at times like these a girl needs her mother, and her father's very sensible,' Esme said.

'I wouldn't phone her without Laura's agreement. I only mentioned it to you when you rang, because, well, I needed to…'

'Of course, you did, and you know I'll do anything I can,' his mother said.

Laura remained motionless; she could hear Colin barking at the back door and Ben moving to open it.

One thing no one had asked Laura, Ben realised as he let Colin in, was what the time was when she first sat on the wall and what it was when Claire found her. Laura's experience as she described it must have lasted for hours, yet if she was hallucinating it might in reality have been only a few minutes. He'd read something about time distortion and made a mental note to ask her, before turning back to his mother.

Laura knew Colin would soon bounce into the hall to see her, but the last thing she wanted at that moment was to see

Esme and to retell everything that she'd been through. Slipping her feet into a pair of Ben's shoes by the front door, Laura quietly slipped out and ran across to her workshop.

'Hi,' Andrea said, as Laura burst through the door. 'I wasn't sure you'd be over today. I'm just getting everything ready for Julie's fitting.'

'Oh yes, good, thank you, I probably won't be working today I just needed to escape my mother-in-law.'

'You look like you could do with a coffee,' Andrea took in Laura's appearance and made her way to the little kitchen without waiting for her to reply.

'Andrea, do you think I'm mad?' Laura asked, following her.

'Well, you look pretty crazy at the moment.'

Laura felt startled by her reply, and then caught a glimpse of herself in the long wall mirror, and started to laugh, she was still in her pyjamas, her hair unbrushed and she was wearing Ben's shoes with the laces undone.

'You're right, good job I didn't interrupt Ben and Esme, she'd be having me sectioned by now.'

'Seriously though,' Laura asked Andrea, when they were sitting sipping their coffee. 'Do you think my mind's going?'

Andrea looked out of the window for a few seconds before replying.

'I think you've been through a really bad time and you're still grieving. I'm not sure about the other things; they all seem pretty weird, but sort of isolated. I mean in here when we're working, you're brilliant, creative, clear-headed, so who knows, the human brain is a complex thing.'

'I don't feel ill, sad yes, losing Poppy was the worst thing ever but I feel I'm coping with it, I can talk about her and look at her photo. What happened the other day when I was out felt real, I mean the people were real, well seemed real, yet how could they be?' Laura asked.

'I have no idea; it sounds like the plot of a sci-fi film, some sort of time warp. Who knows, these things could be real, in years to come people might flit backwards and forwards through time at will. That could be fun.'

'What like 'Doctor Who' or 'Back to the Future',' Laura laughed.

'I'd go back to Shakespeare's time, watch the plays like they're meant to be performed,' Andrea said. 'I could join his troupe.'

'Do you like Shakespeare? You're full of surprises, anyway they didn't have female actors in those days.'

'What about Shakespeare in Love, I could pretend to be a man like what's her name?'

'I didn't know you were so into films,' Laura said. 'Anyway, I'd go back to the time of Henry VIII so I could see the clothes.'

'You're so predictable, I bet you'd be taking them apart to see how they're made.'

The door opened and Ben popped his head round, seeing Laura with Andrea laughing and drinking coffee, he stepped inside.

'Mum called in, she's just gone, I thought you were still in bed,' he said.

'Sorry! Did I give you a fright when I wasn't there?'

'Just a bit, but I got more of a shock when I realised my shoes were missing,' he grinned towards Laura's feet, still encased in his too big shoes. 'I thought we could take Colin for a walk together, if you're up to it, or are you working?' he asked.

'No, I'm not working today. You're ok with Julie, aren't you?' Laura asked Andrea.

'I'm fine. You go for a walk; blow the cobwebs away.'

'Ok, let me go and get dressed first,' Laura stood up, took her and Andrea's mugs into the kitchen then followed Ben out.

'Thanks Andrea, see you tomorrow,' she called over her shoulder.

Andrea watched them cross the drive to the house. She felt

a growing concern for Laura, but also felt hopeless. All she could do was help keep this side of her life as stress free as possible.

Ben took Laura's hand as they walked across the field, still crunchy with the remnants of morning frost. Colin ran on ahead.

'Where did you go from here?' Ben asked.

He was hoping that by retracing Laura's steps they would be able to lay the ghosts of that day to rest. He was highly sceptical about William's story and Laura's experience being linked but decided to keep his thoughts to himself. Colin showed no reluctance about the route they were taking and bounded on ahead.

'This is where I stopped when I felt a migraine coming on,' Laura sat on the wall over the stream, but hung on tightly to Ben's hand, if she was going anywhere again, he was going with her. She closed her eyes. Nothing happened, everything was as it should be when she opened them. She took a deep breath, the air didn't have the special freshness she'd noticed before, too much pollution around she supposed. They walked back down the lane and Laura tried to remember the way, but everything looked so different, it was hard to imagine the wood covering most of the fields and going right up to the cottage. They walked around the side of their cottage, Laura pointing out changes and where she thought the door, that the girl ran through was. There was a trellis with an old wisteria climbing up the middle of the wall now, so it was hard to imagine. In fact, as she looked again, Laura realised that many more changes had been made to the cottage over the last couple of hundred years.

'Maybe we can find an old photo,' said Ben.

Laura nodded, but wasn't certain she wanted to have her vision, or whatever it was, confirmed. She felt muddled and a little afraid, but she wanted to take Ben on her journey, she needed him to believe her, even though she wasn't now sure she believed it herself. They crossed the lawn to the big oak tree after which the cottage was named. It looked old enough, but she couldn't work out the distance from the house, it seemed too close, but the old wood might have made it feel further away.

'This tree must have been in the middle of the wood, all the others have gone, but I think the girl ran this way, I was back nearer the house behind another tree,' she said. It all felt less likely and more like a dream the more she talked about it.

Ben squeezed her hand. One oak tree must look pretty much like any other, especially after two hundred years, but he kept his thoughts to himself.

'Come on, we might as well carry on now we've started,' Ben said, getting the feeling from Laura that she was about to go back inside the cottage. Colin on the other hand was raring to go, having felt shortchanged coming back home so soon after setting out on his walk.

They walked through Laura's supposed wood, across what now was a field and eventually came out onto the road where Laura thought the men on the cart picked her up. The road was now metalled and quite busy with traffic, so Ben put Colin on his lead, and they walked along the verge until the castle came into sight.

'It's just the same,' said Laura.

'Well, I don't suppose castles change like houses do. It's been here since, what did they say on our tour, the twelfth century, or something. Anyway, hundreds of years,' Ben said.

'I suppose so,' Laura tucked her arm through Ben's as they carried on towards the meadow. 'This is where the fair was,' said Laura, holding wide her arms to take in most of the meadow. Fairs and country shows were still held in the meadow so the idea could already have been planted in Laura's subconscious.

Laura showed Ben where she thought she was sitting when she spoke to George; there was still a slight rise in the ground, but hardly high enough to have given her a vantage point over the fair. There were fewer trees along the banks of the river now, and the river itself was back to the small stream she was familiar with.

They walked back until they reached the bridge again and sat side by side without speaking for a few minutes.

'I don't suppose you can remember what the time was when you set off and the time when Claire …?'

Ben felt Laura stiffen, he reached out to put his arm around her, but before he could hold her or finish his sentence she was on her feet.

'You think I made it all up, don't you? Well, I didn't, and I don't care what you or anyone else thinks.' She turned her back and was striding along the lane before Ben could grasp what was going on.

'Laura, Laura, wait,' he ran after her surprised by how far away she was in such a short space of time. 'Stop, Laura please. I do believe you,' he caught her arm and she whirled round eyes blazing. Ben took a step back. For a moment he thought she really did look mad. Laura recognising the fleeting look of horror on his face suddenly deflated and started sobbing, throwing herself into Ben's arms.

'It's all right; I didn't mean to upset you, I promise. I was just, well you know trying to make sense of it all.'

'I know, I've been trying to do the same.'

He handed her a tissue and led her back to the bridge, they sat down again, this time Ben's arm was tightly around Laura's waist.

'I don't know exactly what time, it was afternoon, and then Claire picked me up later in that afternoon, so I suppose, oh I don't know, you'll have to ask Claire.'

Ben strained to hear her quiet words, and then inwardly shrugged, what difference did it make, it happened, or something happened, so whether it was in Laura's mind or real, the main thing was to try to get her back to normal.

'Never mind, it's not really that important, I was just wondering that's all. Come on let's go home,' he reached for her hand and pulled her to her feet, calling to Colin. 'I do believe you by the way,' he said, planting a kiss on her nose.

'I'll guess we'll never really know if you are the Chinese lady,' said Ben, on their return home. 'But it's an interesting story of William's,' he smiled at Laura, determined to keep it light. 'We'll have to remember that next time we go to a fancy-dress party.'

To his relief she laughed. 'Pity I didn't have my camera to take some photos, as proof. Anyway, whatever it was I'm glad to be back where I belong.'

Life, relatively quickly, to Ben's surprise and relief, settled back down into a fairly normal routine, although they both dwelt from time to time on what happened, but kept their thoughts to themselves. Laura took to walking Colin in the opposite direction, just in case there was something strange about the bridge. She was certain she'd read something, or was it on the television, about time cracks that people could in theory slip through. It sounded daft, probably fiction, and she didn't mention it to Ben, he was worried enough about the state of her mind. Laura knew he was trying hard to keep everything normal, but she occasionally caught him looking at her in an anxious questioning way, just fleetingly. As soon as he caught Laura's eye he smiled or made some casual comment, and so they continued, both trying hard not to give the other any cause to worry.

Chapter 26

'Hello again!'

Andrea swung round; she was going to be late; she didn't have time to chat.

'Have you broken down?'

Andrea recognised the man, he was the one who gave her a lift home, the very first time she ventured out this way. She wracked her brains for his name, but nothing came and really, she didn't have time to stop, although she remembered how kind he'd been and much she'd liked him.

'It's Andrea, isn't it?' he asked.

'Yes, sorry I don't…'

'Adam,' he said. 'So, can I help?'

'I've stupidly run out of petrol, and now I'm going to be late picking Ralph up.'

'Ah Ralph, of course, the little man. OK, where do you need to be?'

'The nursery. It's not far, just down the road really. I could walk but I'll be charged extra if I'm late and I was already cutting it a bit fine.'

'Jump in! I'll drop you at the nursery, then I'll go and fill my can up with petrol.'

'Really?' Andrea asked, climbing in. 'That's the second time you've rescued me, I'm very grateful.'

Adam smiled, 'I was hoping I'd see you again,' he said.

Andrea looked across at him he looked genuine. Her heart did an involuntary little flip, he really did have a lovely smile, but she couldn't quite believe he was as perfect as he seemed, and why would someone like him be interested in someone like her.

They reached the nursery only just inside the allotted pick-up time, much to Andrea's relief and she jumped out.

'Thank you so much, I'll be fine now; don't put yourself out.'

'Don't be daft, you can't walk to the petrol station, then back to your car with a heavy can and Ralph,' Adam said.

'No, I suppose not.'

'Right, tell you what, give me your keys and I'll go and get the petrol, fill your car up and drive it back here, then you can put Ralph in his seat and drive me back to my car.'

'Are you sure?' asked Andrea, already fishing in her bag for her keys.

'Of course,' he melted her with another smile. 'I won't be long.'

Andrea sat on the wall, musing again about Adam and wondering why he was going out of his way to help her, she wasn't used to such altruistic behaviour, and she couldn't help wondering what he might want in return. Then she felt ashamed of being so suspicious, but in her experience men, particularly classy men like Adam, didn't put themselves out for the likes of her, especially when there was a baby in tow.

One of the nursery staff on her way out, stopped to chat. She sat on the wall and charmed her way into Andrea's affections by telling her what a beautiful baby Ralph was. She knew that of course, but it did her good to hear it from someone 'official'. Andrea always felt a bit of an outsider here amongst all the middle class married mums. She never told anyone where she lived, just that she worked locally, and mostly they were too busy to press for more information.

Adam was as good as his word and before Andrea started to wonder where he was, he was back. Ralph was settled into his car seat and Adam slipped over into the passenger seat, ready for Andrea to return him to his own car.

'Thank you so much, I was in such a rush this morning I

forgot I was running low. That's the first time I've ever run out,' Andrea said and started the engine.

'Well, I'm glad you did,' Adam replied.

They chatted easily as Andrea drove and sat in her car for quite a while when they reached Adam's, before he opened the door and got out. He made a move to get into his own car, and then turned round.

'Have you ever walked along the river?' he asked, leaning back through the driver's window.

Andrea shook her head.

'Well how about coming over on Saturday and we can take Ralph for a walk, then I cook a mean chilli if you're up for it?'

'Yes, no, I mean I haven't been along the river, and chilli sounds great. Thank you,' Andrea said. They swapped details and with a wave they parted. Andrea's heart was beating just a bit faster than normal, and she sang loudly to all the way home, much to Ralph's surprise, who gurgled loudly with delight in response.

'OK, spill the beans!'

'What, sorry?' Andrea looked up at Laura surprised.

They were busy tracing patterns onto expensive fabric and concentrating hard on what they were doing, so for once, chatting was at a minimum.

'You keep humming and smiling to yourself, not that you aren't usually happy, but I just get a feeling…' Laura grinned, and Andrea blushed.

'Well, do you remember the estate agent who you bought the cottage from?'

'Vaguely, young bloke, can't remember his name or much about him, why?' Laura replied.

'His name's Adam, he certainly remembers you,' Andrea laughed. 'I think you've been his most glamorous client to date.'

Laura looked confused, 'Are you buying a house?' she asked.

'Blimey no, I can't ever imagine being able to afford to buy my own place. No, I've been out with him several times over the last few weeks.'

'Tell me more, in fact I think we need a break, you can tell me everything over coffee.'

They carefully smoothed and covered the fabric making sure it wasn't going to slip onto the floor, before going downstairs to the little kitchen.

'He sounds worth hanging onto,' Laura said, as they washed up their mugs after Andrea had satisfied Laura's curiosity.

'What about Ralph's dad, won't he mind?'

Laura had never enquired about Ralph's father before, and Andrea never mentioned anyone, so she assumed he was well off the scene, but she wondered if he might be lurking in the background.

Andrea snorted.

'Him! Less said about him the better.'

Laura looked enquiringly at Andrea, intrigued now to know more, but she bit her tongue and refrained from asking. Luckily, Andrea continued, now on a roll.

'He was a flash bastard,' Andrea screwed the tea towel round the inside of the mug with such force Laura assumed she was imagining it to be the mystery man's neck.

'Used to bring his car into the garage, always wanted me to work on it, said I had a delicate touch. Chatted me up something rotten and I guess I just fell for the sweet talk. Makes me cringe to remember. Hopefully I'm not quite so naive now,' she said, as she pulled the tea towel out of her mug and reached for Laura's to dry.

'Does he know about Ralph?' Laura asked.

'Oh yes, he knows about him but doesn't want to know him. Gave me some cash, I think he thought I'd get an abortion but then when I kept him, Ralph I mean, he just set up a fund for when Ralph grows up and buggered off back to his wife.'

'Wow, did you know he was married?'

Andrea gave Laura a strange look.

'No, of course not, I wouldn't have touched him with a barge pole if I'd known. Billy wanted to do him over, but I told him he wasn't worth the effort. Anyway, he's gone, I've no idea where he lives and I'm quite happy never to see him again.'

'What about child support and that sort of thing?' Laura didn't really know what that sort of thing was but knew from the newspaper that absent fathers were supposed to pay.

'I can manage without his money, just. So, I prefer it that way.'

'Are you certain Adam's not married?' Laura teased, trying to lighten the mood again.

'First thing I asked him, before I got in his car. No, not really, but I'm certain he isn't.' Andrea laughed. They returned to their current task, with Andrea not only feeling lighthearted about the state of her own life but feeling relieved that Laura seemed more her normal self. Since Laura's weird experience Andrea thought she seemed quiet and distracted, so it was good to hear her laughing again.

Chapter 27

Andrea looked at her phone; it was a text from Adam.

'That's mysterious,' she said to Laura. 'Adam has a proposition for me, he wants to meet me at the nursery later.'

'That sounds exciting.'

Laura remembered when Ben used to surprise her with spontaneous outings and mad plans when they first met. Not all of them completely successful but always full of laughter. That all felt a long time ago. It felt now as though they were treading on eggshells around each other. Perhaps she should do something to surprise him for once. She was lost in thought until Andrea spoke again and brought her back to the present.

'I wonder what it can be.'

'I can't wait to hear about it; mind, if his proposition is a job, I refuse to let you go!' Laura grinned, but realised she was only half joking.

'Don't worry, there's nothing I'd rather be doing.'

Adam was waiting beside his Jeep when Andrea arrived at the nursery to collect Ralph.

'Follow me,' he said kissing her on the cheek and tickling Ralph under the chin.

'Where are we going?' Andrea wasn't sure whether to be wary or excited.

'Not far, literally around the corner.'

About two hundred yards along the road Adam turned into a long drive. He stopped, jumped out and beckoned Andrea in, indicating for her to park next to him. Andrea lifted Ralph out and looked around, confused as to why they were there.

'So?' she queried, inwardly feeling a bit disappointed. She wasn't sure what she was expecting, but it certainly wasn't a load of old buildings.

'See that row of converted stone sheds? Well, they're actually old cow stalls.'

Andrea looked to where he was pointing across the drive, and up a small path to a low building that looked like it now had three front doors.

'Come and have a look,' Adam led the way up the path. 'They're mine,' he said. 'I'm trying to get into property development, and this is my first project.'

'Oh, I see,' said Andrea, trying hard to sound interested.

'So, what I wondered, was if you and Ralph would like to live in one of them?'

Andrea's mind was whirling. It would be perfect, close to nursery and her work, but before she allowed herself to hope, she knew she would not be able to afford it, and then there was her mum. Although her mum would probably welcome having her flat back to herself, or at least her bedroom back, because Billy was still in the other room until his sentencing.

Adam was already opening the first front door at the left end of the building.

'Come on in.'

Andrea looked around the beautifully converted space; it was small but was cleverly divided into an open plan kitchen and living area, then going through a door there was a small lobby area with a bathroom, one double and one single bedroom.

'It's beautiful, but I …' Andrea's voice trailed off she didn't want to say she couldn't afford it, she wanted it so much. She almost felt angry with Adam for tempting her, when he must know she didn't have much money.

'I haven't completely finished the other two yet,' Adam said. 'So, here's my proposition, I was thinking of renting them all out as holiday cottages, but if you would like this one and felt you could take on the management of the other two, bookings, cleaning, changing the beds, that sort of thing, then you could have it rent free. Rent in lieu of salary sort of thing.'

Andrea gaped. Her mind was buzzing, surely, she could manage the upkeep of two small cottages and still work for Laura. She really wanted to keep her job going, it was her dream job, but on a couple of occasions over the last few weeks, she had wondered what would happen if Laura's health deteriorated and she was forced to close the business, at least temporarily. Although nothing had been mentioned, it was purely an anxiety of Andrea's.

'How much time do you think it would take?' she asked Adam.

'Not too much, the other two are smaller than this one, I'll show you in a minute and the bookings would be difficult, but mostly I thought it would be great for you and Ralph, nearer to nursery, nearer to Laura…' he walked across the room and straightened a picture. 'And nearer to me of course. We could spend much more time together.'

Andrea turned away a lump suddenly in her throat, she swallowed hard not wanting to cry but she could feel her emotions bubbling up and about to spill over.

'Hey, what's the matter,' Adam looked at Andrea's back and reached out to gently touch her shoulder. 'Sorry, am I speaking out of turn. I don't mean to push or anything, there's no strings attached, promise.'

Andrea turned round and smiled at his anxious face. Adam relaxed slightly.

'It's just that I'm not used to people, well men especially, being so thoughtful,' she bit her lip to stop it trembling and wiped at her eye. Ralph suddenly gurgled and held his arms out towards Adam, lurching forwards so quickly Andrea nearly dropped him.

'Steady there, come here little man,' he pulled the now beaming Ralph into his arms. 'Well, *he* seems to like the plan!'

Adam sat down in one of the two armchairs and bounced Ralph on his knee.

'I would like us to see more of each other,' Andrea sank onto the arm of the chair and watched Ralph's delighted antics as Adam tickled him. She could hardly believe that this was happening to her.

Adam sat Ralph down on his knee and reached out a hand to Andrea.

'I was talking to my mum about you, and Ralph, of course. She'd love to meet you both.'

'Are you sure? I mean we're not really…' her voice trailed away. She took a deep breath, why should she feel inferior just because she was a single mum and came from Greenville. She would do as her mum always told her and hold her head high.

'Don't worry, anyway mum's not at all like the rest of her family.'

Andrea wasn't sure what he meant and didn't like to ask what the rest of his mother's family was like.

'OK, yes thanks. I'd like to meet her.'

Her heart was pounding so hard she put out her hand to steady herself, she would like, was hoping, that their relationship would develop. Meeting his mother seemed to suddenly take it to a whole new level.

'I wouldn't want to stop working for Laura,' she said, bringing the conversation back to his proposition and onto ground where she felt more secure.

'No, of course not and if this got too much then we'd have to re-think. I don't mean you'd have to move out or anything like that, but I'm certain it will be manageable.'

What did she have to lose, Andrea thought, it couldn't be that difficult and she was used to hard work. She realised this was Adam's way of offering her the cottage rent free, but in a way that maintained her dignity.

'I don't know what to say, it's amazing.'

'Then say yes,' Adam stood up and encircled Andrea and Ralph with his arms. 'I'm sure it will all work, I've been thinking about it for days, I can't see any problems. So, is it yes?' he asked.

'Yes, I'd love to live here.'

Ralph squirmed and started to get restless, Adam passed him back to Andrea, with a final tickle and kiss on the top of his head.

'I need to take him home,' she jiggled the now grizzling Ralph up and down. 'And I need to talk to my mum, let her know my plans. It'll be a bit of a shock for her, but I think she'll be pleased.'

'Of course, no rush, but we could get you moved in over the weekend if you like?'

Adam quickly showed her the two other cottages, while Ralph's protests grew louder; they would be perfect holiday lets. He explained, over Ralph's squawks, that he thought the cottages would appeal to walkers, bird watchers and people just wanting a bit of peace for a few days. Mostly couples rather than families, she assumed. He was right they should be easy to keep clean, Andrea felt certain she could manage it all. They made their way back down the path to go their separate ways, stopping to kiss goodbye, a more meaningful kiss, and a tingle ran down her spine.

'I'll ring you tomorrow,' Adam called.

Andrea was right, although her mum protested weakly. She was clearly relieved to be able to claim back her space and was looking forward to visiting Andrea and Ralph in their new home. Just a couple of days later, Andrea and Ralph were installed. Laura and Ben, armed with flowers and champagne were their first visitors. They made all the right noises about what a lovely place it was, and how convenient for work and nursery. The four of them sat in the tiny garden drinking and laughing until the cold evening broke up the party. Ralph, fast asleep in his cot didn't murmur, now with the luxury of his own room he was sleeping through the night.

'I predict that Adam will be spending more time there

than he does in his own flat, before long,' Ben said, as he and Laura headed back home.

Ben was right, Andrea and Adam's relationship quickly grew deeper, and he was becoming a permanent fixture not only in the cottage but also in Andrea and Ralph's lives.

The holiday bookings were initially slow, but it was early in the year, and there were more booked in for Easter, mostly walkers, as Adam predicted, and people interested in the history of the area. Andrea created a book for each cottage with details of attractions and suggestions for places to eat. Laura let her take off-cuts of fabrics and she made cushion covers and bed throws, for her own home as well as the holiday lets. It was the first time in her life she had a place to call her own and she took immense pride in keeping everywhere immaculate, including filling the small garden with plants and flowers.

Her mother visited and although she was pleased for Andrea, she clearly felt uncomfortable with the open fields and having wildlife in such close proximity. Her life was back in the hubbub of the city and the estate.

Feedback from the first visitors was very positive and managing it all was no problem for Andrea. Her old life seemed like a distant memory as she adapted quickly to her new surroundings, only occasionally experiencing a shiver of fear in case it all fell apart.

Chapter 28

Once again Laura woke up in the middle of the night, it wasn't the gradual dawning awareness of being awake that usually came at that hour, it was wham, bang, full blown alert awakeness. Every part of her body was tingling, her ears were straining so hard they almost hurt, but she didn't move. She lay rigid under the duvet. She didn't want to hear again the sound that she knew must have disturbed her. She tried to think of a song or something trivial to occupy and distract her mind. She turned to look at Ben; he was asleep, breathing deeply and rhythmically, and she envied him his peace.

She gasped, there it was again, quite faint but an unmistakable cry, it could only be the cry of a baby. It seemed so real; she was certain it *was* real. She dug her nails into her thigh, it hurt, she was awake, and the cry was real. It was exactly the same cry she heard from outside the cottage on that strange day.

Lying stiff as a ramrod she forced herself not to get up to walk the short distance along the landing to the nursery. Laura knew if she did get up it would be the same as on previous occasions, the room would be empty and the crying would stop, and she didn't want to wake Ben. He was beginning to lose patience with her. He tried hard to conceal his irritation, but she knew, could tell from his suppressed sighs and over calm reassurances that he was frustrated by her continued nighttime hearings. Eventually, but after a few minutes of tense quiet, silence fell again and she fell back into a restless sleep, disturbed by strange and incomprehensible dreams.

Ben stirred; it must be early as it was still dark, although the light from behind the curtains seemed unusual. He checked, Laura was asleep beside him, but he could tell from the tangle of quilt that she wasn't sleeping peacefully. It must have been her tugging the quilt that woke him. He got up and went into the bathroom. It was cold, too early for the heating, he stopped to look out of the window before getting back into bed, it was snowing, that would account for the light. He watched for a moment as big heavy flakes swirled down and were gently covering the lawn in a soft, white blanket. He felt a surge of excitement, he loved snow. There was something magical about it in this country. It was different to the snow where they went skiing. Here it was unexpected and unpredictable. It was also different to the slushy grimy mess of snow in the city. He resisted the urge to wake Laura up to tell her and climbed back into bed, hoping the snow would still be there in the morning.

'I'll go and make a cup of tea, you stay there,' Ben whispered to the waking Laura a couple of hours later.

He quickly hopped out of bed and pulled on his dressing gown. He forced himself not to look out of the window; he wanted to save the revelation until he was downstairs. He made his way first into the sitting room. He could hear Colin stirring in the kitchen, eager to see him and be fed. He walked to the French doors and threw the curtains back; the sudden whiteness made him blink, but the garden was a picture, a veritable winter wonderland.

Then Ben caught his breath, a chill ran down his spine, and he shivered, but not with cold. Leading from the wall to the left side of the doors, going across the lawn all the way to the big oak tree, was a single set of footprints in the snow. Human footprints! No, that's ridiculous he thought, it must be an animal. He stood rooted to the spot for several seconds then rushed into the kitchen, opened the back door, pulled on his boots and ran, hotly pursued by an over excited Colin, who was equally excited and bemused by the snow, across the lawn to the footprints. Without thinking or even examining them more closely he started scuffing them over. Colin thought it was a great game and helped by bouncing around him. Ben's only thought was to erase the footprints before Laura saw them. As he reached the tree Colin backed off, hackles rising and making a low growl.

'Colin, here, don't be silly,' Ben called him back before he started barking.

The snow continued to fall, and Ben hoped the fresh snow would muffle the tracks before Laura came down. He went back into the kitchen, put the kettle on and sank into a chair feeling quite shaken. There must be a logical explanation; he just couldn't fathom out what it was. The footsteps went from the middle of the wall, where Laura said she saw a door. No, it was ridiculous, he mustn't get drawn into Laura's hallucination, or whatever it was. There was only one explanation, they must have been animal tracks, he didn't really look at them properly if he had, and not panicked, he would have known they were animal tracks. He worked hard trying to convince himself, but in the end decided to give up trying to work it out, before he sent himself mad.

Laura was like an excited child when she saw the snow and all thoughts of her nighttime waking were temporarily pushed to the back of her mind.

'I can see you and Colin have already been enjoying yourselves,' she said looking at the now indistinct area of disturbed snow where the footprints had been. 'You should have woken me.'

'I think it'll be here at least all day so you won't miss out, we can have a snowball fight later.' Ben pulled on his coat he felt the need to be out of the house and didn't want Laura to pick up on his agitation.

'Are you going to work? Have you had breakfast? What about the roads?'

'I must go into the bank. Apparently, the main roads are fine, and I can see that cars have managed to get along the lane, so it should be fine. I won't be long.'

'We can go for a walk when you get back,' Laura said, raising her face to receive Ben's goodbye kiss. She pottered about the house, worked for a while on a design, then decided to bake a cake. Something about the snow was bringing out her inner cook. She looked in the cupboards, and then looked in her few cookery books, mainly gifts from her mother, to find a cake that fitted her ingredients. Coffee and walnut sponge, without the walnuts, it would have to be. She weighed and sifted occasionally looking up to check the snow was still falling and imagining Ben's face when he returned to the aroma of homemade cake. She was just putting her rather sloppy mix into the oven when she heard it.

A baby crying.

There it was again. In the daytime. Never before had she heard it in the daytime. She shakily placed her cake in the oven slammed the door shut and leant against it, every sense on high alert. Colin was by the door to the hall, hackles up and growling almost inaudibly. No, it couldn't be, she must be imagining it, she thought.

'Colin, here come and have a biscuit.'

Colin looked back at her hearing his favourite word, well second favourite after walk, but didn't move, instead he barked and pawed at the door. Laura slowly opened the door and Colin ran to the stairs barking.

'Colin, stop it,' she caught his collar and tried to smooth his hackles. She couldn't hear anything and was about to return to the kitchen when the clear, pathetic mewl of a baby reached her from upstairs. Trembling, she climbed the stairs and made her way along the landing. There it was again, definitely coming from inside the nursery. She stood on the landing feeling as though all her blood was draining from her limbs, she was unable to move, and she began to feel faint. Colin pushed passed her and nearly knocked her off balance, but his movement was enough to focus her, and she grabbed the windowsill to steady herself. Colin stood growling about a foot outside the door. The crying wasn't any louder now

Laura was upstairs; it seemed somehow like a distant echo.

Trembling, Laura took a deep breath and flung the door open just as a real shriek of a cry reached her ears. She yelped herself, shuddered and stepped into the room, it was silent, too silent. The snow piling on the windowsill diffused the light and she presumed muffled any outside sounds. Laura shivered, the air inside the room was icy cold, despite the heating being on. There it was again, but quieter now, and seemed to be coming from the cupboard. Against all her instincts Laura flung open the cupboard doors - nothing. A surge of adrenaline flooded through her, and she raced from the room, nearly falling over the still growling Colin, to where Ben's toolbox was on the floor in the spare bedroom, left from his aborted attempt to put up a shelf. She grabbed a hammer and ran back to the nursery; another cry spurred her on; she attacked the cupboard with all her might smashing through the backboards and ripping off the doors in a frenzy.

Chapter 29

Ben entered the kitchen and sniffed approvingly at the baking cake. He called for Laura but instead of a reply, he could hear Colin barking madly upstairs. Instinctively knowing something was wrong. He leapt up the stairs and stopped dead when he saw Laura, like a mad woman, demolishing the cupboard.

'For Christ's sake Laura, what are you doing?' he yelled, to make himself heard over the banging and Colin's barking. She stopped and turned wild eyes towards Ben.

'The baby, the crying it's coming from in here,' she turned back and surveyed the splintered wood across the room. 'Listen,' she whispered.

'No, there's nothing to hear; nothing. There is no baby. This is getting bloody ridiculous. I've had enough. It's about time you pulled yourself together Laura, I mean it, I can't take much more.'

Ben turned and ran back down the stairs. 'Colin come,' he called, and seconds later he banged the door behind him and was striding down the lane with Colin by his side. After a few minutes he stopped and leant over putting his hands on his thighs and taking in deep breaths of the cold air. His heartbeat so hard in his chest he feared he was having a heart attack. Slowly he recovered, climbed over a stile and walked blindly through the snowy landscape, his emotions in turmoil. He couldn't cope anymore. Laura was becoming more like a stranger, and he seriously wondered if she really was mentally ill. He couldn't keep pretending she would be all right. Everything was starting to unravel, and a knot of fear lodged in his stomach.

As his paced slowed he unexpectedly started to think about Andrea, calm down to earth Andrea, he couldn't imagine her flying into an hysterical rage, he tried to imagine kissing her, then pulled himself up short. What was he doing? He felt disgusted with himself and shook his head to dislodge the image of Andrea's broad smile. Then to his horror found that tears were streaming down his face. He stumbled on, nearly tripping on the uneven ground that was hidden underneath the smooth blanket of snow. He should go back, he would have to be strong to help Laura through this, if he could. They were in it together. He would stand by her whatever.

'Ben! Hi, is everything all right?'

Ben looked up surprised to hear his name being called. He was behind the church and Aiden Jones, the vicar, was just climbing over the low wall into the field.

'Short cut to the vicarage,' he said, as an explanation as to why he was in the field, and to cover his concern at the sight of the tearful Ben.

Ben blew his nose; he didn't know whether to be embarrassed or relieved to see Aiden.

'You look like you could do with a hot drink, I'll be putting the kettle straight on if you fancy coming back with me.'

Ben hesitated. 'What about Colin?' he asked.

'Colin's very welcome,' Aiden bent to stroke Colin's now wet head. 'I should think he'll welcome a biscuit as well, follow me let's get into the warm.'

He pushed open the ornate wooden front door of the vicarage and showed Ben into a small comfortable room off the main hallway that Ben assumed must be his study. He wondered how many distraught parishioners' footsteps he was following in.

'Make yourself comfortable, hang your coat on the back of the door. Tea or coffee?'

'Coffee please.'

Ben tried, unsuccessfully, to stop Colin shaking himself, sending droplets of water everywhere. He dabbed at the obvious damp patches with a tissue and the sleeve of his jumper then sank into a comfy old leather armchair, one of a pair. The room was furnished in a mismatch of styles; a large rickety looking table was pushed into one corner with Aiden's computer and piles of paper heaped on it. The walls were lined with shelves crammed full of books, Ben looked at the ones closest to him and was surprised by the range of topics. The vicar was obviously a Le Carre fan, as well, it appeared, to have an interest in sport of all kinds, and the first and second world wars. There was a small, glowing woodburner in the fireplace, filling the room with comforting warmth. Ben stood up, not only drawn to the heat but to a photo on the mantel-piece. He was studying it when Aiden returned with a tray wafting the delicious aroma of proper coffee. He put the tray on the coffee table.

'I thought we could do with a drop of this as well to warm us up,' he said lifting a brandy bottle. 'Goes well with the coffee.'

Ben carefully put the photo back on the shelf and sat down watching him pour both the brandy and coffee.

'That's my wife and son,' Aiden said, nodding towards the photo and handing Ben a mug. 'She died twelve years ago from cancer,' he said.

'I'm really sorry. Does your son still live with you?' Ben was surprised, he'd assumed Aiden was single, the proverbial celibate priest, or was that Catholic. Yes of course it was, he suddenly felt very ignorant about religion and fidgeted beginning to feel uncomfortable in the presence of a vicar.

'Darren, he's at Durham doing law, final year.'

'He wasn't called to the Church then?'

Aiden laughed. 'Good grief no; we have interesting debates about philosophy and the likelihood of God's existence when we get together. He sees religion as a form of social control and an outdated doctrine. Actually, Susie, my wife, held very similar views,' he took a slug of brandy and chuckled. 'I do wonder sometimes if they're on the right lines, not that I'd ever give Darren a hint of that.'

Ben relaxed, impressed and surprised by Aiden's openness. He studied his companion while he took some sips of both coffee and the warming welcoming brandy. He must be about mid-fifties he reckoned, greying hair but still quite a lithe, athletic-looking physique. He had soft grey eyes that sparkled, and an easy smile, in a face that you could readily trust.

'Really, do you sometimes have doubts?' Ben asked.

'Well, I don't know about doubts, I just accept things. I don't analyse or need to have an explanation for everything in the way Darren does.'

'Sounds like he'll be a good lawyer.'

Aiden nodded and continued. 'My parents were Christian missionaries, so I grew up with religion all around me, it was just a given. I never questioned it. I didn't want to follow in their footsteps, missionary work I mean, times were changing, and missionaries were less welcome, but I did want to minister to people in the broadest sense, so becoming a vicar seemed the logical step.'

'How long have you been vicar here at St Michaels?'

'Let me think, it must be nearly ten years; it was for Darren's sake really. I'd always been in inner city parishes before, but after Susie died it got harder, being a single dad and all that, so we came here.'

'No regrets?' Ben asked.

'About us coming to live here? No none, people here have just as many concerns and worries and they give birth, marry and die just the same. I feel accepted here, part of the community. It's a good community.'

Ben nodded, whether it was the brandy or the warmth of Aiden's kindness, he wasn't sure, but felt an overwhelming desire to tell him everything that was happening with Laura. After a few moments comfortable silence Ben started to speak.

'Do you remember when we met in the pub you said other

people reported hearing a baby crying in our cottage.'

'Of course, I'm sorry, here I am rambling on about me. How is your wife?'

Ben told Aiden everything, from losing Poppy right up to the scene he recently walked out of.

He listened without interrupting, then after a few moments reflection he told Ben what he knew about Oak Tree Cottage. It was all hearsay of course, just stories other parishioners had told him, but it did seem that some of the older locals thought the cottage was haunted. He'd never paid much attention to their tales. There was a vague story about a young girl and a baby, many years ago, centuries probably, dying in unnatural circumstances. Someone, he told Ben, was rumoured to have been hung in a tree, but he emphasized that it was all a bit vague and there was no substance to the stories.

Ben listened and thought he was going to be sick, the girl, the tree; it was all as Laura described.

'Are you sure?' he asked, but he must have spoken so quietly Aiden didn't answer.

Instead, Aiden continued, the only first-hand information he could tell Ben was that no one stayed in the cottage very long, some people came and went before he even knew their names, and it seemed that there hadn't been a child living in the house for many, many years. The latest couple, the people who Laura and Ben bought from were French; they visited the church once for a Sunday service. They had seemed quite edgy and mentioned to Aiden after the service that they had heard strange noises in the cottage, a bit like an animal crying, but they weren't certain.

'Is that why they sold?' asked Ben twiddling his wedding ring round his finger. He was beginning to think they too must sell up.

'No, I don't think it was. I think it was financial problems. I didn't really get to know them, but I did hear that his business went bust. I think they went back to France.'

'Do you believe in ghosts?' Ben asked. Aiden tried not to look surprised by Ben's question.

'Ghosts? In the Halloween sense, no, but I think sometimes there might be unquiet souls.'

'So, do you think Laura, and other people who lived there, could have heard the cry of that baby?'

'I wouldn't like to say definitively, but I think there are a lot of things in this world that we don't understand.'

Ben nodded and for several moments neither of the men spoke.

'I don't know what to think, what to do, how to help her,' Ben sipped his coffee and blew his nose on a tissue fished from his pocket. 'Everything seems to be going wrong, well not everything, Laura's business is going well but she's, well she's sort of...' he blew his nose again.

'She hasn't lost a baby before.' Aiden passed Ben another tissue and was rewarded with a weak smile. 'I'm not an expert but I would imagine her emotions are in turmoil at the moment.'

'What about her hearing and seeing things, I don't know what to think. Could it be unquiet souls?' Ben didn't mention the footsteps in the snow. 'Do you think we should move, I don't want to, but if the problems are in the house not in Laura's head...?'

Aiden didn't reply, for a moment he watched Ben who was twisting the tissue tightly round his fingers and was touched by the anguish and look of fear on his face.

'I'd be happy to come and bless the house if you think it might help.'

'But we aren't believers and I'm sure Laura wouldn't agree. I'm sorry we just aren't religious,' Ben moved to stand up. 'I should go.'

'You're a kind, caring man Ben. Lots of people, who profess to be Christian or any religion for that matter, don't have your compassion. Some people sit in church every week, but there isn't an ounce of humanity in them. I don't care whether you believe in anything or not, I can feel your pain and, well, if I can help,' Aiden looked directly at Ben, and Ben knew he meant it.

'What would a blessing mean, would it work, would Laura need to be part of it? Sorry, lots of questions.'

'I don't think Laura would need to be involved, particularly if it's happening outside of her mind.'

'And the believing bit?'

'You mean believing in God?'

Ben nodded.

'I can bring the belief, you can provide the coffee,' Aiden leant across and touched Ben's arm. 'I can't guarantee it will work but it won't do any harm, and if it settles some restless energy then everyone will be happier.'

'OK, perhaps I can suggest Laura goes to stay with her mum or a friend,' Ben stood up, feeling like he needed a good blast of cold fresh air. 'It's time I got back to her. Thank you, Aiden. Talking has helped.'

'I'll walk as far as the church with you,' he said, gathering the mugs and glasses on to the tray. 'Let me know if, or when, you'd like me to come round, just give me a ring,' Aiden picked up a compliment slip with his contact details from the table and gave it to Ben, who pushed it deep into his coat pocket. The two men walked back in silence, through the snow, which had now stopped falling, only stopping at the church gate to shake hands and wish each other a good day.

Chapter 30

Ben cleared up the ruins of the cupboard and tried as best he could to reassure Laura that everything would be all right. He tried, again, to convince her that he did understand and, more importantly, from Laura's point of view that he did believe her.

He kept quiet about his meeting with Aiden, but mulled over what he had said, particularly the offer of the blessing. He was becoming even more sceptical as time passed, but what did they have to lose? He liked him and where was the harm; even Aiden said it would do no harm, so why not? It was worth a try.

The opportunity didn't immediately arise for Ben to suggest that Laura paid a visit to her family or a friend, and he didn't want her to suspect he was up to something. Superficially, life carried on as before, almost at times getting back to normal, but not quite. There had been no further episodes of crying, and Laura seemed outwardly to be more relaxed. The main anxiety that continued to linger with Ben was that Laura, either didn't want to, or wouldn't, talk about what happened that day. While she might appear more relaxed, he felt as though they were living with a time bomb.

'I think I need to go to London for a couple of days,' Laura said, one evening as they were eating dinner.

'Oh, right, for work?'

'I need to look at fabrics and there's a textile trade fair coming up. I thought I'd contact Vicky to see if I can stay with her; she'll probably be going anyway. I'll contact Anya to see if she's free as well.'

'Good idea,' said Ben, mentally crossing everything that Aiden would be available to come and bless the house while Laura was away.

Before Laura finished paying for the taxi, Vicky was down the steps outside her Primrose Hill flat and gathered Laura into her arms.

'Laura, darling, how are you, let me look at you? Oh my God Laura, I've been so worried about you. It's so wonderful to see you, come in, come in.' Vicky picked up Laura's small bag and ushered her up the steps into the spacious shared hallway of the large, converted house. Vicky had lived here as long as Laura could remember, and it must now be worth a small fortune. Laura smiled to herself at Vicky's gushing but genuine welcome, she was just the same.

Some people thought Vicky was affected, but Laura knew her better. She was a small, slightly eccentric fifty-something, who was never known to underplay an emotion. She always regarded Laura as something of a protégé, which was true to some extent. Almost viewed her as she would a daughter, if she had ever got round to having one. Laura loved and respected her, and it was true Vicky taught her more about design, fabric and dressmaking in their time together than Laura ever learnt in college.

'Come on through, Rufus is rustling up a pasta dish of some sort, but we can have a glass of wine and catch up first.'

Laura followed Vicky through the garden flat, it was small, beautifully decorated but always slightly chaotic, with papers all over the floor and swatches of material pinned to a big board leaning up against the fireplace. A laptop was open on the coffee table with a note pad covered in scrawling writing next to it.

Rufus, a large bear of a man, appeared dressed in a flowery apron with his hands encased in bright red, silicone oven gloves. He was a handsome man of about sixty with a mop of dark grey hair, and the confident air that men who are sure of their position in life wear so easily. Rufus was one of those men you couldn't help but like and Laura smiled in delight to see him. She had known him for as long as she'd known Vicky, but what he did for his work continued to remain a mystery. Even when she asked Vicky the reply was a vague description that meant nothing to Laura, and made her think even Vicky wasn't sure, but whatever it was he seemed very successful, judging by the trappings of their lifestyle.

'Laura sweetheart, lovely to see you,' he removed his oven gloves and leant over and kissed her cheek. 'I won't bombard you with questions now, I'll leave that to Vicky, we can catch up over supper.'

'I'm not bombarding her. Anyway, Laura come on let's go into the sunroom, we have a lot of catching up to do,' Vicky said, already armed with a bottle of red and two glasses. Laura smiled at Rufus and caught his wink. She felt so at home here with two of her dearest friends.

The sunroom was rather a grand term for a small room with big windows overlooking their postage stamp of a lawn, but in this part of London it was heaven. The evening sun, currently struggling between the two houses backing on to theirs, landed perfectly on a spot where, in the summer, lounger chairs would be placed, making it a haven of peace and warmth. It made Laura realise how much space she was now used to at Oak Tree Cottage.

Vicky launched straight in, wanting to know all the details of Laura's labour, the eventual stillbirth, and more importantly how Laura and Ben were coping. Once she'd gathered her emotions together Laura found it a huge relief to have someone be so open, instead of pussy footing around worrying about whether they would upset her. It wasn't that Vicky was insensitive, far from it, and despite never experiencing anything like it herself she was very empathetic in her manner. Laura found herself talking nonstop about every last detail and every emotion she had been through, although she didn't elaborate on her strange experiences, those could come later.

'Poor darling, sounds like you've been on a roller coaster.'

Laura nodded.

'It's been so good to talk. I don't think I've ever spoken quite so frankly about my feelings to anyone, not even Ben,' she said.

'You must, it's good to talk, even when it's hard, and he's probably feeling equally as raw. Promise me you will talk to him?'

Laura nodded, twirled her wine glass between her fingers and stared absently out of the window. She was so absorbed in her own feelings she never really gave Ben's grief proper consideration. Rufus joined them, pulling Laura out of her reverie. He topped up their glasses before sinking into a chair beside Laura.

'Here's to you Laura,' he raised his glass. 'I'm so glad you've come to stay; Vicky has been getting in a stew over the demanding Celine and her wedding dress. Maybe now she'll talk about something else.'

'Not just her dress, the whole entourage; honestly Laura she's a nightmare, you know Celine the actress?'

'Was she the one, the blue dress…?' Laura giggled.

'Don't mention the blue dress, yes the very same, but I don't want to discuss her now, we'll save that for tomorrow. I'm hoping to find something at the trade fair to meet her eccentric demands. Now let me tell you about Gordon Rivers, I bet you haven't heard?'

'No, I'm sure I haven't,' Laura shared a conspiratorial smile with Rufus.

'Well…' Vicky settled back and regaled Laura with the antics of a mutual acquaintance who designed theatre costumes, and the mess he found himself in both professionally and personally when he became involved in a production that went bankrupt. Rufus threw in the odd comment, usually immediately contradicted by Vicky, and although the events were obviously disastrous for those involved, by the end Laura was wiping tears of laughter from her cheeks. The whole evening passed in the same vein, laughter interspersed with delicious food and probably too much wine. Laura went to bed that night feeling lighter of spirit than she had in weeks.

The next couple of days passed in a whirl of fabrics, designers and accessories at the trade fair. Vicky attended on the first day and introduced Laura to several useful contacts. The second, and more successful day for Laura, was spent on her own, identifying new suppliers and gathering swatches of a wide range of fabrics; buying pieces of equipment to supplement what she already owned, and particularly some soft grip scissors, including a left-handed pair for Andrea. She also bought several varieties of embellishments, one of which Laura was certain would be perfect to use as a clasp on Lucinda's overdress.

Chapter 31

Just as she was about to leave the trade fair, Laura received a reply to a text she had sent to Anya earlier, asking if she was free for a coffee that afternoon. She was, and Anya suggested meeting in a wine bar not far from the trade show. Laura looked at her watch and with a spring in her step set off to meet her friend.

She arrived just as Anya was walking into the wine bar, and stopped in her tracks, staring. Anya was pregnant. Laura was certain; that bump couldn't be anything else. She felt as though she had been punched in the stomach, she leant against the wall trying to catch her breath. Why hadn't Anya told her, prepared her? Gathering her thoughts Laura knew why, probably Anya wouldn't want to upset her by telling her over the phone, but Laura wished she had. She was probably being oversensitive, but Laura was hurt and irrationally felt angry and betrayed. She took a big gulp of air, it took all her will power to compose herself before going in, she told herself she wasn't upset that Anya was pregnant, not really, she was surprised, more upset and actually a bit guilty that her friend hadn't felt she could share her news. She smoothed down the front of her coat, of course she was pleased for Anya, of course she was. She pasted on her best smile and pushed open the door. Anya was sitting at a table in an alcove and she stood up to great Laura when she entered.

'Well look at you, how lovely,' said Laura. 'When are you due?'

Anya smiled with relief and hugged Laura close.

'I'm nearly twenty weeks,' Anya said. 'I know it's silly, but I wasn't sure how to tell you.'

'Oh Anya, I'm delighted for you, and Stephen of course, how is he?'

Laura gulped her wine; she needed to quench her feelings and give herself courage to keep going. She watched while Anya sipped sparkling water. All Laura could think about was that Anya was pregnant and it wasn't fair. She tried hard, and overall, successfully, to conceal her feelings, but surprised herself by how bitter she felt. Every time she looked at Anya, the glow of her skin and the unconscious way she kept resting her hand on her bump caused Laura's stomach to tie itself in a knot of jealousy. They chatted, almost like old times, but not quite. Anya did most of the talking. Not only was she pregnant, but they were in the process of buying a house in Surrey, closer to Stephen's parents she explained, yet still easy for him to commute to London. It had a nice big garden; it wasn't a cottage as pretty as Laura's, but it suited them perfectly. Laura was happy for her to ramble on; she just smiled and nodded in the right places, asking occasional questions. Anya, so wrapped up in her own situation didn't seem to notice Laura's uncharacteristic quietness.

Eventually, Laura made excuses to leave, drinking wine on her own was no fun and she wanted to return to the sanctuary of Vicky's flat.

'You must come and stay with us again soon,' Laura said, as they parted to go their separate ways.

'Or you must come and see our new place, you can give me some ideas about colour schemes.'

They hugged and kissed; Anya was reluctant to agree to visit Oak Tree Cottage again. Even the thought of going back made her shiver involuntarily, and she instinctively didn't want to take her new baby there.

'Take care; keep me up to date with everything. Love to Stephen,' Laura waved, smiled too brightly, and hurried around the corner before her façade broke.

Laura arrived back in Primrose Hill drained and tired, and relieved to be able to discuss fashion and the trade show with Vicky, rather than babies and houses.

'Do you believe in ghosts?' she asked late into the evening after a couple more glasses of wine. Unaware that she was echoing Ben's question to Aiden.

Vicky emphatically didn't, but Rufus was more circumspect, and they both listened attentively as Laura described the happenings at Oak Tree Cottage, occasionally exchanging glances with each other as her story continued.

'Darling, I'm sure it must be your hormones, your emotions running wild,' said Vicky at one stage.

'But it's not all the time, it just happens out of the blue. Even people in the village think our house is haunted,' Laura said.

'Well, there you are,' said Vicky. 'Autosuggestion, it happens when you're in a low state.'

Rufus coughed to conceal a laugh, he knew Vicky didn't know what she was talking about, but it somehow seemed to make sense to Laura, which he supposed was the main point.

'Yes, positive thinking is the way forward, push village tittle-tattle out of your mind,' he said, and was rewarded with a sceptical warning look from Vicky who thought he was mocking her.

Laura nodded.

'You're probably right,' she said. 'I need to pull myself together,' she started laughing, but wasn't really sure why, and soon all three of them were laughing together. Whatever the reason it worked as therapy and Laura really did feel happier.

'We've got a bit of news as well?' Vicky glanced at Rufus and received an affirming nod.

Laura sat forward in her chair, all ears; she knew it couldn't be anything to do with babies.

'We're buying a little place in Italy, with a possible view to retirement, but for lots of holidays in the meantime. So, you and Ben must use it.'

'With or without us,' Rufus leant over and touched Laura's arm. 'With us would be more special of course.'

'Tell me more, it sounds wonderful, except the bit about you possibly retiring out there.'

'Oh, that won't be for ages, I can't prise Vicky away from her dresses. I keep telling her Italy is the home of fashion, but well …'

A faraway look came into Rufus's eyes and Vicky reached over and gently touched his hand. Laura got the impression that retirement was possibly closer than they let on. They chatted late into the evening and Laura fell into bed with the slightly giddy feeling of having drunk too much, something she hadn't done since before becoming pregnant. She was delighted when Rufus suggested asking Ben to join them for the weekend; it was late so she would contact him tomorrow.

Chapter 32

Ben dithered in the hallway not knowing what to do, he watched anxiously as Aiden made his way upstairs, preceded by a very agitated Colin.

'Why don't you go and put the kettle on Ben?' Aiden suggested from the landing.

'Yes, OK, if you don't need me.'

Ben detected a note of nervousness in Aiden's voice, or was he projecting his own feelings? Anyway, a sceptic breathing down his neck was the last thing he needed while he did whatever he needed to do. Ben headed towards the kitchen pleased to have a purpose.

'Ben, can you call Colin down.'

'Sorry, Colin here boy, come and have a biscuit.'

Colin slunk reluctantly down the stairs, not even responding to the promise of a biscuit with a wag.

'Well, boy, you're sensing something strange going on, aren't you?' Ben said to Colin once they were inside the kitchen, with the door closed. He stroked Colin's silky fur surprised to feel that his hackles were raised.

'It's OK boy nothing to worry about, Aiden knows what he's doing.' Ben's words were as much to reassure himself as Colin. Colin responded with a sigh and lay on the floor staring intently at the door.

Doing something like this was a new experience for Aiden as well, he wasn't at all sure if this was the right thing to do, but like he'd confidently said to Ben before, he supposed it couldn't do any harm. He drew on his inner faith he desperately wanted to help this young couple and hoped his faith was strong enough. He opened the nursery door and was immediately struck by the change in temperature within the room. He shivered and stepped inside, glancing at the window to check it hadn't been left open. It hadn't. He crossed himself and pulled a small book from out of his pocket.

'May the God of peace
Bring peace to this house…'

Aiden continued to read the blessing aloud as he walked around the nursery. He moved from room to room until he found his way back to Ben in the kitchen. Ben looked up expectantly; he was surprised by the drained look on Aiden's face.

'I've done what I can,' he said.

'Thank you,' Ben wasn't sure what he should say or do, this felt way out of his comfort zone. 'I'm really grateful, what can I do to repay you?' he asked after a pause.

'Tell you what,' Aiden smiled. 'Why not turn the kettle off; you can buy me a pint in the pub.'

'Sounds good to me, come on Colin,' Ben grabbed his coat and soon they were all walking at a pace down the road.

Well, guess I must be off,' Aiden said, draining his beer. 'Thanks for the pint, Ben. Take care, and let me know how things are, you know, with Laura.'

'No, thank you Aiden, I appreciate everything.'

Ben left the pub shortly afterwards and received a text from Laura on his way home, suggesting he join her, Vicky and Rufus, in London for the weekend. He could think of nothing he would like to do more, and within an hour Colin was lodged with William and Claire for the weekend, and he was on his way to the station.

The weekend was a huge success, Laura was her normal, relaxed self. They met friends for brunch in one of their old haunts, went to an exhibition, and out for dinner with Vicky and Rufus. Conversation and laughter flowed all weekend, and it was with a pang of regret that they hugged Vicky and Rufus goodbye late on Sunday afternoon, with promises to return soon and of reciprocal visits. As the train drew nearer their station both Ben and Laura fell quiet, neither really looking forward to going home. Not for the first time Ben wondered if a mistake had been made moving to the country and he was beginning to think again that they should move back to London.

They delayed their return home by calling in to collect Colin and stopping for coffee with William and Claire. So, it was quite late when they turned the key in the front door. Ben wasn't quite sure what he was expecting, but everything felt calm and normal as he stepped into the hall. Colin bounced into the kitchen and sat on the mat waiting for a biscuit.

'I think I'll go straight up, I'm exhausted,' said Laura, turning to the stairs.

She was surprised when she reached the top to see the nursery door ajar, Ben must have been in there. She hesitated, then walked across to close it, but instead something made her push it open, and as she stepped inside the warmth in the room struck her.

'You've done something to the radiator,' she said, as Ben came into the room and stood beside her. He put his arm around her shoulder and kissed her neck but didn't reply. Could that be Aiden's work or was it a coincidence? He wasn't quite sure which he preferred, but Laura was right there was a definite change to the atmosphere and temperature in the room. He allowed himself to hope.

Chapter 33

'You look tired Laura,' Lady Carlton-Prior said, as Laura carefully helped her out of the simple, elegant, deep ochre evening dress. Not a colour everyone one could carry off, but it suited Lady Carlton-Prior's complexion perfectly.

'I'm getting over a migraine, it always leaves me a bit wiped out,' Laura replied.

She wasn't getting over a migraine but was actually feeling decidedly queasy, and she didn't want to have Lady Carlton-Prior jumping to conclusions, before Laura herself reached that conclusion.

'Ah yes, my husband suffers, damned nuisance, aren't they? Knocks him off his feet for days.'

Laura smiled to herself; she was starting to develop a bit of a soft spot for Lady Carlton-Prior, or Alex, as she'd asked Laura to call her. Laura found calling her Alex uncomfortable, so now she didn't really call her anything, except Lady C-P in her head and when talking to Andrea.

'Yes, they certainly are, luckily I don't get them too often. There we are,' Laura said, smoothing the fabric of the dress before hanging it back on the rail and drawing the curtain.

'I'm delighted with it, thank you Laura, you really are a clever girl,' Lady Carlton-Prior said, oblivious of how condescending she sounded, as she watched Laura carefully handling the dress. Laura smiled, she knew the colour would suit Lady Carlton-Prior despite her Ladyship's initial reservations that it was too dark for her and would make her look old. She didn't look old at all, in or out of the dress, and Laura guessed she could only be in her late-fifties, sixties at the most. She was lucky enough to have beautiful skin and a good bone structure that should keep her looking good even when she did reach old age.

'How will you wear your hair?' Laura asked.

'Up I think, don't you?' she asked, and Laura agreed. 'I have some beautiful gold and deep amber earrings that will look just right with it. I do wish you would talk to Lucinda about her hair, she wants to leave it all straggly.'

'I'll leave you to dress,' Laura said, going through to join Lucy and Andrea, she had no intention of trying to persuade Lucy to wear her hair any other way than the way she wanted.

Lucy and Andrea were deep in conversation about an aspect of the bridesmaid's dresses. Andrea was becoming a real asset, and Laura 's confidence in her was growing daily, she could overhear her reassuring Lucy that the dresses wouldn't be too flouncy or frilly and that we would make sure they flattered each of the girl's figures. The bridesmaids were an eclectic mix, chosen, Laura presumed, mainly by Lucy's mother, as only one of the four was a friend of Lucy's, the others being assorted distant relatives. They were a mix of shapes and sizes and the same style dress would certainly not fit them all, so Andrea's suggestion of different individual styles in the same fabric really went down well with both Lucy and her mother. This wasn't a new idea for bridesmaids, but Laura was pleased when Andrea thought of it herself.

'Where on earth did you get that brooch?' they all looked up startled at her tone of voice as Lady Carlton-Prior swept across the floor, jabbing her finger towards Andrea.

'It was a present.' Andrea instantly flushed to the roots of her hair, and instinctively put her hand up to cover the delicate marcasite brooch, depicting three swallows in flight.

'That's as maybe, but my sister lost a lot of jewellery in a robbery last year and she had a brooch very like that one.'

'Mother!' Lucinda glared at her mother.

Lady Carlton-Prior lowered her hand and Andrea fled upstairs before she could say anything else.

'You must remember it Lucinda, you always liked that brooch as a child didn't you recognise it, you must have?'

'No, I certainly did not.'

'Well…' Lady Carlton-Prior started, but another warning glance from her daughter made her stop.

'I think we had better go mother. Thank you, Laura, I'll see you soon, Andrea's given me my next appointment,' Lucy, looking equally discomfited as both she and Laura, steered her mother out of the door, continuing to admonish her as they went towards their car. As soon as the door closed Laura raced up the stairs to Andrea. She was sitting, motionless with her head in her hands.

'Are you OK, what was that all about?'

'How could he do it to me?' she raised a tear-streaked face to Laura.

'Who, what?' Laura sat on a corner of the desk, next to Andrea.

'My brother gave me that brooch for Christmas. I know he's a fraudster and probably a money thief, but well, I didn't think he robbed houses as well. How could he, then give it to me, the bastard,' Andrea started sobbing uncontrollably.

'He might have bought it in good faith,' Laura said, and noticed when Andrea looked up that the brooch was no longer pinned to her top. She reached out and squeezed Andrea's hand.

'Even if he didn't steal it, he must have used dirty money, so it amounts to the same thing.'

'Come on, let me make us both a cup of tea.'

Andrea sat staring at nothing in particular, while Laura bustled about in the little kitchen making tea. She hoped this incident wouldn't put Lady Carlton-Prior off recommending her, and then immediately chastised herself for being selfish. This wasn't about her or her business. What she needed to do now was support Andrea. Her feelings for Lady Carlton-Prior were now less favourable than they were an hour earlier, and of course she would stand by Andrea, after all even if the brooch was stolen it wasn't Andrea's fault, and Lady Carlton-Prior's reaction was completely out of order. They drank their tea almost in silence; Laura tried to engage Andrea in conversation about other dresses they were working on, but with limited success.

'I thought at the time it was a bit too tasteful for him to have chosen, but it was so pretty I didn't want to think about where it came from. It's the nicest present he's ever bought me. What do you think I should do with it?' Andrea asked, eventually.

'With the brooch?'

Andrea nodded.

'Well, I don't really know, nothing probably, at least not at the moment.'

'D'you think she'll call the police?'

'I don't know, I hope not but I suppose she might. Although it should be down to her sister.'

'Oh well, looks like Billy's going to go down anyway, they might just as well add this to it. I wonder what else he's done. No, I don't, I don't want to even think about that.'

Laura looked at Andrea, touched by the pain and bitterness in her voice, her home life and experiences were so far away from hers, and yet Laura felt closer to her than many of her other friends. She guessed Andrea was also itching to go and find her brother so she could give him a mouthful of abuse.

'Do you think he will, go to prison I mean?' Laura asked.

'After this I hope he does, I could kill him.'

The two women finished their tea and started clearing up; Laura couldn't see any benefit in carrying on, as neither of their minds would be fully on work.

'You go on home, there's nothing much else to be done today. Go and talk things over with Adam,' Laura said.

'Adam? What will he think? I haven't told him too much about Billy yet.'

'He's going out with you, not Billy, and you're not responsible for your brother. Go on you'll feel better tomorrow.'

Laura kept her fingers crossed, not really sure what tomorrow might bring, especially if Lady Carlton-Prior did go to the police, but she hoped Andrea would feel better after talking to Adam.

Laura carried on after Andrea left, trying to create a pattern for a new commission, but her mind wasn't really on work. She wondered how this would all pan out, could Andrea be implicated in receiving stolen goods, surely not. She was totally innocent. Laura really knew very little about the law and let her imagination run wild for a few moments. She was worried about Andrea but in one way she felt grateful to have something other than her own anxieties to think about.

Chapter 34

Laura decided to pack up for the day and was just about to go across to the house when a scrunch of tyres on the gravel made her go to the window. She expected to see Ben returning, but her heart gave a lurch when she saw Lady Carlton-Prior's Range Rover pull up outside. She felt slightly sick, her returning so soon couldn't be good news. Laura felt a wave of relief that Andrea wasn't still there, perhaps she would be able to prevent the situation getting out of hand. Persuade Lady Carlton-Prior not to take it any further, unless she had already of course. Laura opened the door and waited while Lady Carlton-Prior climbed out, she was alone and looked harassed.

'Laura, oh dear, where's Andrea I must speak to her?'

Laura was surprised by how ruffled Lady Carlton-Prior seemed, she was flapping her hands and almost pushed Laura out of the way in her haste to get through the door.

'Where is she, where's Andrea?' she asked again.

'She's not here I told her to go home, she was quite shocked by your accusation.'

Laura looked at Lady Carlton-Prior, she looked dreadful.

'Are you all right, would you like to sit down?'

Lady Carlton-Prior was pacing around the room; she sat down at Laura's request then like a jack-in-a-box sprang back up again.

'Oh dear, I was hoping to see her. Oh dear, I've made a terrible mistake.'

On hearing those words Laura relaxed a little.

'Please, Lady Carlton-Prior, do sit down and explain,' said Laura, sitting down herself and hoping that her action would encourage the clearly stressed woman to sit down as well. It did, Lady Carlton-Prior sank into a chair. Laura thought she looked on the verge of tears.

'Oh Laura, I've been such a fool, Lucinda's really cross with me,' she looked up at Laura, who nodded in encouragement.

'I rang my sister, straight away after we left here. I was so certain that brooch was one of the ones that was stolen from her.' She took a deep breath before carrying on.

'But it isn't hers. She lost a lot of jewellery in the burglary, but the marcasite brooch wasn't taken. Apparently, it's always pinned on one of her jackets and she was wearing it at the time,' she looked up at Laura again. 'I accused poor Andrea, oh dear I feel terrible, that poor girl what will she think. I just, well I just assumed the worst, and I didn't stop to think. Lucinda's so cross. My sister was horrified as well, when I told her. I must see her to explain, Andrea I mean.'

'Andrea was very upset thinking that her brother, well you know…' Laura felt some sympathy for Lady Carlton-Prior, who was genuinely mortified by her behaviour, but Laura didn't want to let her off the hook too quickly. 'I think she was going to see her brother straight away, to challenge him.'

'No, I must try to stop her, I feel I must see her to apologise as soon as possible, can you ring her?'

Laura dialled Andrea's mobile but it just went to voice mail. Lady Carlton-Prior's agitation increased, she jumped up and started pacing again. Laura wanted to laugh and part of her felt she deserved her pain and would happily have strung it out for longer, except she knew the sooner Andrea was told the quicker she would be out of her misery.

'I can give you her address, she doesn't live far away.'

'Yes, please Laura, if you wouldn't mind, I really feel I must put this right as soon as I can.'

Laura wrote Andrea's address on a piece of paper and gave Lady Carlton-Prior detailed directions, then watched as she drove out of the gate scattering gravel everywhere in her haste.

'Adam, what on earth are you doing here?' Lady Carlton-Prior asked, looking around confused, perhaps she'd misunderstood Laura's directions.

Adam pulled the door open wider and gaped in surprise.

'Aunt Alex, what are you doing here, more to the point?' Adam asked, knowing full well what his aunt's visit must be about. He'd gone straight round to see Andrea when she called him in quite a state but was surprised to now see his aunt on the doorstep.

'I'm looking for someone called Andrea, is she here? Do you know her?'

'Yes, she is here, she lives here, but she's quite upset,' Adam replied.

'Yes, yes, I know, that's why I'm here. Laura gave me her address.'

Adam stood aside to let his aunt pass. Andrea was standing in the doorway to the sitting room a look of total bemusement on her face.

'Aunt Alex?' she mouthed to Adam, her eyebrows quizzically raised so high they nearly disappeared into her hairline, as Lady Carlton-Prior stepped into the hallway.

'Andrea, my dear, I am so, so, sorry, I hope you can forgive me.'

Andrea looked even more bemused.

'Sit down aunt,' said Adam, thinking that both women looked as though they were about to fall down in shock.

'My sister, Geraldine…'

'What's going on?' Andrea interrupted, before she flopped onto the small sofa and looked from one to the other, this was getting surreal.

'Geraldine, I rang her straight away, her marcasite brooch wasn't stolen, she was wearing it, it was on her jacket, so it wasn't in the house.'

Lady Carlton-Prior was gabbling, not at all the composed

aristocrat Andrea knew from the studio. Andrea stared at her, she was still smarting from the earlier accusation, but the words slowly sank in and began to make sense. She didn't know whether to laugh out loud, cry, or swear; in the end she just sat open mouthed.

'You remember the burglary don't you Adam?' Lady Carlton-Prior asked, turning for support to her nephew.

Adam nodded, but said nothing. He was not only angry with his aunt for accusing Andrea, wrongly, as it turned out, but also because he hadn't explained his family connection to Andrea when she previously spoke about the 'posh' family for whom they were making dresses.

'Some of her jewellery was stolen but not that particular brooch. I'm so sorry Andrea, I was a bit hasty. I feel dreadful. Please can you forgive me?' she asked, looking directly into Andrea's eyes that were also rapidly filling with tears.

Andrea swallowed hard. 'Of course, I can, I'm just relieved it wasn't my brother, I mean relieved it wasn't him who stole it, or bought stolen goods. I was delighted when he gave me that brooch, it was tearing me apart thinking it was stolen.'

'Thank you, Andrea, you are very kind,' she reached across and touched Andrea's arm, her smile wobbling uncertainly.

Andrea returned a beaming smile; relief made her magnanimous.

'Adam could you make us all a drink please?'

'So, you and Adam are... friends?' Lady Carlton-Prior looked between them, trying to weigh up this new situation, before Adam left to put the kettle on.

'Yes, we are aunt, close friends, very close,' said Adam, before Andrea could reply.

'Do you live here as well Adam, your mother never said?'

'No, Andrea lives here with another young man, Ralph, I live in my flat.'

Lady Carlton-Prior opened her mouth and then closed it again she decided to bite her tongue. Before Adam could wind his aunt up further, Ralph let out an almighty howl. Andrea jumped to her feet to fetch him and after a couple of minutes returned and with a grin plonked Ralph into Adam's arms.

Lady Carlton-Prior gasped, and the decision this time not to say anything was involuntary, for once she was speechless.

'This is Ralph, and no, he's not mine,' Adam said, reading his aunt's mind.

'I'm a fool aren't I Adam?'

Again, Adam didn't reply but just smiled sadly at his aunt.

'Well, I had better go, don't worry about the drink,' she leant over and took both of Andrea's hands in hers. 'I hope you won't think too badly of me. I need to think before I speak in future. Actually, Lucinda's told me that on many an occasion.'

'Of course, I won't think badly of you, it was an easy mistake,' Andrea said, winking at Adam as they followed Lady Carlton-Prior out into the small courtyard garden and watched her climb into the Range Rover. With a toot on the horn, she was gone.

'Well,' said Andrea, grabbing Adam's hand. 'What a relief, but I think you've got some explaining to do. Aunt Alex indeed.'

Chapter 35

'Right, let me get this straight, Adam is Lady Carlton-Prior's nephew and he never told you?' asked Laura.

'No, well I suppose it never came up; aunts aren't high on our list of topics to talk about. I talk about work but not client's names, well I might have mentioned the Carlton-Priors, but I don't think so, so there's no reason to make the connection, but it was a surprise.'

'Was it Adam's mum who was burgled?'

'No, apparently there are three sisters, Lady C-P is the eldest, Geraldine the youngest, and Adam's mum Grace in the middle. It was Geraldine who was burgled. Adam said his parents haven't got anything worth taking.'

'Aren't they all, you know aristocrats or at least wealthy?' Laura asked.

'I'm not sure what the three sister's background is, but Adam says he comes from quite an ordinary family, well not ordinary by my standards, but not in the Carlton-Prior league. Adam's mum is a nurse and his dad's a physiotherapist with the football club, and Geraldine and her husband are both solicitors, so pretty posh I guess,' Andrea replied.

'Sounds posh to me too,'

'Billy will be welled chuffed if I tell him I'm going out with someone with connections to the football club, but I won't tell him, or he'll be badgering me to get him free tickets all the time.'

Laura suddenly started to giggle, why she wasn't sure, but soon they were both almost helpless with laughter.

'Someone's having far too much fun for a Wednesday morning,' Ben said, coming into the kitchen with Colin close behind.

'Sorry are we disturbing you, we just came over for a drink, I've run out of milk over there?'

'No, I just came to get a coffee, what's so funny?'

'Nothing really, only Andrea's going out with Lady Carlton-Prior's nephew,' both women collapsed in giggles again. Colin barked, excited by the jovial atmosphere and hoping that there might be a biscuit or better still a walk in it for him.

'No, you're right, I can't see the joke, but carry on, sadly some of us have work to do,' he poured his coffee, planted a kiss on Laura's head and left the room, reluctantly followed by a disappointed Colin.

'Laura where are you; I've got a coffee for you?'

'I'm in here,' Laura called from the nursery.

She was leaning on the windowsill looking out at the garden. Blossom was on the trees, and shrubs were bearing the fresh green of new leaves. The sun was shining, and Colin was chasing up and down the lawn. She turned to Ben and smiled.

'What are you doing in here?' he asked, handing her a steaming mug of coffee.

'Thanks,' Laura looked at it and put it on the windowsill, she couldn't face it.

'Everything ok?' Ben asked.

'Yes fine, I was just wondering how soon we should bring the cot back from your parents' house.'

Ben looked confused, and then the penny dropped.

Laura picked up the test stick from the sill and silently passed it to Ben.

'It's positive,' he said, barely above a whisper. He held the stick, staring at it mesmerized for a moment, then lifted Laura in his arms and twirled her around.

'Don't, don't, I'll be sick,' she laughed.

'This is amazing news, are you sure?'

'Yes, very sure, I've suspected for a few days, but now with this,' she indicated the stick. 'I'm certain, oh Ben, it will be all right won't it?'

'Yes, it will be perfect this time, but you need to book an appointment straight away, do it today, promise?'

'Promise,' she replied. 'Let's keep it to ourselves for a bit, though.'

He nodded, suddenly overwhelmed with a mix of emotions ranging for ecstasy to terror.

'That looks pretty.'

'Oh,' Laura, startled, jumped to her feet and put her hand to her chest, stretching and rubbing her back at the same time.

'The tubs and window boxes,' Elsie, who was casually leaning on the gate, nodded towards the containers that Laura was filling with annuals.

'Sorry, I didn't see you coming,' Laura tucked a strand of hair behind her ear and hoped that Elsie was just passing not actually coming to see her. 'Were you, um did you ...'

'I was just out for a walk dear, the doctor has told me to take more exercise, good for the circulation, you know. He said I'm a marvel for my age, but I just needed to walk a bit more, so I thought where shall I go and you know I haven't been along this way for ages. So enough about me, how are you my dear?'

'Good, yes, very well thank you,' Laura nodded and smiled.

'I see the wisteria's coming back, I thought that died a long time ago, no one seemed to be able to get it to grow.'

'Yes, Ben's cut it right back. Kill or cure we thought.'

'He must have green fingers I'll say, it's been on its last legs for years.'

Laura wiped her hands on her jeans and walked over to the gate, not really wanting to engage in conversation but didn't want to appear rude.

'He's a novice gardener, well we both are really. Ben's thinking of starting a vegetable patch in the back.

'My Gerald's your man for vegetables. I'm sure he'd love to give your Ben some advice he just has to ask.

'Thank you, that's very kind,' Laura followed Elsie's gaze towards the house, she had a strange expression on her face and Laura began to wish she would continue with her walk and leave her in peace. Elsie nodded knowingly and looked at Laura. 'The house looks um, let me think, relaxed, yes relaxed that's the word my dear. Very pretty, well done.'

Laura turned back towards the house; it did look lovely with the sunshine warming the mellow stone, and the flowers and shrubs all thriving in the borders under the windows and around the front porch.

'My parents have been advising which shrubs to plant for a good display.'

'It's more than that dear it's the feel. I think you'll be happy here, at last someone will be happy here.'

Laura was about to reply but Elsie was already starting to walk slowly along the lane.

'I must get on, keep up the good work,' she called over her shoulder.

Laura watched her until she disappeared out of sight around the bend in the lane. Was she right, was there something different about the house? Laura felt more at peace than she had for months, but she assumed that was to do with… She rested her hand on her stomach, pleased that Elsie missed her bump, she can't have noticed. Laura smiled; she was sure Elsie wouldn't have been able to resist saying something if she thought Laura was pregnant.

Chapter 36

'What a lovely day,' Andrea said, looking out of the window as Laura drove along windy roads through beautiful countryside towards Crowbury Hall. 'I hope it stays like this for the wedding.'

The car, with the back seats down, was full of garment bags containing all the completed dresses for the Carlton-Prior wedding. Laura felt nervous she always did at this final stage, when it was almost too late to change anything. She would be happy once they were all out and hanging up again, but Andrea was right it was a beautiful day and overall, she felt at peace with the world.

'How would you feel about doing a fashion design course?' Laura asked.

'What you mean a proper college course?'

'There's one linked to the university that you can actually do most of from home, you have a tutor and have projects to do, but it's a good course and leads to a proper qualification. I was looking at the details the other day.'

'I'm not sure, do you think I could do it? I'm not sure I could afford it anyway,' Andrea said, but she was interested and wondered if there was a way.

'I'm certain you could do it; you have such good ideas, and your workmanship is really excellent. Don't worry about costs, I can cover those from our funds. I just thought together we could develop the business a bit more, I mean we can do that anyway, but if you enhanced your skills…'

'Wow, really, I'd love to if it's possible.'

'We could expand the range; bring in new lines, more than just wedding dresses. We'd need to do more on the marketing side as well,' Laura said, starting to feel excited herself.

'How about a children's range?'

'Children? I hadn't thought of that, but yes why not, you could try it out as a project. The only thing with children's clothes is getting the cost right, there's so much competition.'

They were so deep in conversation, bouncing ideas off each other that neither noticed the sign for Crowbury Hall, before they'd sailed past the entrance. The road was narrow, and Laura struggled to turn the car round, fearful of ending up in a ditch with her precious cargo of dresses. Laura drove slowly along the winding driveway until, turning a bend next to a small copse, the hall came into view.

'Wow look at that,' said Andrea. 'It's like something from a period drama. Perhaps your man on horseback will come riding into view.'

'Oh don't. I don't think I'll ever forget about that. Except now it just seems like some sort of nightmare. I do worry a bit, though, you know, in case it happens next time.'

Andrea touched Laura's arm. 'I'm sure everything will be fine this time,' she said, mentally crossing her fingers and kicking herself for even mentioning it.

'Yes, thanks. I feel different this time, not so frantic about making sure everything's perfect, getting the right things, everything matching and top of the range.'

'It'll be perfect without all the stuff,' said Andrea.

'I know that now, mainly thanks to you.'

They exchanged smiles and carried on along the drive.

The Hall was quite imposing, but not overpowering or bleak, and the sunshine made the many windows sparkle. Towards the back they could just see where a marquee had been erected. There were people everywhere, rushing in and out of the front and side doors with arms full of boxes, shouting and gesticulating to each other as they went about their business. Chairs and tables were stacked in a pile against the wall, presumably waiting to be installed in the marquee.

'Looks pretty chaotic,' said Laura, parking as close to the front steps as she could. 'We better take them in a few at a time,' she said, nodding towards the dresses.

'You take Lucinda's, I'll bring the bridesmaids and come back for Lady C-P's.'

With the garment bag draped across her arms, Laura mounted the steps to the open front door. More people were rushing around inside, Laura stopped not knowing quite where to go.

A young, smartly dressed woman stepped briskly up to her.

'Ah, these must be the dresses. Are you Laura? I'll let her Ladyship know you're here,' she said, without waiting for Laura to reply.

'Laura, and Andrea,' Lady Carlton-Prior said as she entered the hallway and spotted Andrea coming in just behind Laura. 'Come with me,' she led the way up the sweeping staircase.

Once the dresses were hanging properly Laura relaxed and turned to smile at Lady Carlton-Prior, who to her surprise appeared dishevelled and looked as though she might have been crying.

'Is everything all right?' Laura asked.

'No, it is not. Lucinda's being ghastly; she says she's not going through with it. She says she never asked for all this and, oh I don't know, I just don't know,' Lady Carlton-Prior slumped into a small chair in the dressing room, which was bigger than Laura's bedroom, and put her head in her hands. 'I just don't know what to do. She can be so difficult, no thought for me and all I've done for this wedding.'

Andrea was smoothing out the dresses, but Laura could tell from her shoulders that she was struggling not to laugh. Laura bit her lip, the last thing she needed now was a fit of the giggles.

'Where is Lucinda?' Laura asked.

'In the grounds somewhere, probably by the lake, it's where she goes when she's in a strop.'

'Would you like me to go and find her? I'd rather like her to try on her dress before I leave.'

'Yes, please that would help. If you can persuade her to come in, and at least participate in something. Oh, there's a scroll or something on the hall table for her, could you take it?' Lady Carlton-Prior stood up slowly and walked to the window, her shoulders slumped as she stared out at the melee below in the grounds.

'Don't worry; I'm sure it's just last-minute nerves. We've seen it all before, haven't we Laura?' Andrea surprisingly composed gently touched the older woman's arm.

Laura winked at Andrea over her shoulder as she made her way out to find the errant Lucy.

Chapter 37

She walked out into the sunshine towards the direction of the lake, the gardens looked stunning, and she wondered how many people were employed to keep them looking so good, wouldn't Elsie just love to wander round here, she thought.

A little flutter in her stomach made her stop and smile, she wished she could just enjoy a stroll around the grounds herself soaking up the warmth, but she soon spotted Lucinda, not far off sitting on a seat in an arbour.

'Hi,' she said, sitting down next to her.

'Hi.'

'Things not going so well?' Laura stretched out her legs and looked towards the lake.

'Not going well? It's a bloody nightmare. This is everything I didn't want, it's my wedding but it's turned into mother's pomp and glory show,' Lucinda looked like she was about to explode. 'I've got a good mind to boycott the whole thing.'

'What was your vision?' Laura asked. 'By the way your mother asked me to give you this,' Laura handed Lucinda the scroll.

'My vision? Mother never asked me about my vision. I wanted something small, no fuss, something meaningful to me and Ed. This is all mother, not me,' she waved her hands towards the marquee and battalions of scurrying people. 'It's all about being seen and being the best. I seem to be irrelevant in her plan.'

Laura found it quite hard to believe that Lucinda allowed her mother to totally ignore her wishes. In all her dealings with her Laura never considered Lucinda to be a shrinking violet.

'What about Ed, what did he want?'

'Oh, he didn't want a big fuss either, but he's quite happy, but he's not here every day with mother going on and on about the most trivial details,' Lucinda suddenly stopped and looked at Laura. 'You must think me the most ungrateful brat,' she said.

'Not at all, you're not the first bride to feel that everything's being done to her, not for her, or with her. Your mother is genuinely worried you're going to call it off though.'

'Really, she's not just playing the drama queen, as usual. Dad's got the right idea he's gone to London for the day.'

Laura didn't really know what else to say, she just hoped after all her hard work the dresses would get worn. Deep down she was sure they would, Lucy was just having a wobble. They sat in companionable silence for a while. Laura raised her face and momentarily closed her eyes to absorb the warmth of the sun's rays. She could easily have nodded off but was roused by Lucy untying the scroll and laughing out loud when she read it.

'What is it?' Laura couldn't help asking when she looked at Lucy, who was brushing a tear from her cheek, but she was smiling from ear to ear at the same time.

'It's from Eddie,' she said, handing the scroll to Laura and searching her pockets for a tissue.

Laura read the scroll, as Lucinda wandered off blowing her nose and using her phone. The scroll was a mockup of a wedding invitation, inviting Lucinda to their 'proper' wedding in just over a week's time, on the beach in Vanuatu. All you need are flip-flops and a sarong it said. Vanuatu, Laura had heard of it, an Island in the South Pacific.

'Is that where you're going for your honeymoon?' she asked, when Lucinda returned and sat next to her, all smiles.

'Yes, Eddie spent some time there a couple of years ago. I've just spoken to him, he says this will be our official wedding and we should enjoy the day, all this,' she indicated the marquee again, 'as an amazing party with all our family and friends.'

'Well, I suppose that's what it's all about, this is for everyone to celebrate with you, but this,' Laura touched the scroll. 'This is your special private ceremony.'

'I suppose I'd better go back to the house and put mother out of her misery, and you'll be wanting me to try on my dress I expect?'

Laura nodded, she wondered about offering to run up a sarong, she could see it in her mind, white fine silk edged with embroidery and beads, but she kept quiet. Lucy probably wanted to buy one from a local woman, something authentic to the country.

'There's Andrea, probably looking for us,' Laura watched as Andrea scanned the grounds.

'Did you know Andrea's going out with my cousin?'

'Yes, I didn't know he was your cousin until, well you know.'

'Until my mother made such a scene about Andrea's brooch.'

Laura nodded and was about to get up.

'The brooch was stolen.'

Laura sat back down and stared at Lucy.

'But I don't understand, your mother …'

'It was one of a pair. My aunt was so annoyed at my mother's histrionics she told her she was wearing it at the time. I don't think mother knew about the other one, neither did I until my aunt contacted me.'

'But, why, what about Andrea?' Laura felt confused and suddenly deflated.

'The guy who burgled her house has been caught and convicted. It was obvious Andrea was innocent, so there was nothing to gain by causing her more distress.'

'Her brother bought it for her; she was so relieved that it wasn't stolen. Mind you he's about to go to prison for fraud.'

'Don't say anything to her, will you?'

'No, of course not, but what about your mother?'

'She has no idea, and my aunt certainly won't say anything.'

'Actually, I haven't noticed her wearing it since that day.'

'Laura, Lucinda, there you are.'

Andrea was hurrying round the edge of the lake towards them.

'Come on let's go and put mother out of her misery,' Lucy stood up and waved to Andrea. 'We're coming.'

Lucinda spent a few moments alone with her mother and instantly the whole atmosphere of the house lifted. Shortly afterwards Lady Carlton-Prior joined them all in her daughter's dressing room and cooed about how beautiful Lucinda looked and how clever Laura was making trousers look so special and glamorous. Laura was tidying up and making sure all the garments were in order when Lucy came up behind her.

'Is that a little bump I can see?' she asked.

'Yes, due around Christmas,' Laura replied.

'I'm so pleased for you. This has turned out to be a day of good news after all. Mother have you noticed?'

Lucy indicated Laura's bump and before she knew it Laura was clasped in Lady Carlton-Prior's arms.

'Oh, how wonderful, I'm so pleased. This really is a happy day.'

'Thank you,' Laura wriggled out of her arms and smiled. 'Ben and I are delighted.'

Lucy and her mother walked down the stairs with Laura and Andrea.

'We'll see you tomorrow, about nine-o-clock. No not there, those need to be in the marquee.' Lady Carlton-Prior, back in full organising mode, swept across the hall to direct some poor unsuspecting tradesmen.

'She's happy now,' Lucy grinned and raised her eyebrows.

'See you tomorrow, have a good night.'

Chapter 38

Laura sat on the bottom stair; she was interested but couldn't get over enthused by the builder discussing plaster while he tapped the wall in the hallway. They had always planned to have a downstairs toilet put in, but her heart hadn't been in it before. Of course, a family house needed a downstairs toilet, but she couldn't contemplate it when they weren't a family. They weren't quite a family, yet, she thought, but Ben was right, better to get the mess over with now, rather than when a new baby was in the house. She shivered slightly, she hardly dared to imagine bringing a baby into the house, and no matter how many times the professionals reassured her, there was always that nagging fear.

'What do you think Laura?' Ben asked, assuming she knew what was being considered. 'Lawrence is suggesting we take this wall right back to the stone to give us a bit more space, and then there'll be room to fit a small cloakroom in that corner, it means we might get away with not taking any space from the dining room. What do you think?'

Laura nodded her agreement, but the thought of all the dust didn't thrill her.

'I'll put a sheet up over the stairs to contain the mess,' Lawrence said, as if reading her mind. 'You can see this wall's been lined and plastered over, several times by the look of it, it's got some really old stuff under here,' he pushed a screwdriver into the wall and a shower of dust came out of the hole.

'It's quite deep, the previous occupants probably changed the lay out at some time or might just be stone walls went out of fashion or something, but I reckon it'll be like the one in your sitting room,' he said.

'What if it isn't?' Laura asked.

'Well, if it isn't, I can do a better job of covering it over again. Give you a smooth finish and still gain a bit of space.'

'Sounds OK to me,' she looked around the hall checking that everything that could be, had already been removed.

'Good, I'll get started, John my apprentice should be here soon, so we'll have it all off in no time,' he said, and with that he started pulling huge sheets from a bag to pin across the stairwell.

'Coffee, tea?' Ben asked.

'Tea, strong, two sugars please.'

'What are you doing today,' Ben asked Laura, who started to flick idly through the newspaper, once they were back in the kitchen.

'Andrea and I are going to look over her project and then do some stocktaking, and then I want to upload some new photos to my website. I need to show a bigger range of styles. What time will you be home?'

'Not sure, but not late. Right, I'd better get going and don't overdo it,' Ben drained his cup, leant over to kiss Laura, almost knocking her coffee out of her hand, picked up his jacket and keys and was away. He smiled to himself as he climbed into his car and backed out of the drive, Laura was looking radiant and he was quietly confident that this time everything would end as expected.

Andrea arrived shortly after Ben left. 'What's going on in there,' she asked nodding towards the hall, where bangs loud enough to make the whole house shudder were emanating.

'We're having a downstairs loo put in.'

'Sounds like they're knocking the place down.'

'I know he's taking some plaster of a wall first. Come on let's go over and get started, get away from the racket and dust.'

They spent a very productive morning going through

Andrea's project, she was nervous about submitting it, but Laura was certain she was heading for a distinction. Her ideas and designs were so original and her enthusiasm for the course knew no bounds. Laura felt, through Andrea, the thrill again of being a student, only this time she wasn't the one having to take the exams. They spent another hour sorting through fabrics and threads making sure everything was back along the wall on the purpose-built hooks, racks and shelves, strategically placed to house everything they needed, in a neat accessible way. Then they made a list of items they needed to replenish. Laura wanted everything organised before the baby came. She knew Andrea would keep things ticking over, and she would be on hand if there were any queries. Andrea felt certain Laura wouldn't be able to keep out of the workroom for long, but she was secretly looking forward to having a bit more responsibility, even if only temporarily.

'What do you think about moving this?' Laura turned a screen so that Andrea could see, but before she could make any comment, Lawrence came bursting through the door.

'Ah don't touch anything, you're covered in dust,' Laura got up and flapped at him to go back out of the door, with her following right behind.

He looked as white as a sheet, or maybe it was just the dust.

'What is it? I'll just be in a minute,' she said to Andrea, still herding Lawrence away from her pristine space.

'Come and see this, quickly.'

Laura followed the seemingly agitated Lawrence back into the house; it took her a while to realise what was different. Everything was muted by the light grey dust, but then she realised there was a door, where there hadn't been a door before.

'What's that, how... where did that come from?'

'It's an old door, years old, it must have been boarded up, and then bricked over and plastered, then forgotten about.'

'But where does it go, there's no door on the other side,'

Laura took a step closer; the door was open and there was a dark void beyond.

'It's an old cellar, and…' he swallowed. 'There are bones down there.'

'We haven't got a cellar. What do you mean bones?' Laura could feel panic rising through her body.

'It's not a very big cellar; it's been closed off for decades, longer even,' Lawrence hesitated in amongst the rubble, he didn't want to look scared in front of Laura, but the thought of human bones hidden for years really spooked him.

Laura took a step closer.

'Do you want to come and see?'

'I'm not sure,' Laura took a step back. 'What sort of bones are they, animal probably?'

'Small bones but looks like a baby to me.'

'No, no it can't be. Close the door; I'll ring Ben. No, I'll get Andrea,' Laura raced back across to the workshop. 'Wait there.'

'What is it, you look like you've seen a ghost?'

'Quick, there's a cellar, a body, a baby.'

'What, where? Slow down are you sure, do you need to call the police?'

'Bones, old bones not a real body, a baby's bones. Quick, please come. I can't look.'

Andrea followed Laura; she really was losing it this time she thought.

'OK, come on, let's have a look.'

Andrea enjoyed a bit of drama but was more concerned that Laura was getting herself in a state. She followed Laura into the hall; Lawrence, the builder, was standing in a pile of rubble outside an old battered looking wooden door that was half shut. Andrea was surprised how anxious he looked, and the dust made him look as though he himself was a ghost. She grinned and he smiled weakly back.

'Come on where are these bones then?'

Lawrence looked across the top of Andrea's head towards

Laura. Laura nodded. He pushed open the door and hesitated.

'There's no light, must be pre-electricity but I've got a torch,' he switched the torch on and shone it down the narrow stone stairs. Andrea leant forward to look over his shoulder.

'You go first, I'll be right behind,' she said, winking at Laura.

'I'll come as well,' said Laura, feeling more confident behind Andrea.

'Careful, the steps are quite worn, don't slip.'

The three of them descended into the cellar, a musty stale smell wafted up to greet them.

'It's surprisingly dry,' said Lawrence, falling back on his builder's assessment skills, touching the walls.

It wasn't very deep, only about eight steps down to the brick-based floor. Lawrence stooped to stop his head knocking on the ceiling. He shone the torch around; the small square space was completely empty apart from some old bits of wood, a broken earthenware bowl and an old wooden crate or storage box of some sort.

'In there,' Lawrence played the torch on the box and instinctively stepped back as Andrea moved towards it.

'Shine the torch closer,' she said, and lifted the lid. 'My God, you're right it does look like a baby's remains. It's tiny, must have been newborn.'

Laura peeped over her shoulder and shuddered.

'How tragic, what should we do?'

'I think I better ring Ben before we do anything.'

'I don't know, what do you think we should do?' Andrea turned to Lawrence.

'Well, I vaguely remember something like this happened to a mate of mine when he was on a job, I'm sure he said they rang the police. Shall we get out of here?' Lawrence was already turning to follow Laura back up the stairs.

Andrea closed the lid of the box.

'Poor little mite,' she whispered, and followed the others.

'Ben says ring the police,' Laura said, pushing her mobile back into her pocket. 'He's coming straight home but will be a few hours.'

'You better ring them as the house owner,' said Lawrence.

'I'll make some tea,' Andrea said, already crunching her way across the rubble to the kitchen before waiting for an answer. Laura nodded at her retreating body, pulling her phone out again.

Chapter 39

By the time Ben pulled into the drive a police car was parked by the door and blue tape was across the front door. He was filled with a feeling of dread and hurried round the back looking for Laura. He found her with Andrea on the patio with a young-looking policeman, who appeared to be about to leave.

'PC Wilson,' the policeman said, holding his hand out to Ben. 'I can stay and explain if you want,' he said, looking at Laura and surreptitiously at his watch.

'That's OK, you go, I can explain everything to Ben.'

'Well, if there are any queries give me a ring, but it's not really a police issue anymore.'

'Thank you, I think we can sort it from here.'

'Bye then, thanks for the tea.'

'I'll make a move as well now Ben's back. See you tomorrow,' Andrea said and walked round the side of the house with the policeman.

Laura turned back to a very puzzled, worried looking Ben, who was flopped in a chair.

'What on earth?' he asked. 'Are you all right? Come on sit down and tell me what's going on.'

'Well,' Laura took a deep breath and filled Ben in on all the details, from when Lawrence called her about discovering a cellar containing bones, to the police arriving, followed by a forensic archaeologist, and eventually being told that the bones were well over one hundred years old and basically it was down to them to dispose of them in a respectful manner.

'They were exceptionally prompt and efficient. Do you want to see?' Laura asked.

Ben nodded and stood up amazed at how cool Laura was being about it all.

'Are you sure you're ok?' he asked.

'Yes, I'm fine now, but it was a bit of a shock,' she led the way round to the front of the house. 'It's better going this way to stop all the dust getting into the kitchen. It was lucky the forensic chap was available straight away.'

Ben followed, not certain what to expect. The policeman must have removed the blue tape on his way out, as it was now crumpled in a ball by the door. He stood in the hallway for a moment surveying the scene. Lawrence was right about making it bigger. There was wood, concrete and old plaster on the floor, which must have been used over many years to initially block the door then smooth the wall over. He crunched his way over to where Laura was standing by the open door.

'Lawrence wasn't allowed to touch anything so no clearing up has been done, he said he'd sort it tomorrow,' she said. 'Look how old this wood is,' Laura touched the door.

Ben nodded, ducked under the frame and peered down the steps.

'There's no light, Lawrence thought it must have been blocked up pre-electricity.'

Laura handed him the torch and followed him down.

'Over there,' she pointed at the box.

Ben hesitated, he felt as though the dry dusty air was going to choke him, every fibre of his body wanted to rush back up the stairs and close the door on whatever was lurking down there. Instead, he followed Laura's direction and crossed the small space to the corner where the box was sitting with its lid askew from recent disturbance. Ben shone the torch and looked into the box. He felt strangely emotional as he looked at the tiny bones that had been hidden away for so long. He didn't say anything, but Laura's strange experience, and

Alan's story, all seemed to fit, but he had no idea how or why, and if he was honest, he didn't want to think about it too deeply. It was, surely, just a bizarre coincidence.

'We can't leave it here,' he said eventually.

'No, the policeman said we should dispose of them with dignity, or something. Do you think that means burying them in the garden?'

'Definitely not, no way!' Ben was horrified at the thought. 'I'll speak to Aiden.'

'Aiden?'

'The vicar,' he explained.

'I didn't know you were on first name terms with the vicar,' Laura said.

'I've met him in the pub a few times, nice guy,' he said. 'Anyway, I think the little thing deserves a proper burial, don't you?

'Yes, of course,' she started to cough.

'Go and get some air, the dust's getting into your lungs.

Ben closed the door and picked up several of Lawrence's discarded tools before following Laura into the fresh air. She was sitting on the step of her workshop, apparently lost in thought. She shifted slightly to make room for him next to her.

'You remember my weird experience?'

Ben nodded; how could he forget.

'This could be that baby, the bones I mean. I don't understand how or what happened that day, but it felt real and there was a baby, what do you think?'

Ben looked at her, he was tired and anxious and the last thing he wanted was for Laura to get herself worked up again.

'I don't know. To be honest I don't know what to think about any of it.'

'In a way I hope it is that baby, it sort of fits everything together, and now we can lay the baby to rest. It won't be part of the house anymore, does that make sense?'

'Hello there.'

A call from the gate disturbed them, before Ben could respond to Laura. Ben heard Laura groan under her breath and looked up to see an elderly lady looking over.

'I'm not disturbing you, am I? Only I heard the police were here and I was, well I don't want to intrude you understand, but I did wonder if everything was all right?'

'Hello Elsie, yes everything's fine thank you. We're just having some work done and the builder found something we needed to get checked.' Laura walked towards the gate but didn't invite the older woman in.

'Oh right, yes, I see. I needed to go for one of my walks and I thought I'd just come this way; you know to see… So, everything's all right is it?'

'The builder found some old bones, but there's no problem, we just needed the police to check them,' Ben put his arm around Laura's shoulders. 'It was nice of you to be concerned. Come on darling we need to get everything sorted.' Ben steered Laura away and they walked around the side of the house leaving Elsie to gape at their retreating figures.

'Well done,' Laura whispered, as they rounded the corner of the house, and to his relief Laura didn't resume their previous conversation.

A couple of weeks later after making enquiries and double checking with the police, Ben, Laura, Andrea, Adam and Lawrence all stood round a tiny hole in a corner of the churchyard while Aiden gently laid a small box, especially bought and lined with silk by Laura, into the ground. Aiden said a prayer and Laura and Andrea both placed flowers on the little mound of earth.

'Poor little thing, I feel relieved that we've been able to do the right thing,' Laura said, as she stared at the tiny grave.

'Aiden, will you join us for a drink in the pub?' Ben asked, once all the formalities were complete.

'Good idea, I'll join you in a few minutes,' he said, turning to go back into the church.

A couple of hours later, after what turned into quite a wake, with William and Claire being in the pub as well, Ben and Laura made their way back along the lane with Aiden.

'Well, this is me,' Aiden nodded towards the gate to the vicarage. 'Take care the both of you.'

'We will and you, thanks Aiden. Goodbye.'

Later that evening Ben and Laura stood in their new cellar, Lawrence had fixed up a light and now the place had been thoroughly swept it seemed to have potential. Laura placed a rose, made from the same ivory silk used to line the box, on the spot where the bones were found.

'Do you think it would be sacrilege to turn it into a wine cellar?' Ben asked, he still felt slightly uncomfortable when he thought about the baby being incarcerated down there, but he was more of a pragmatist and wanted to use the space rather than keep it as a sort of shrine. To his relief Laura agreed.

'No, I think it's perfect for a wine cellar; it's not really big enough to use for much else is it? Now the baby is decently buried I feel the house is properly ours. No more ghosts.'

'No more ghosts,' he repeated, and led the way back up to their new enlarged hallway.

Chapter 40

'Do you believe in God?' Ben asked.

Laura stopped peeling the vegetables for dinner and turned to look at Ben. He was sitting at the kitchen table with the newspaper spread out in front of him.

'I'm not really sure, why do you ask?'

'Nothing really, I was just thinking.'

Laura wiped her hands and pulled out the chair opposite him, it seemed such a strange question to ask out of the blue, that she felt she needed to work out what was behind it.

'Is something bothering you?' Laura asked.

'No, just thinking about everything, I suppose.'

'Do you, believe in God I mean?'

'I don't know, I've always sort of thought not, but…' he paused. 'Everything's been so strange, I was just wondering.'

'I've not really thought about it properly. I suppose if someone asked me about religion, I'd say I was C of E, but it's more of a default position. I'm not sure I believe in a God as such, you know an all-seeing presence. I think I might be more humanist, but I don't really know. It's not something I've dwelt on.'

'What about the baby's bones and your strange experiences?' Ben asked.

'What's that got to do with God? Even if it wasn't just in my mind, I can't see how it has anything to do with religion. Have you been talking to Aiden about it?' Laura looked at Ben slightly puzzled.

The more she thought about it, the more Laura felt she didn't believe in God. She'd gone to Sunday school as a child, but that was more because all her friends did. She and Ben were married in the local church near her parents' house, but again, that was more because it was what everybody did, rather than anything to do with faith. If there was a God why was he so cruel as to take Poppy from them, she thought, but didn't say anything out loud. She couldn't quite follow Ben's train of thought about her experiences and the baby's bones in the cellar. Perhaps he was just looking for answers, and where there aren't clear answers perhaps that's when people turn to God or religion.

She reached across and squeezed Ben's hand.

'I think everything will be OK now,' she said.

'Yes, I think it will be, it's just I've been thinking about something that I can't quite work out.'

Laura looked at him, his brow was furrowed, and he did look quite anxious. She hoped he wasn't sickening for something.

'I'm sure everything will be OK,' she repeated.

Ben nodded, and then he proceeded to tell her about his visit to Aiden after Laura smashed up the cupboard, and how he came and blessed the house when Laura was in London with Vicky.

'Why didn't you tell me before?' Laura asked. She wasn't quite sure how she felt about it. 'What else haven't you told me?'

'I wasn't sure what you'd think, and I didn't want to upset you even more,' Ben replied. 'I told him we weren't really believers, but he said that wouldn't matter, so I thought it was worth a go, after all it couldn't do any harm. I was just thinking about everything, and after his blessing the house felt better, you felt it didn't you? You said the nursery felt warmer and even Colin stopped growling on the landing.'

'Yes, it did, but surely… Now I'm confused,' she said.

'I was just thinking, how could Aiden walking round the house saying a prayer make a difference, and it did make a difference, even to you and you didn't know about it.'

'There have been so many strange things going on, I'm not sure what to make of any of them anymore. Maybe Aiden settled a restless soul, or maybe it was just coincidence, who knows? Do you think it was God?' Laura asked.

'I'm not sure, I don't even think Aiden's sure, it's just all very thought provoking, some things just seem beyond our comprehension. Anyway, another thing I was thinking was maybe we should have the new baby christened, I know we never talked about it before, but what do you think?'

'I suppose it is sort of expected, our parents would probably like it,' Laura said. 'But if Aiden knows we aren't really believers he might not want to do it.'

Ben nodded, that thought had momentarily crossed his mind as well, but he'd dismissed it.

'You're right about our parents and I'm sure Aiden won't hold our doubts against the baby, but we'd have to check it out with him. And in a way it would be a thank you to him for everything.'

'Yes, I guess so, let's think about it nearer the time.' Laura stood up and went back to the sink with all sorts of answerless questions going round in her mind.

Chapter 41

Laura walked down the lane and after scanning around to check no one was about went into the churchyard. There wasn't any reason to be surreptitious; she just wanted to look around quietly on her own. The discussion about religion with Ben unsettled her, not that she was looking for answers about religion in the churchyard. She was thinking more about the baby whose bones lay in their cellar for so long, and the people who lived in the cottage all those years ago, and she thought maybe there might be answers on the gravestones.

Before doing anything, Laura laid a flower on the grave of the unknown baby, she felt a pang of regret that Poppy didn't have a grave she could visit. Ben dealt with all the administration at the time, and the hospital arranged the funeral, a cremation, presumably with other babies. Laura at the time hadn't been in a fit state to give it much thought, Poppy was dead that was all that mattered, but now she wondered if it they'd done the right thing. If anything goes wrong this time, she thought, unconsciously laying her hand on her stomach, there will be a proper funeral. She shook her head to stop herself thinking such things, this time everything was going to be fine, she couldn't, no wouldn't, contemplate any other outcome.

Wandering around randomly reading inscriptions, Laura was surprised at how big the graveyard was for such a small village. She remembered a history project when she was at school, which entailed searching the graveyard at home for local mariners who had lost their lives, and along with information in the museum they were able to build a picture of the person, their families and their lives. Laura hoped she could do the same now, but it soon became apparent it wasn't going to be that easy, for one thing she didn't know the names of the people she was looking for, nor did she know the year or even the decade they lived or died in.

When they first moved to London, she and Ben spent a fascinating afternoon on a guided tour of Highgate cemetery. The tombs there were, of course, far more elaborate than the simple headstones here, and their occupant's lives were already well documented. The people who lay here were, now all these years later, mostly anonymous. Laura looked for the graves that appeared to be the oldest and started reading names and dates.

Many of them were badly worn and almost indecipherable but there seemed to be several key groups of names, Cooper, Brown, and Harris, in some cases there seemed to be generations of the same family buried beside one another. Her quest seemed fruitless; the family from her cottage could be any of them. She wondered if William's great-grandfather's great uncle was buried here. If she knew the date, he died she could at least have a guess at the decade, the girl she saw running from the cottage and her baby died. She was certain that the girl was the baby's mother and could only speculate as to the circumstances that led to the scene she'd witnessed. In her own mind, and kept to herself, Laura was convinced that she had witnessed a real scene. She didn't know how and tried not to dwell on the logistics, but she could think of no other explanation.

Laura leant against the wall staring at the jumble of gravestones, then pulled out her phone and rang Claire, who didn't seem the least surprised by Laura's request. She could hear her calling to William in the background asking his great uncle's name. Walter William Thompson was his name and he died in 1836. Laura felt a wave of excitement that date would fit. So, she was looking for the grave of a young girl who died sometime before the eighteen twenties. Laura tried to remember what she looked like; she must have been about sixteen, possibly younger but she couldn't have been much older.

After about five minutes of examining the oldest graves, Laura found Walter Thompson's grave. The headstone was old but the engraving still clearly visible, Walter William Thompson, Farmer, died 16 April 1836, and below Walter's name was engraved the name of his wife Clara, who died five years later in 1841. She traced her fingers around Walter's name and wondered if he really was one of the men on the cart. Did she really meet him? It all seemed so improbable, yet she couldn't shake off the conviction that it really happened, every aspect of that incident remained vivid in her memory, she could replay it in her mind just as though she was watching a rerun of an old film.

Laura looked at the nearby graves and decided that several must be the graves of Walter and Clara's children. She must ask William if he knows more about them. None of the ages or dates on the graves fitted what she was looking for, but she didn't really know what that was.

'Laura, hello; sorry I didn't mean to make you jump,'

Laura turned to see Aiden threading his way through the gravestones towards her, and suddenly felt a mixture of guilt and embarrassment at being found there.

'How are you?' he asked.

'Hi, yes fine thanks, I was just, well I thought it would be nice to see if I could find out more about the people from the cottage.'

'Difficult without knowing their names,' he said. 'Do you mind me asking how it would help, to know who they are?'

Aiden slowly led the way towards a nearby bench at the side of the path, Laura followed, and they sat side by side in the sunshine. Neither spoke for a few minutes.

'I'm not sure, I just felt I wanted to know who the baby

belonged to, if it was the girl, well Ben spoke to you didn't he about what happened.'

'Yes, he did, he told me about the crying and your strange encounter,' Aiden didn't say more he wasn't sure what else Laura knew.

Laura didn't mention that she knew about the house blessing, but she couldn't help wondering what else Ben had told him, maybe she would ask Ben later.

'I thought I might be able to find a gravestone for a girl about the age of the one I saw, the one who I think must be the baby's mother,' she nodded towards the baby's tiny grave, Aiden followed her gaze.

'Pretty flower,' he said.

Laura nodded, 'I made it out of silk, I put one in the cellar as well.'

'It's possible the mother, if she killed herself, won't have a headstone,' Aiden said.

'Oh, I didn't think of that, what would have happened to her?'

'It's possible she could be buried here. They used to bury people who committed suicide in unmarked graves at the edge of churchyards during the night, but that could be anywhere as the churchyard boundaries have changed over the years.'

'What about her parents, or parish records, don't they record births and deaths?' Laura asked. Aiden felt he needed to tread carefully with Laura, he didn't want to thwart her, but he wasn't sure this search was entirely a good way for her to be channeling her energies.

'Well, there are parish records, not here anymore, all in the archives now,' he said. 'But it's likely the baby's birth was never registered and without names it would be very difficult.'

Laura looked down at her hands, of course the baby wouldn't be registered, why hadn't she thought of that. You don't register a birth then hide the baby. She sighed, and was about to stand up, but Aiden continued.

'The information contained in records before the mid eighteen hundreds is a bit sketchy. Same with the census, I think, the first one covered the early eighteen hundreds but there were big gaps and probably poorer agricultural workers weren't recorded in detail. You might find something on your house deeds, it's possible they go back that far.'

'It's not as easy as I hoped,' Laura said. 'I just felt the need to know.'

'Something tragic obviously happened. A baby wouldn't be left in a cellar in normal circumstances, but I'm not sure archive records would ever give you answers.'

'You don't think, the baby was alive when it was put down there, do you?' Laura asked. Aiden looked at Laura and thought about what to say. He wondered just how emotionally fragile she was, with everything she'd been through and now being pregnant again. She could be quite delicate. All his instincts were telling him to treat her with kid gloves. Yet when he looked at Laura, he saw a strong, stable, woman who was just looking for answers to help her make sense of everything. In a strange way she reminded him of Susie, not to look at, of course, but Susie always wanted to know why, she would have encouraged Laura to search all the archives for answers. He smiled to himself.

'What are you thinking?' Laura asked.

'Honestly?'

Laura nodded.

'I was thinking how like my late wife you are; she would want to know everything like you.'

Before Laura could reply Aiden continued.

'In answer to your question, I don't know, I want to believe the baby was dead before they put it in the cellar, but it's such an odd thing to do, it's almost too cruel to contemplate.'

'Maybe no one outside the family knew she was pregnant, so they had to hide the body.'

Aiden noted that Laura referred to the baby as a body, so he wondered if subconsciously she was convincing herself the baby wasn't alive. He took his lead from her and carried on as thought the baby was already dead. Whatever she had, or had not, imagined previously, and he was sure Ben told him Laura heard a baby crying when a girl ran out of the cottage. The hidden baby was real, and he shivered inwardly thinking about it, his gut instinct was that the baby was left alone in the cellar to die.

'Yes, that's possible,' he said.

'Elsie, you know the lady that lives in the cottage a little way passed the shop?'

Aiden nodded, he knew Elsie well, she was a regular every Sunday, a bit of a gossip, but basically harmless.

'Well Elsie mentioned a rumour about incest, do you think the baby could be a result of incest?'

'Goodness,' he wondered what other tales Elsie had been filling Laura's head with. 'I don't think that's anything anyone will ever know. I'm certain that any stories Elsie might tell are just that, stories not facts. In any case it makes little difference to us now, the past cannot be changed.'

'What did you think when Ben told you what I experienced?'

'Well, there are so many things that happen in this life that we can't adequately explain, and your experience strikes me as one of those. I don't suppose you will ever really know, but I do think that if it felt real to you then in some way it was real.'

Aiden stopped talking, he felt he was waffling and not making much sense. He was desperate not to make matters worse and was greatly relieved when he looked at Laura and she was nodding.

'I think you're right, maybe I need to just accept it as something unexplained and stop looking for answers,' she said.

'The important thing, is that the baby has now been laid to rest in the proper place, and you and Ben can get on with building your family in your lovely home.'

Aiden cast a quick glance at the clock above the church door and catching the subliminal message Laura stood up.

'Ben told me about you blessing our house, when I was in London,' she said. 'Thank you it seems to have worked.'

Aiden just smiled; he didn't say anything but was pleased Ben had eventually told Laura. They walked together towards the Lych-gate both deep in thought.

'All the best for the new arrival, not long to wait now I guess?' he said before they parted company, Aiden back into the church and Laura back along the lane to home.

'Thanks Aiden, no, just a few weeks now.'

Chapter 42

'Ben!'

Ben looked up; Laura was bent over clinging to the back of a chair.

'What is it?' he leapt to his feet and rushed to her.

'Ugh, what's that?' he said, as he slipped.

'My waters have gone, quick do something the baby's coming.'

'No, it can't be,' Ben said, whirling around in a panic. 'We'll have to go to the hospital. Now.'

He quickly pulled his socks on and shoved his feet into shoes, then noticed Laura was in her nightie with bare feet.

'Here quick put these on.'

'They're wellingtons,' she started to protest, but was overtaken by another contraction. As it subsided, she pushed her feet into the boots and arms into the coat Ben was holding.

'I'll ring the hospital from the car,' Ben said. Eventually they got into the car and away, but not until after Ben ran back to make sure Colin was in the kitchen and pick up his phone and keys. The journey was everything nightmares were made of, traffic lights, thirty-mile limits, and pouring rain. Laura was groaning telling Ben to hurry and Ben felt as though every movement was being made in slow motion. He was consumed with panic; this wasn't how it was supposed to be. This time everything was going to be calm and safe, everyone had told them so. He reached across to hold Laura's hand to try to reassure her, but she shook it off shrieking at him to put it on the wheel and just get her there.

Once they arrived at the hospital, Ben parked outside the door in an emergency space, this was an emergency after all, and bundled Laura out of the car into the welcome arms of a midwife waiting at the door of the delivery suite, alerted by Ben's frantic call.

'I'll go and park the car,' Ben said, rushing back out.

'Don't leave me,' Laura called.

'Right back,' he replied, running back to the car. An instinct to keep running and not stop swept over him, but he knew he must be strong for Laura. The midwife smiled to herself, she had witnessed many agitated parents arrive at the unit, usually with hours to spare, but she wasn't sure she'd admitted anyone dressed in a nightie, wellies and old gardening jacket before.

'She's having a caesarean next week,' Ben said, as he rushed back into the room. 'It's all arranged, for Thursday.'

'Not now, this baby's in a hurry, not waiting until Thursday,' the midwife said, turning her attention back to Laura.

'Here put this on,' a nurse, with student midwife on her badge, handed Ben a blue gown and paper hat.

He stuffed the hat in his pocket and quickly pulled the gown on over his jumper and jeans, before rushing to Laura's side.

'Are you ok?' he asked.

Laura ignored him and grabbed the gas and air; she held the mask tightly over her face and took deep breaths. Ben pulled strands of her hair away from her face, which was bathed in sweat, and then rested a hand on her shoulder. He felt helpless and slightly sick, everything reminded him of the last time, he was even certain it was the same room. It wasn't supposed to be like this. At every appointment they had attended up to this point the doctor and midwife had reassured them that Laura would have an elective caesarean before she went into labour. It was supposed to eliminate even the miniscule risk of the baby dying in the same circumstances as before. It never crossed either of their minds that the baby might come early. Was it too early, he wondered, was that a problem? He was about to ask but was distracted by the midwife.

'Good girl Laura, now nice deep breaths and a big push.' The midwife was calm, and in control. Ben started to sway, he was going to faint, it was too much.

'Sit here and put your head between your knees,' the student midwife, recognising the greenish pallor of Ben's complexion, gently pushed him into a chair by the side of the bed before turning her attention back to Laura and the other midwife. He couldn't do this, not again. Ben thought he was going to be sick.

Laura woke at the first sound of a cry; she climbed out of bed, careful not to wake Ben, who didn't even stir. He was sleeping the deep sleep of the slightly traumatised and emotionally drained. Laura leant over to kiss him but changed her mind; she didn't want to wake him. She slipped on her dressing gown and slippers and made her way along the landing to the nursery. She pushed open the door and switched on the lamp, the room glowed in a soft warm light. Laura went to the cot and reached in to lift out her beautiful baby girl, who's crying momentarily stopped as she snuffled into Laura's shoulder.

'It's all right, mummy's here,' she whispered into the baby's warm downy hair. Mummy's here,' she said again, as she sat in the small green velour nursing chair and prepared to feed her perfect daughter. She smiled up at the pink rabbit with the long floppy ears sitting on the shelf. Could anything ever be more wonderful, she thought.

Chapter 43

Almost Thirty years later

'Laura, hello.' Lucinda stood up as Laura entered the room. 'How are you,' she stepped forward, reaching out her arms embracing Laura and kissing her on both cheeks.

'Lucinda, how lovely to see you, it's been so long,' Laura smiled, delighted to see her old client. 'Are you living back in England now?' she asked.

'Only temporarily, probably a year and then we'll go back. We're at the Hall so I can help mother with dad, in between work assignments.'

'You're living in Canada, aren't you?'

'Yes, Vancouver, have you been there?'

Laura shook her head.

'It's beautiful you should visit,' Lucinda said.

'One day perhaps,' Laura said, turning towards Andrea who was making adjustments to a toile being worn by a tall young woman. 'This must be your daughter? She looks so like you.'

'Yes, this is Caroline. Everyone says she looks like I did at her age, except for her colouring of course, that comes from Ed's side,' Lucinda smiled fondly up at her daughter.

'Hello Caroline,' Laura moved forward extending her hand. 'Lovely to meet you,' Laura looked with a touch of envy at the girl's long shiny red hair and clear pale complexion. 'I love your hair, but I bet you hate it?'

'I used to, I think I've grown into it now,' Caroline smiled the same open smile as her mother.

'Caroline's getting married while we're over here,' Lucinda said.

'That dress is going to look wonderful, so elegant.' Laura said, looking at the drape of light muslin that Andrea was busy tweaking. 'Have you thought about fabric?' Laura asked Andrea.

'We've got two contenders. 'See which one you prefer.'

Andrea picked up two swathes of fabric and draped one over each of Caroline's shoulders.

'I prefer this one,' Caroline said, stroking a beautiful heavy pale ivory silk.

No one replied.

'If you want my honest opinion,' said Laura, catching Andrea's eye and slightly nodding head, before continuing. 'I think the other one compliments your colouring more.'

'I agree,' said Lucinda, and Laura had the distinct impression that Lucinda's preference might not sway her daughter.

'Come and look in the mirror,' said Andrea.

She draped the fabrics alternately around Caroline's neck and shoulders, it was obvious to the onlookers that the pale ivory drained all the colour from her complexion, whereas the slightly deeper, oyster coloured antique silk, lifted her complexion and looked wonderful with her hair.

'This one makes me look a bit washed out doesn't it?' Caroline said, looking sadly at her favourite. 'I can see this one suits me much better.'

Everyone nodded in agreement.

'I think it will look stunning,' said Laura, and Caroline beamed at her. 'Are you wearing the family veil?' she asked.

'Oh yes, of course, I want to keep up the tradition,' she replied.

Laura smiled; Caroline might look like her mother, but Laura sensed she wasn't quite the rebel her mother once was.

'OK not much more to do, then you can take this off,' Andrea said, turning back to the task in hand.

'Now Laura, I wonder if you could make an outfit for me?

I haven't anything suitable for the mother of the bride,' Lucinda said.

'Of course, come through to my room and we can do some drawings.'

'Nothing too outrageous mother,' Caroline called, as Lucinda followed Laura out of the room.

'Of course, not darling,' Lucinda called back, smiling conspiratorially at Laura. 'Well, this is a bit different from your little cottage,' Lucinda said, looking around the large busy workplace.

'We grew out of the cottage workshop, we've been here about eighteen years now, it's been perfect for us. 'Now can I get you a tea or coffee while we talk outfits?'

'Oh yes please, strong coffee. Was I this difficult when I came with my mother?'

Laura laughed out loud but didn't reply.

'OK, you don't need to say anymore. I remember getting into a strop with mother. I'm trying hard not to be too much like her now.'

The two women spent a very convivial time sipping coffee, chatting about all sorts, including dresses, of course. They eventually came up with a design that Lucinda was delighted with, an Audrey Hepburn style dress with a plain bodice and lace flared skirt, with a loose three-quarter sleeved coat over the top, with the same neckline. Laura transferred the design to her computer and tried different colours for Lucinda to consider. The advances in technology had made life much easier for her.

'I'll do some proper drawings and send for some samples so you can see the real thing,' said Laura, when Lucinda became totally indecisive.

'Oh, that looks lovely,' Caroline said, when Laura showed her the images. 'Perfect, well done mother.'

'Well done Laura,' Lucinda said.

'Apparently Sir Carlton-Prior is quite incapacitated after a stroke, that's one of the reason's Lucinda has come home for a while. That and some conservation project her husband's working on,' Andrea told Laura, as they sat on the terrace drinking tea, before going back to work.

'That's a shame, strokes are so awful. Caroline's a beautiful girl, isn't she?'

'She's lovely and so easy to work with,' Andrea replied.

'Not like Lucinda in her day,' said Laura. 'Mind to be fair it was Lady Carlton-Prior who was more challenging.'

They both laughed at the memory.

'Do you remember that brooch?'

Laura looked at Andrea and wondered if Lucinda had after all this time told her the truth.

'The bird brooch, of course, I haven't seen you wear it since.'

'I haven't got it anymore. I gave it to a charity shop a couple of days after that fateful day.'

Laura wasn't sure what to say, she opened then closed her mouth and looked at Andrea.

'It was stolen, you know. I don't know why Lady Carlton-Prior's sister said it wasn't.'

'It was one of a pair,' said Laura, without thinking.

'You knew? Why didn't you say anything?'

'Lucinda told me the day before her wedding, she asked me not to say. Anyway, it wasn't Billy who stole it; they'd caught the actual burglar. So there didn't seem much point telling you. How, I mean when, did you find out?'

'The day after the accusation, I still had doubts. Even if it wasn't Lady C-Ps sister's brooch, I just couldn't imagine Billy going into a shop and buying such a thing, so I thought it must have been stolen by someone. I decided to confront him, he said he didn't steal it and I believed him, apparently he bought it from a friend of a friend, someone he didn't really know.'

'Why didn't you say anything?' Laura asked.

'Too embarrassed, and too angry with Billy I suppose. He was going to prison anyway so I just donated it to a charity shop, hopefully some good came from it.'

Laura sipped her tea and wondered where the brooch was now.

'If Lucinda knew, did her mother?' Andrea asked.

'I don't think so; no, I'm certain she didn't. I got the impression Lucinda's aunt was annoyed with Lady C-P for making a scene, so she told her she was wearing the brooch, but didn't tell her there were actually two of them.'

'It seems like a lifetime ago, seeing Lucinda again brought it back.'

'Yes, doesn't it just. We must be getting old, making a wedding dress for our first client's daughter.'

They sat quietly both reflecting on their lives and all that had occurred during the intervening years.

'Once we've finished our tea shall we look at the selection for the show so far, then we hopefully can identify the gaps?' Laura's mind was already back on work and the prestigious London fashion show they were involved with.

'Yes, it shouldn't take too long now; I think we're almost there. You haven't forgotten I'm having a few days off?'

'No, how is your mum?' Laura asked, remembering that Andrea's mum was now very frail.

'She's settling in well, her room is very nice, overlooking the garden. She says it's the poshest place she's ever lived. Anyway, I'll go straight to London on Wednesday, I'll check out the venue again and I think I've found a couple more models,' Andrea said.

'I'll put my brain to work on the publicity material and check the invitations. By the way do you think Jenny's ready to mentor a student, we've got two from the design course coming in three weeks?' Laura asked.

'I don't see why not; she's proved herself to be very capable.'

'Hmm I'll ask her; I suppose we can help if she struggles.'

'I'm sure she'll be just fine,' Andrea said, picking up a magazine and flicking through. 'Look I meant to show you this earlier.'

Andrea opened the magazine and passed it across to Laura.

'Under the photo,' she said.

'That's Abigail Devlin isn't it?' Laura said, 'She's wearing one of our dresses.'

'Read the blurb,' Andrea said.

Laura read out loud:

'Oscar hopeful Abigail Devlin looking stunning in an understated elegant L&A Exclusive gown, featuring their trademark quirkiness of design.'

'Wow that's good and just in time for the show,' Laura studied the photograph, the original dress was one of her designs, but the adaptations were down to Andrea.

Before Laura locked up that night she wandered around the now silent workshop and could hardly believe how far they had come. She rarely had the time, or desire these days, to look back. It must be talking about the past with Lucinda. She reflected how different work was when she started out on her own. The risk she taken employing Andrea, then a complete amateur, and now a respected designer in her own right. Now look at them, dressing film stars on red carpets around the world and one of their outfits was even worn at a Royal wedding. She thought about the comment in the magazine, Andrea was definitely responsible for the quirky edge. They made a good team she thought, as she turned the key and set off for home.

Chapter 44

'Mmm those look good,' Chloe said, leaning over to look at the cakes Laura was taking out of the oven.

'We'll have one with some coffee when they've cooled down a bit,' Laura smiled at her daughter. 'The other one I'm taking over for Esme later.'

'I called in to see Gran the other day she was pleased to see me, but I wasn't convinced she really knew who I was. How do you think she is?' Chloe asked.

'Coping, I'd say, but only just, she's getting very forgetful, I'm not sure how much longer she'll be able to stay in that house on her own.'

'And what about you, mum?'

'What about me?' Laura knew exactly what Chloe was getting at, but she wasn't ready to move on just yet. She busied herself with the cakes, turning them out onto racks, and then put the coffee pot on the hob.

Chloe smiled indulgently, looking at her mother's back and decided not to pursue that conversation, for now.

'Has Andrea told you about Ralph's uncle?'

'Billy? No, I haven't seen Andrea for a couple of days. What's Billy done now?' Laura asked.

'He's been caught drink driving, the night before last, I think. Andrea thinks he'll probably lose his job.'

'He's so irresponsible, what was he thinking, especially now he's got a family?' Laura hoped Andrea wasn't going to bail him out again.

'Well at least he didn't cause an accident,' Chloe said, and then sensing her mother tense leapt to her feet. 'Oh mum, I'm sorry I didn't think,' Chloe crossed the kitchen to put her arms around Laura, who had given an involuntary gasp and turned pale. 'I'm sorry are you OK?' she said patting her mother on the back.

'Yes, yes I'm fine,' Laura let her gaze rest on the smiling photo of Ben, dressed in his cricket whites, standing in pride of place on the dresser. He'd become a stalwart of the cricket team. How she missed him, it was like a physical ache in her heart.

'Now then how about a slice of cake, even if it is still warm?' Laura said, disentangling herself from her daughter's arms and reaching for plates. She cut them both rather large slices and set them on the table, poured the coffee and sat down with a determined smile fixed on her face.

'Ralph and I were wondering if you would like to come to Cornwall with us next month. We've rented a place for a week, it's just a short walk to the beach.'

'That sounds lovely, yes I'd like that very much.'

'Good. Andrea and Adam are hoping to come down, for a few days at least. It'll be lovely to all be together.'

Laura nodded, it would be lovely, but for Laura all being together just emphasized the yawning gap left by Ben. She glanced at the calendar, a eighteen-month, two week and three-day gap to be precise.

'Is the beach dog friendly?' Laura asked standing up to pour herself a glass of water.

'Of course, it's one of the few that's dog friendly all year round, so Stan and Lily will be able to wear themselves out running around.'

As if on cue Stan started barking, and Lily, Laura's nearly three-year-old granddaughter, came running down the garden crying loudly. Laura smiled as Lily burst through the door dressed in a pink tutu, green chunky jumper and wellington boots, her blonde hair struggling out of a red bow on top of her head. The girl has style, she thought, but more like her other granny's than mine.

'Nasty tree, nasty, crying, I don't like it,' she said, quite distraught and pushed her head into her mother's lap. Chloe made soothing noises and stroked her hair.

'Poor Lily, did you hurt yourself on the tree, never mind, let me see.'

'Nasty tree, bad,' she said again.

'There, never mind poppet,' Chloe said, lifting her daughter onto her knee. 'It must be the wind humming through the branches, remember like it used to, I used to say it was singing,' Chloe addressed this last comment to her mother.

Laura was standing by the sink, staring out of the window. She gripped the glass she was holding so tightly it shattered in her hand, but she barely noticed the water soaking into her blouse quickly followed by drips of blood, as the shards of glass cut into her hand. She became aware of a feeling as though an icicle had been thrust into her chest. She was gasping but remained rigid, staring into the garden. She felt bile rising in her throat and thought she was going to be sick. She could see Stan, he was standing rigid under the old oak tree, hackles raised, and she could tell even from this distance that he was growling, his lips were drawn back in an uncharacteristic snarl. As if in slow motion, the hairs on the back of her neck one by one stood on end.

'Mum are you OK? Here let me take that,' Chloe released her mother's grip on the glass and pushed her hand under the tap, carefully picking out tiny pieces of glass.

Laura didn't speak; she just submitted to Chloe's ministering, who eventually, after rummaging through her bag, carefully stuck a bright pink Mister Man plaster on her mother's palm. Lily stood, thumb in mouth watching, she instinctively knew that granny needed mummy more than she did at this moment.

Chloe engulfed the still shaking Laura in her arms before leading her to a chair, where she crouched down beside her. She'd never seen her mother like this before. She knew that her mother had lost a baby before she was born but was completely unaware of the events that followed.

'Mum are you all right, what is it? You look as though you've seen a ghost?'

After many minutes trying to compose herself, Laura turned to face her daughter; she nodded, and tried to smile but only succeeded in a slight contortion of her lips.

'Yes, I'm fine, don't worry it's nothing. Really, I'm fine. Just a funny few minutes,' she said, but deep down she knew. She wished Ben was here.

'You're right,' she said. 'I think I am ready to sell the house, after all. It's time to move on.'

Printed in Great Britain
by Amazon